AN EXPERIMENT IN LEISURE

AN EXPERIMENT IN LEISURE

Anna Glendenning

Chatto &Windus
LONDON

1 3 5 7 9 10 8 6 4 2

Chatto & Windus, an imprint of Vintage, is part of the Penguin Random House group of companies whose addresses can be found at global.penguinrandomhouse.com

Penguin
Random House
UK

First published by Chatto & Windus in 2021

penguin.co.uk/vintage

A CIP catalogue record for this book is available from the British Library

ISBN 9781784743970

Typeset in 11.8/15 pt Adobe Garamond
by Integra Software Services Pvt. Ltd, Pondicherry

Printed and bound in Great Britain by Clays Ltd, Elcograf S.p.A.

The authorised representative in the EEA is Penguin Random House Ireland, Morrison Chambers, 32 Nassau Street, Dublin D02 YH68.

Penguin Random House is committed to a sustainable future for our business, our readers and our planet. This book is made from Forest Stewardship Council® certified paper.

MIX
Paper from
responsible sources
FSC® C018179
www.fsc.org

For Saba

During the years when I found it necessary to revise the circuitry of my mind I discovered that I was no longer interested in whether the woman on the ledge outside the window on the sixteenth floor jumped or did not jump, or in why. I was interested only in the picture of her in my mind: her hair incandescent in the floodlights, her bare toes curled inward on the stone ledge.

Joan Didion

I can't remember the day I started calling dinner 'lunch' and tea 'dinner', but I know that it happened, because that's what I call them now.

Lynsey Hanley

7. Finally, we arrive at the fascinating and philosophic question: can one eat one's cake and have it?

Donald Winnicott

The lights turn on as you walk: tailbone in, steeple fingers, thumbs flush with the diaphragm. You ring the bell and de-germ. Hello Debbie (light blue). Hello Sandra (navy).

Michael's at the far end. You give him a nod. You tidy his shelf. There's a Leeds United cap up there, peak bleached and split, and a small bottle of Davidoff Cool Water, and a photo of him in Tenerife with his second wife. Red Bull bumbag, mirror Oakleys, big blue parrot on a perch.

He has a diary now.

4.4 All entries should be made in black ink.

4.10 Avoid jargon and abbreviations. Try to relate what you write to how you would normally verbalise the information.

4.12 If there are any concerns about how to describe an aspect of care or an event, please consult a member of the Diary Team for advice.

You take the pen. *You're yellow*, you write, *and I know what your toenails look like.*

You spray him with Davidoff Cool Water.

*

These are your Sundays. On Sunday nights you go back to London. Weekdays you sit on a collapsible chair with Caroline, General Manager, Association for Office Stationers. You watch her open tabs, writing down the things she's saying on small orange Post-it notes. You lean in with your wide-legged trousers and your goose-pimpled ankles and your hankering Clarks suede brogues. You lean in. Then you fold the chair, make her a Nescafé, place it by her mouse mat and walk away. For this she swivels her chair and watches, though when you turn she'll be looking at her screen. She'll push her forehead with the heel of her hand and say *right*, *THINK*, *Jesus Christ* or: *done*.

*

Rebecca calls on a Tuesday night.
    'Hello?'
    'Hi. It's me. Tash's phone.'
    'Oh, hi. Happy New Year.'
    'Yeah. Wait a sec.' Her trainers echo in the stairwell, gloss-painted concrete.
    'Hello?'
    'Hang on.' Keys.
    'What's going on?'
    'It's Dad—'
    'Shall I come up?'
    Door. 'Ah fuck.'
    'What's happened?'
    'Smudge's had a meltdown. Fuck's sake.'
    'What's happened?'
    'Little fucker. Smudge! Smudge mate. Come on mate.'
    'Rebecca.'
    'Look I've got to go.'
    'Shall I come up?'
    'Tash? Tash! Tash have you seen this?'
    'Tomorrow?'
    'Yeah.'

*

You book a quiet coach aisle seat to Leeds, take a bowl of cemented Weetabix through to the kitchen. You live in Islington with Matthew and Adam, Hornsey Road. This is your life.

It's a galley kitchen. At the far end there's a table you found by the bins off Sunnyside Gardens, custard Formica, plus two sprightly stools with black leather tops.

You kill the big light, take a stool and sit the other opposite. That one's for Rebecca.

You clear your throat and take your phone out, screen up. Close your eyes, tap it with your index finger.

'Testing.'

Cough out the frog.

'Testing.'

You shared a room as kids, Rebecca in the top bunk and you underneath. You shared a room and a Furby and a pair of Babyliss crimpers. Once you woke up early and she crimped your hair for school, layer by layer. She showed you the back with a miniature mirror, spray-painted silver and glue-gunned with little glass shells. Once the Furby woke up in the night and you couldn't work out how to stop it. She climbed down the ladder and took out the batteries.

You message Caroline. *That's fine*, she says, *you're having a tough time*, then you make a fresh bowl of Weetabix, coat it with sugar, watch it bloat, throw it in the bin. You go to your room. You lie prostrate on the bed. You stay there for a while before heading to the floor.

JANUARY 2015

The train pulled in to Leeds with a kazoo over the tannoy. *Right on time, ladies and gents!* Right on time. I left the station, wandered dazed up to the lights, crossed the road and found myself in an atrium, a great big glittery packhorse suspended from the ceiling. I went to Urban Outfitters, Leeds Trinity Urban Outfitters. I tried on a pair of faux-herringbone trousers and a cobalt velvet jacket, stood for a while in the cobalt blue with my hand on the changing room rail. *Remember he loved his wife,* I mouthed. I wasn't in love and I wasn't his wife.

Down Boar Lane, then, to the bus station. Booth twenty-two. Grey metal chair. I sat down but my coat wasn't long enough and the cold hit me hard, right up in the belly. I went to Greggs.

'Oh, hi. Hi. Could I have a coffee please?'

Nod.

Pause.

Shrug.

'Oh. Oh, erm, large please.'

Milk?

'Oh, yeah, black please. Yeah. Thanks. Thank you. Thanks. Thank you.'

*

Back at my booth I drank it quick, lid off, chin in the steam. Then I needed a wee.

'Can I—?' I said to the woman with the yellow traffic cone. She carried on mopping, eyes down.

'Erm. Excu—. Could I just? Could I? It's just I—. Sorry. Sorry.'

She looked up, took one of her earbuds out. 'Speak up, love!' Outstretched arm. 'All yours.'

I hovered over some more cold metal, stainless this time, stainless. When I emerged she'd left a dry route out.

'Oh. Oh, thank you. Thank you so much. Sorry.'

She nodded, both buds back in now, her voice louder with it. 'Take care, love.'

In the booth I made a coffee sleeve concertina, ripped off the coupon for Mum, and forty minutes later came the X84, sweeping and arrogant as a needed bus will be. I needed another wee.

The Headrow was rammed with paper bags and drawstring bags and ropey exultation, Christmas lights. At the Merrion Centre a man got on with a toddler. She was arching her back out of her chair, crying in Spanish. He stared at her in silence, first with bemusement and then, as she hit her stride, with accusation.

Otley. Home. Mum was still at Center Parcs with Jackie and the girls, Pamper Sesh for Jackie's January birthday. *Back tomorrow xx.* I let myself in with the outhouse key, dumped the bag of trouser, walked to Asdas for some bits and then on, along and down the hairpin bend to the new estate: Garnett's, they called it, Garnett Wharfe, what was the paper mill. There was a trail of *Help to Buy* flags lining the way. They had Labradors on them.

It was bitter now, newsworthy. I saw five frozen spiderwebs. No one else, nobody bar Mrs Miller, the primary school lunchtime supervisor, the one with the red-raw forearms. I was stuck to the tarmac.

'You're better on the grass.'

I nodded.

She walked on.

I moved to the grass.

*

I went back into town the next day, to Jimmy's. Rebecca drove up from Sheffield and we met on the ward. It was time, they said. They were turning him off. We said goodbye in turn – his wife, Rebecca, me, his wife.

Would we like to stay with him for a while, Sandra asked; it would take several hours before he lost his breath. Rebecca had her chin to her chest. Alison was shaking her head. Michael was softer without his plastic, calmer. He had a two-day stubble, three- or four- in the hard to reach bits. I doused myself in Davidoff.

Alison was his wife. On the corridor I asked her for her number. 'One L?' 'One L, love.' Rebecca was a few metres down, pacing on the phone to Tash, and Alison was clutching her cross-body bag, feeling the shape of its innards like that kids' game we used to play with the sheet. *What's this, Grace, can you feel it? Can you tell? Scissors!* I liked her coat and I told her. 'Thanks,' she said. 'It's a coatigan.' 'It's lovely.' 'Thanks.' Then she hugged me, light and quick, pausing with her chin on the back of my shoulder – not a rest or a press but a hover – before pulling away. She waved goodbye to Rebecca. She had her purse, yes. She had her keys. Bye.

*

I walked with Rebecca to her car, a red Twingo named Dawn.

'I'll give you a lift to Mum's.'

'Are you sure?'

'Get in.'

'Oh, thanks.'

She put on Heart FM, the heating full blast, and a new pair of owlish specs out the glove box. 'Arty and cool,' she said.

'Nice.'

'Two for one, so.'

'They're nice. I like them.'

She nodded. She reached down to her right. 'Werther's?'

I did a mini whiplash movement. Vigorous nod.

'Take two.'

She stopped at the top of the cobbles, engine still purring.

'I won't come in.'

'No?'

'It's late.'

'Stay over?'

'It's late.'

'Then stay.'

'No.'

'Please?'

'Some of us have got work.'

'I—'

'*No* Grace.'

'Alright! Chill.'

'Fuck off.'

'Sorry. Sorry. Drive safe?'

'*Yes.*' She started cursing at the radio.

I reached behind me for my rucksack, opened the door.

'Take care, yeah?'

I nodded.

'Be nice to her.'

'I—'

'Bye, Grace.'

'Bye. Love you.'

'Bye.'

Mum was in the kitchen running a bowl.

'You said you'd be home for tea.'

'Sorry.'

I took a step towards her.

She put her Marigolds up, back still turned.

'Microwave,' she said.

'Oh. Thanks.'

There was a cling-filmed plate of sausages in there, four hunks of peeled Maris Piper, dash of English mustard and half a boiled broccoli the colour of moss.

'I pricked it for you.'

'Aw. Thanks Mum.'

She dropped her knife and fork and spoon from a height into the metal container on the draining board, the thing with the circular holes, one by one. The noise was appalling.

'I really appreciate it, Mum.'

She drained the bowl.

I shut the microwave.

'Mum?'

She did a heavy shrug, poked her sodden tea towel into the cat's bum tea towel holder.

'Look Mum I'm sorry bu—'

'You could have called.'

'No reception Mum.'

'WhatsApp.'

10

'They—. Look, I don't know how to—. They turned him off, Mum.'

Pause. Three seconds.

'*Christ.*'

She put both hands on the side for a moment, very still, crouching forward ever so slightly as though she'd like to vault the counter, her fingers scrunched into fists. Then she brought herself upright very slowly, head right up, let her shoulders drop, right hand to her crucifix, heavy exhalations. She turned back round as I made to hug her, sorting out her Nivea Creme, returning her rings.

'Mum?'

She shook her head and went upstairs.

I stayed very still. 'Come on Mabel,' I heard her say, 'out,' and Mabel touched down from a six-inch height with a sleepy sullen plop. The landing light went. I listened. Mabel did two steps down, little wallop of belly, then she paused, her signature move, licking herself off, looking back at the door, waiting, judging then taking the rest of the stairs. Mum's door clicked.

I went to the top of the cellar steps. Mum had left the immersion on for me, for a while, enough for a full bath. I turned. Mabel.

'*What?*'

She looked up at me. She looked away.

I ran a bath, washed the smell of postponed body from the insides of my nose, a smell of yeast. When I was a prune I got out, put on Mum's snowflake dressing gown and went downstairs. I gave Mabel the sausage, chucked the rest, tight wet coil of cling and all, fiddling the bin so she wouldn't see. I boiled a bottle, locked Mabel in, kettle at the wall, bed.

*

11

There was a note in the morning, *LOVE YOU BUNNY*. Mum had a banana out the side of her head and I had my big blue glasses and she'd drawn us there together in a love heart. Michael's kept on for a while, a surprising while, the best part of a day, then he died.

*

A week later they held the funeral. I went back up the day before, dumped my stuff and walked, back to Garnett's, over the iron bridge, up Newall, bit of Weston, Billams Hill, Tittybottle Park, Ilkley Road, Bradford Road roundabout. That took about an hour, an hour at pace, and Otley's pretty flat if you leave off the sides, though truly it's a valley, a dale. To the south there's the Chevin – prehistoric ridge, big stones with carvings, massive height. In winter the sun has trouble getting over it.

Mr Parker used to joke there were dragons past the Chevin, south. *This is a local town for local people. Metal birds*, he'd say, his hand a cross up at the sky.

I crossed the bridge up over the bypass and sat on a bench on Birdcage Walk, the one with the permanent waterlogged drain, wrote Michael a poem. The odd car came by. Some of them swerved the drain. Some splashed on through and splattered my shins and I winced and cursed but I nodded. I was one of life's splashers. Rebecca? Rebecca swerved.

In the morning we followed the hearse up Otley Road to Lawnswood Crem. Rebecca sat next to me, Alison in the back. We were silent. It was raining, hard. When we stepped out and onto the gravel a man in a pinstriped waistcoat handed Rebecca a golf umbrella, bowed his head. He must have been high-ranking, stood here with the daughters, but the last session was running over and he couldn't do much about that. 'Busy time of year love?' Alison asked and the pinstriped man said, 'Yes, yes love,' and he re-bowed his head. We waited for twenty minutes as the crowd of umbrellas thickened across the gravel. I was wearing a pair of Rebecca's emergency pumps. Black, Primark. My toes were gone.

I read out my poem. It was short, sweet, a thing about Elland Road, the strips he'd bought us in '98. I made the last line overlong for a laugh and there was one, diffuse and distressing. I sat back down.

The reverend continued a few moments then opened it out to the floor. Tony stood up and talked about MotoGP. Rossi, Pedrosa, Lorenzo, loved 'em our lad, bloody loved 'em, and what about our lad Bradley! *Go on Bradders!* Laughter. Laughter to fade. Then we all trooped out to the Faces.

'Poignant,' Aunty Jan said, touching Tony's arm. It was 'Ooh La La'.

'Ronnie Wood's the vocal on this one. Rod didn't show at the studio that day so it's Ronnie, it's Ronnie singing this one, love, and not many people know that.'

'Right, love.'

'Not many people know that.'

He turned to me. He squeezed my arm.

I nodded.

At the wake Jan served her corned beef slice, corned beef slice and sliced beef tomato with a sprig of thirsty parsley (curly). Trish had let us have the run of the golf club, half-price bar.

'Tragic,' she said to Graham in the foyer, 'barely gone forty.'

'Int it, love,' said Graham. 'What yer havin'.'

*

I left early for my super off-peak return. Jan put a top slice in foil for me, some Dolcelatte and a flask of milky tea.

'Oh. No, no I can't take your flask Jan.'

She shook her head and pressed it to my chest.

A man came over in a pale blue shirt, lightly soiled with multipack vol-au-vent. 'You're his twins then.'

'Yes. One of them. Nice to meet you.'

'Jesus.'

Mum walked over as he backed away.

'I'll come see you at Easter, Mum.'

'Right.'

She held my foil while I rechecked the front pocket of my rucksack. 'I will.'

'Will you?'

'Yes, Mum.'

She gave me back my foil.

'I'll try.'

'I love you, love.'

I swung the rucksack over my shoulder, pulled the straps and wriggled the weight out.

'I do, love.'

'I know. You too.'

I found my seat, retrieved the Moleskine and propelling pencil. I crossed out some recently mistaken epiphanies.

London. No one was home. In my room the wall was black and wet in the corner where the bed was. The sheets now, too, and the mattress. I sighed, and then I climbed on top in my coat and hat and I slept. I liked this about myself.

There was a cast-iron clang in the morning, the letterbox. I went down, took the pizza ads out to the recycling and sat on the bench, Siobhan's bench, Siobhan from flat one. I watched my fingers turn to wax, and when they were done I went back up and stared out the window. I noticed a man in the garden. He put Siobhan's birdbath on its side and rolled it in some wadding. I looked deeper and there was another one, another man. He was dismantling the fence with an electric screwdriver.

I went back down.

'Why are you doing this? Will you stop?'

'We're landscape architects.'

*

Matthew came home the next day. I didn't know where from. I'd been for a walk up the Haringey ladder and when I got back there was a pair of new Asics by his door and a dinner plate of coke in the kitchen. One line, bit wonky. He must have run for the 91 and bashed it with his hip. I perked it back up with my pinky and popped some on my gum.

15

Erm, no.

I swilled.

I went back to bed.

I'd tried pulling the bed into the middle of the room to get away from the damp but then I couldn't really move myself around so now it was in its former position, hovering an inch or so from the wall, hospital style, headboardless. I didn't want to wonder if Matthew would come home so I put my headphones in, though he did come home and I heard, Matthew and the woman he'd most recently fallen in love with. Jessica. She was gentle in his company, gentle and sad.

Matthew was a management consultant. He liked ergonomic runs, turning women into angels and withstanding contradiction. I liked *Elle* magazine. *Elle* and *Vogue*. It used to be *i-D* but that intimidated now. *Elle*, *Vogue* and sleep.

Jessica left early and Matthew knocked. 'Come in babe.' He sat on the end of the bed. He felt weird, he said, why did she leave so early, and I reminded him she did shifts didn't she, weekends. Maybe she had work. She'd be at work. He didn't know.

'Grace?'

'Yeah.'

'Seriously, do you think she likes me?'

'It's work Matthew, that'll be it, she'll want to change her knickers.'

I handed him a malted milk and showed him Victoria Beckham.

'I think she's ugly,' I said, handing him the mag.

'She's not. She's incredibly successful. And hot. That's impressive.'

'Obviously. What I mean is: a world in which she has to look like this, like this,' I said, tracing her ribs with my index finger, 'that's ugly.'

'You're being petulant,' he said, then he flopped forward and groaned. 'I feel *weird.* I love her. I love her Grace. I feel weird.'

I patted his head.

*

Adam was next. He'd been in Central America for a month. Matthew made him a banner. *BEING A DICKHEAD'S COOL,* it said, then underneath I'd added, smaller: *we missed you.*

'We all play synth,' he sang from the corridor and then he nudged my door open. An illustrated tin of IPA rolled down the carpet.

'Can I come in?'

'Hi darling.' I extended my arms and fluttered my fingers from down on my throne, a yoga brick pushed up against the radiator. I was burning off the moisture from some rained-on layers of wool.

He sat on the carpet. 'Thanks for my banner.'

'Glad you like.'

'I—. Matthew told me,' he said.

I nodded, pointing at the tin. 'This for me?'

He nodded.

'Cheers.'

'Cheers.'

Adam had been to Ally Pally en route, to his parents', so we ate his mum's mushroom lasagne then we drank, hard. When I went to break my seal the bathroom bulb was stark, crude without its lampshade, and the walls were their sickly teal, filthy, and I was a man among men.

I went back through. Adam was stood up, phone on charge, saying we should all go out, out-out, Elephant and Castle, but Matthew and I were tired so Adam went out-out alone. He didn't mind. He was a techno head, though clean now (ish). Matthew and me stayed in and analysed his recovery. 'His internal resources were brittle,' I said. Matthew nodded.

We watched three eps of *Green Wing* on the laptop then Matthew turned it off, the apple so graceful in its fade. We brushed our teeth in concert, downed our pre-bed water and went to bed. Separately, now, though at one stage my envy was lust. Tonight too, a bit.

Matthew had a careful body. No superfluities, fine motor skills and tremendous biceps, though sometimes he seemed too compact, too big for someone so small, and that made him clumsy, and he never used enough Fairy, always too fretful and rash to wait for the bottle to deliver its goods, though in his defence the bottle was more often than not running out, and that was not a Matthew problem, that was structural.

Adam was a medic and better with grease, meticulous, but he cared much less about tone. He had a little belly and he kept it well, under an Aphex Twin T-shirt. He wore chequered beige boxers and his dad's old Blue Harbour slippers and he padded around the flat with great calm, defrosting individual slices of bread, boiling up eggs for multi-day egg mayo pack-ups. He always broke his cereal boxes down into neat rectangles that he stamped on with his slippers. He was responsible for Boris the basil plant.

I didn't think about my body. I was fine with it. I had let it disappear, along with all knowledge of my scrutiny.

Then I stopped bleeding.

*

18

I booked in with the doctor. Her name was Doctor Imogen Barltrop. The buttons on her shirt had turned copper and she was a little bit pregnant. There was a tall grey man in the corner, legs crossed, clipboard on his right knee.

'Is it OK for Dr Watts to join us?'

'Yes,' I said and she asked me why I was here and I said I'd stopped bleeding.

'How long?'

'Three months.'

'When's the last time you had sex?'

'I—. I don't know.'

She looked at Dr Watts.

'I'm not pregnant.'

She weighed me and measured me and migrated me into her spreadsheet. Then she put me on the bed and pressed my lower abdomen, harder and lower than expected. A dash of pubic hair escaped from my trousers. I closed my eyes.

'You can sit back up now,' she said, then she printed something off and handed me it, a piece of paper with the word *amenorrhoea*.

'Have you had any thoughts about the investigations you'd like to pursue?'

I shook my head. I watched my umbrella, which was wet, which was leaking.

'OK. Do you have a partner?'

'No.'

'Do you live alone?'

'No.'

'Are you sleeping?'

'Yes . . . No.'

The man wrote this down.

'You might have polycystic ovaries but I'm inclined to think it's stress. We'll do some bloods and an ultrasound but I'd like to refer you for some counselling, too.'

She printed out a few more sheets, stapled them together. Dr Watts nodded, slowly.

'Thank you,' I said and then again to Dr Watts and then again to the door.

*

The letterbox went.

Q1: How often have you been bothered by having little pleasure or interest in doing things?

Q2: How often have you been bothered by feeling down, depressed or hopeless?

Q3: How often have you been bothered by trouble falling or staying asleep, or sleeping too much?

Q4: How often have you been bothered by feeling tired or having little energy?

Q5: How often have you been bothered by poor appetite or overeating?

Q6: How often have you been bothered by feeling bad about yourself, or that you are a failure or have let yourself or your family down?

Q7: How often have you been bothered by trouble concentrating on things, such as watching television?

Q8: How often have you been bothered by moving or speaking so slowly that other people could have noticed?

Q9: Have you had an anxiety attack?

I found a psychoanalyst. Her name was Rachel. Psychotherapist, strictly, but I preferred analyst.

*

Rachel lived in Notting Hill. I rang a few numbers in my search but that's what cinched it. Notting Hill was London when we were kids, *Notting Hill* Notting Hill, and all Richard Curtis pre-*The Edge of Reason*. He fared well in the Morrisons bargain bin.

I wanted to be Honey and Anna, both. That's what I'd tell Rachel. I was here to be more complex and integrated, with lots of aspects to my character and ultimately real. If I couldn't have that – and I knew I was a child still, Rachel, yes, I know – then I'd settle for some mid-level peace of mind amid the trappings – the light in Hugh's landing, those honey-soaked apricots – though I did believe things would go well. I was ready. We'd do the work and rework my body, too. I'd *occupy* myself. I'd have Keira's command of Keira's jaw, please, and a Bridget timbre, and I'd learn how to pronounce timbre, and I'd cry like Emma Thompson.

The house was on Oxford Gardens, a red brick house with a gable-roofed portico laced with recently weatherproofed wood. For the first session I wore Danish cigarette pants and mahogany socks.

I knocked. Five short raps small gap two more. The door was filled with panes of glass of different colours.

'The latch is broken,' said Rachel, locking the door behind us with a key on a length of string. I didn't understand, I'd never had a door with a latch. She had a steel-grey bob.

'It's a beautiful door.'

'Yes,' she said. 'It is.'

The consulting room smelt of bergamot and painted radiator, indiscriminate heat. There was a bed and a wicker chair. She swept her hand between the two.

'You can go wherever feels comfortable.'

21

'Oh, well . . .'

'People often start with the chair.'

'Can I take the chair?'

'Yes.'

I sat on the chair. I crossed my legs.

'Shall I—'

'I'm going to lay out my terms first. Is that OK?'

'Oh, yes. That sounds great.'

Same room, same time, once a week. If she cancelled I didn't have to pay. If I cancelled I had to pay.

'Ah, I see. That makes sense. You have to cover yourself. It's precarious work this, isn't it? I'd never really thought about that before, but, yeah. That's really interesting.'

A nod.

'Can I . . . Can I begin?'

Another nod.

I found a point on the wall behind her head and tried to count to ten. Much too long. Five.

'Well. Right, well. I've been thinking quite a bit about how I should start so I thought I'd just come out and say it.' Small release of breath from the nose. 'Erm, I've been a bit, well, worried, I'd say, I think worried is the word. Maybe not quite as strong as worried, but well, erm, I know this, this "work" relies on me opening myself back up to my childhood, and I, I don't remember a massive amount of early material, say, like pre-Princess Di? I do remember that. My mum had dolled us up at the crack of dawn that day for some wedding or something, some family do, so I remember that, and I'd say that's my earliest memory, but before that is repressed, like repressed-repressed. I know some people say they remember being three or four but I'm more like six. But, yeah. Sorry. Yeah. Anyway, yeah, that's definitely somewhere I'd like us to, erm, I don't know . . ., "Go"? "Begin"?'

She nodded.

'I've tried not to over-prepare. I just—. I don't know.'

A moment here, a couple of seconds.

'I'm not.' Little nasal ha. 'I'm not sure how to begin.'

'That's OK.'

'I guess that's quite common.'

'Beginnings can be difficult.'

'Yeah, I imagine people find that difficult.'

She looked down and I looked down with her. I watched her boots for a moment – flat ones, ankle boots – and the shape they made of her shins. She was wearing a mauve corduroy pinafore dress. She must have been in her mid-sixties but the boots made her shins look younger, sweet like Red Riding Hood, Red Riding Hood dressed in red wellies. They made me think of Sarah, Sarah the American who wore a red mackintosh and lived in Ben Rhydding. She called it a mackintosh, I remember, and it was a mac. That made her an American. We were seven.

Sarah's house was a mansion, that's what we called it, and she was big too, like precocious. Her dad worked at Menwith Hill. For a few months we'd go there after school, Rebecca and me. Rebecca played with the brothers, a go-kart game they called Wacky Races after the telly, or pool in the basement room with the red glass light bulbs, and I played with Sarah.

'We went to this house every day but, I don't remember why and I don't remember Sarah too much, not her appearance. Dark hair, I remember she had dark hair and it was really dark and it would get matted around her face. It was really interesting, like, like it was a physical presence of how clever she was?'

'She was bright.'

23

'Yeah. Yeah, absolutely. Yes. But I just—. I can't remember her face at all, sorry. I remember her clothes. God. Her clothes had their original hangers. That was a massive deal. I remember she had Marks and Spencer knickers with the days of the week on the front and all the days were extant, oh and the crème de la crème this baby blue hoody with the G A P across the chest. Hmm . . . God it's so odd how it comes back isn't it? She had these patchwork jeans, big flares with the patches in different shades of denim and, like, a long-sleeved top with flared crochet sleeves. She used to put her clothes out on the bed and tell me to take mine off and I'd stand there in my off-white knickers and she'd dress me up.'

Silence.

'I think about that quite a lot.' Fingers. Rug. 'Anyway. She left.' Boots. Shins. 'She went back to America. Probably her dad, but I always felt it was me. I think she told me it was me, that's what I remember, like it was my fault? I think she told me before she went. She didn't, I know she didn't, probably not in reality, I think that would be a bit dark, but that's how I remember it. I think.'

'It was you?'

'Hmm. There was something—.' Breath. 'No. I don't know. When she'd gone though Rebecca started playing with Jenny a lot more. Jenny was this girl who lived down the street and me and Rebecca never really—. I don't know. Sorry. Sorry. Rebecca's my sister by the way. I don't know. I think. I think. Hmm. Sorry.'

'Take your time.'

'I don't know. I don't know why I'm even talking about her, Sarah, to be honest. She popped up but—. I don't know. She'll have popped up for a reason I know. Hmm.'

Silence.

24

'Yeah. I guess I wanted her and her clothes and then I wanted rid of her and then she went.'

Silence.

'I don't mean that I actually think that now by the way. I mean it like fantasy, like phantasy with the P H. Is it Klein who says something like that? Red angry babies who wish death and feel bad. I can get behind that. Kids are dark I think.'

Silence.

'Anyway, Rebecca and I were drifting apart then, so.'

Silence.

'Sorry. Yeah. I'm very—. I guess I'm trying to say I'm ambitious.'

'Yes.'

'That's definitely a thing. That goes right back. Loved my little Puffin books, hand always first up. I sat at the front for carpet time, always, right on the edge of the metal carpet strip and pressing down so like sometimes it properly hurt. I think that's meaningful.'

Silence.

'Sorry. This is a lot of me talking.' Blush.

'That's OK. That's what you're here for.'

Blush. Furtive smile. 'I really remember the feel of that carpet strip coming through now, right through my shoes and socks, the black pumps and those polyester socks with the frills and holes, the ones that make your feet sweat. I was pushy.'

'Pushy?'

'Needy.' Grimace. 'Rebecca was more—. Quieter I guess, more of a beanbags-at-the-back situation.'

'And Rebecca's your sister.'

'Yes.'

'And you did well at school.'

'Yes.'

Silence.

'I was lucky.'

Silence.

'Though I guess I definitely wasn't—. I went pretty hard at it. Definitely wasn't—. Not normal.'

'Hmm.'

'Sorry,' now with air quotes, '"normal" quote unquote.'

'Did you go to university?'

'Yes.'

'OK.'

'Yeah.'

'Did your parents go to university?'

'No.'

'And your sister, she—'

'No.'

'Where did you go?'

'Hmm.' Silence. 'Cambridge.'

'Right.'

'English.'

'OK.'

I nodded. 'But I don't really like to—. Yeah. No. Sorry.'

'You went to Cambridge.'

'I mean, yes, I did, but like, well they gave me a lot of money, so. It was financially . . .'

Silence.

'I'm not, well, I'm not *Cambridge*, not Cambridge-Cambridge.' I screwed up my face. Chin to chest. Blush.

Silence.

'Sorry. I don't tell people much. It was hideous.'

'You don't like people to know.'

'Well, no, I mean I'm not trying to hide my, well, my "privilege" or whatever. I just want to, well. It's a big thing isn't it so you can't just—. You can't just throw it in there.'

Silence.

'No. It—. Hmm. I do—. Well, I try to say it in an out-there, straight-up way and not get, well, not get all weird about it . . . People take that for snobbery I think, sometimes, sometimes I wonder if that's patronising itself, not telling people about it, like I'm playing with weighted dice or, I don't know, it's kind of a dick move in itself that, like, erm. Yeah. I don't know. I don't want people to—. Hmm.'

'You want people to like you.'

Blush. Deep. 'I suppose.'

Silence.

'It's just not a very nice thing.'

Silence.

'The whole Cambridge thing.'

Silence.

'It's. It's hideous. Everything about it. It's minging. I hate it. I'd burn it down.'

'OK.'

'Sorry.'

Silence.

I cleared my throat.

'You went to Cambridge, and now you're living in London.'

'Yep. Yes.'

'And your sister?'

'God. No way. Hates it.'

'Where does she live?'

'Sheffield.'

'OK. Are you close?'

'We're twins.'

'Oh. Interesting.'

'Yeah.'

'Identical?'

'Fraternal.'

'Are you close?'

'Well, we're twins.'

'OK.'

'Would it help to see a photo?'

'Oh. No. No. Maybe at the end.'

'Sorry.'

Silence.

'We don't look alike but we do look related.'

'I don't need to see a photo. It's OK.'

Blush.

'Sorry.'

'What do you do for a living?'

'It's a bit—. Well, it's a bit here and there at the moment. But, yeah, I don't want to make a thing of it, like, I know I'm really lucky, so I, yeah.'

'Do you have a job?'

'Yeah. I did a bit of cash-in-hand for a couple of months when I first got here, at this deli in Belsize Park – posh grilled cheese, coffee. Lots of wide-brimmed hats, Gant . . . It was a bit of a mare.'

'You didn't enjoy it.'

'Well.' A little *ha*. 'People know when their coffee's burnt down here don't they! Don't they just. I didn't know you could burn coffee but, well, I mean I didn't know what a cafetière was until I left home . . . Yeah. Sorry. That's very judgy.'

'It sounds evocative.'

'Oh. Yes. I guess. Hmm.'

Silence.

'It's quite refreshing, I suppose. It is what it is.'

Silence.

'I love all that stuff.'

Silence.

'Coffee. Cheese.'

Silence.

'I sold some Manchego to Helena Bonham Carter once.'

'Oh.'

'Sorry.'

A pause. 'What do you do now?'

'Oh, yes. Yes. I'm an Office Administrator. No. Wait. Admin Assistant. I sell office equipment, me and a woman called Caroline. She's my boss strictly, but—. We—. Well, you know. I don't really believe in all that. She's—. I'd say she's maybe forty-three. Married, no kids. Ten deck a day, on the hour, couple of Costa croissants in the morning. Oh and Trebor, she loves those.'

'It's just the two of you.'

'Yes. She's kind. She's really kind. Yes. Yeah. I think she's quite interesting actually.'

'She takes your interest.'

'Well. I'm not *in it*-in it.'

'I'm not sure I follow.'

'Well, I shouldn't be doing a job like this, should I.' Blush.

Silence.

'I think—. I think I should be doing something socially relevant.' A tremor in my chest. 'I feel bad about it but I think this, this situation, this job situation – work, labour, all of it – like, I think a lot about what it means to be "employed", like what does it mean to be in that relation, like, for the psyche, and to be an "employee", I mean . . . I think about that a lot.'

A nod. 'Though it seems to me you get something from it, your job.'

'Hmm. Yes, in theory. I get tired though. It's all work.'

Silence.

'I mean, of course I totally understand it will come up organically when I "begin", when we "begin". I'm not being, like . . . keeping it from you or anything. Yes. Caroline's . . . well, I'm trying not to get too involved.'

Silence.

'She—. She's kind. And she was really good with the whole Michael thing.'

'Michael?'

'Oh. Sorry. Michael's my dad.'

'Oh. OK.'

'Sorry. Sorry, I should have explained. He's dead.'

'Oh.'

Silence.

'It's fine. Really. He wasn't around.'

Water bottle.

'Can you tell me a bit about your mother?'

'Oh yes. She's great. She's a real character. She takes a bit of work, but yeah. No, we're really close. Really close. She tells me a lot.'

'You're her confidante.'

'I guess so. Or was.'

'That can be challenging.'

'Hmm. I can see that. But it's not that bad really. We're not talking *Grey Gardens*.'

'We can talk about this. It's often better for mothers to submit their problems to their peers, not their children.'

'God, yes, I can imagine that. That's interesting. Yes. That's really interesting actually.'

30

A few moments here, seven, eight seconds, and maybe she blushed too, perhaps she blushed, though it was bloody hot in here and her corduroy was substantial.

'We have to finish.'

I got the Tube at Ladbroke Grove. Five girls got on too, sat in a row. They had rips in the knees of their jeans and jackets with padded panels and cinnamon swirls in cellophane bags, though none of them had all three. One had a pair of Adidas trackies, Adidas Originals. I wanted them.

*

The Adidas trackies came. Originals, off ASOS. Michael had loved all that, Tony said, seventies leisurewear, and this was a tough time, time for a good bit of leisure, this, though when they arrived too big I was relieved. It was nice to pack them back up and wash and dress and have a little reason for a trip to the post office.

I headed up Stroud Green Road, ASOS bag in hand, phone and card in pocket, but the post office was closed so I had to shove it in, shove it in the box and it got a bit stuck so I had to really shove it in and there were quite a few cars coming past and they saw that, the people in those cars and the people out here on the pavement out on Stroud Green Road, but I got it in in the end. I stepped away from the box, looked around. I walked on.

A few steps ahead I checked my phone to check I had it, slipped my hand back in my pocket. The phone was there but the card was gone. No, definitely gone. I walked a few more yards. I stopped. I looked behind me. There it was, on the ground. I thought about turning back to get it. I walked on.

I got in. I cancelled the card. Matthew had forgotten to turn the heating off so I turned the heating off. I got the Henry out and started on my bedroom. *Now then, Grace. Come on. Vroom vroom.* This was OK for a bit but then Henry overheated. I unplugged him, pressed the button that sucked up the cord. The cord disappeared. Then I stood back up and put my palm out to the wall, stood there for a long while. Henry belonged in the cupboard in the hall. Yes, Henry belonged in the cupboard in the hall.

I went to bed.

*

To pay for Rachel I started babysitting, afternoons with baby Sara who lived across the road. We'd walk down to the New River and sit in the gravel and throw rocks and on the way back we'd go see the Greek man for a babyccino. Sara liked to eat the chocolate off the foam then wobble until he replaced the chocolate. She liked chocolate a lot. On the last leg we'd watch the fast trains push through Hornsey station. We'd watch until Sara did a poo then we'd get the 91 home. Sara was perfectly herself, the pinnacle of self-care. Self-care was important, self-love too, and both of these increasingly popular, but Sara was Sara and selfhood was tiring, tiring and inefficient. We'd watch *Peppa Pig* in the late afternoon, waiting to feel realistic.

*

Matthew turned twenty-five. He made a group chat: *Quartercentenary Birthday Bash feat. Matthew.*

Jessica arrived first and drank a lot of punch. The place filled up and I watched Matthew watch her move around the room.

'Grace!' she said, sitting down next to me.

'Hi Jessica.'

'Three things,' she said, holding up three fingers.

'OK.'

'Three things you need to know.'

'Jessica! This is nice.'

'Did you know—. Babies. Babies . . .'

'Babies?'

'Learn to hold on before they learn to let go.'

'Oh! That's fun.'

'And we're free.'

'Oh yes, Jessica, the bars are wide enough to walk through.'

'That's Kafka! Matthew loves Kafka.'

'He does?'

'Drink?'

Five or six hours went by. Someone took Jessica home.

Then Siobhan from downstairs knocked, then Siobhan knocked harder, so I put the big light on: party over. It was cold and damp and the big light was on and Matthew needed to go to bed.

'Come on sweet angel,' I said.

'I love you,' said Matthew.

'I love you too,' I said.

Matthew's door was closed. He opened it and in his bed were two people we didn't know, naked and asleep with the duvet down at their waists.

'Oh shit. Sorry,' I said.

'Beautiful,' said Matthew, 'like swans.'

I nodded. They were half-enclosed. Bloated and warm. A relationship.

*

Matthew and I were solid, went back. Two years maybe. I met him soon after I moved down for good, friend of a friend. After I'd known him a month or so he borrowed his dad's car and took me to a nuclear bunker. It was date-adjacent. There was a pop-up canteen serving curry to a film crew. He bought us both a plate of chicken balti then we sat and had a smoke and a tea on a picnic bench, watching a rooster circle a hen. I'd started my period and didn't have a tampon. I was a vegetarian.

Three or four dates in he took us to the theatre. We were right up in the gods when Matthew dropped his bag of Minstrels. I looked again and he was slumped forward in his seat with a ferocious nosebleed. A big one, with big meaty clots. I stood up and shouted *NOSEBLEED* and it upset him. *I need you to treat me with dignity*, he said, and later we agreed on our lack of romantic connection. Matthew was too brooding and moody and amenable to fantasy; I was too much. Then we got drunk and I asked him to agree I was a superlative friend, though I should not be above the law, and we should and would never have sex. He agreed to agree.

He lived off the Kilburn High Road then. He had no wooden spoon, no chopping board, and the hob was covered in dust. It all felt very hi-res. He had a cold tap that never ran hot and a big black bed that sank like a coffin and his bedroom was always cold because he kept the window open, something to do with his psoriasis. Then his skin got well and he moved in with us and started swaying his dick around. I gave him my blessing, though after six months or so I threw his desert boots in the bin. They'd started to erode with the pursuit of something that was supposed to be fun.

*

Rachel was moving house, just a bit further down the Gardens, so we had a week off, our first break. Breaks are important, she said, and ought to be thought about.

The day her removal men came I dreamt her door was open. I flew my way in, down the hall and up the stairs. Might have bumped into her at any point. How strange that would have been. How unacceptable. They were doing some work up there so there were dust sheets over her dark waxed floorboards and little paintwork tasters on the walls – pelt, cabbage white, Oxford stone – and scraps of bubble wrap and cardboard and I was on the verge of calling her name, outing myself, but I couldn't be sure she was there. Then she came out of the bathroom. She looked at me strong in the face with the face of Rebecca I think, yes, and then straight down at the ground.

That's what she did when our time was up. I'd get up to go get my coat from the coat stand and look back at her and say thank you, have a nice evening. She'd look at me and then at the ground, a true professional.

*

We started back up the next week. The new consulting room door was stiff and didn't click. I pushed it. I shoved it. I folded my coat in two but the coat stand had gone so I went to rest it on my bag, on the floor.

'There's a hook,' she said.

I turned to the door, thinking she meant there was a hook to keep the door shut with, then I saw there was a hook on the back of the door.

I told her I felt I'd been here before. I'd flown here. I'd been here in my head. I told her it was a coincidence.

'I don't deal in coincidences,' she said.

35

Silence.

'Sorry. Yes. Sorry. I mean, I don't either.'

Silence.

'I think I was being ironic there, like, "ooh, what a coincidence!" Where it's actually not a coincidence. That's really why I wanted to, well—. Well. That's what I meant to say.' Blush.

Silence.

'Sorry.'

Silence.

'Can I use the couch?'

'Go ahead,' she said, and I got on the couch.

We listened to my stomach whining for a bit. I should have been Ophelia in the river now, floating up here on the couch, but this always happened, these high-pitched lengthy whines. Always, especially with apples. I knew that but I loved them and I'd been giddy and gone mad, picked up a Braeburn from the man on the corner while I tried not to be so eager arriving because I wasn't eager. I was relaxed. I just wanted my full fifty minutes pound-a-minute Rachel. I was awake.

I had a routine now. I'd get there ten minutes early then loiter by the man on the corner, eye a bunch of herbs or an avo or a pomegranate, sometimes pop into Tesco Express. Then I'd go up and round the corner and I'd slow-walk the Gardens, watch the second hand just nudge thirty seconds past the hour, then I'd knock.

I tried to abide with the apple and Rachel, tried not to distract her with some new bit of speech but well.

'Do you find things move a bit, well, quicker, with the couch?'

Silence.

'God . . . Sorry. I don't mean to be mercenary.'

'This work takes time.'

'Yes. Yes. Sorry. I understand. Sorry.'

'We're bound by your unconscious, and the unconscious, each unconscious, has its own dimensions. It doesn't know time as something to fill or waste or economise.'

Fill, waste, economise, I sang in my head on the Tube. *Fill, waste, economise.*

*

A month in and I was still dry-eyed. I'd lie silent, rotating some explanations, my rings from finger to thumb. *Maybe we don't have a therapeutic alliance. Maybe you're just thinking too much about how to be a different person. That's not the point, is it? Maybe you're trying too hard to remember, against the tide. That's not the point, is it?*

'I'm not sure I'm doing this right.'

'Why do you think that?'

'I thought I might have broken down by now.'

'Do you want to break down?'

'No. I wonder quite a bit though, I often wonder like, when that happens, like, how it works in time. Is there a general time frame?'

Silence.

'I guess . . . Yeah, I guess I find it really interesting, like, how the analyst goes about getting a patient cared about, contained I think is the right word here? Though, yeah, I know that concept's kind of suffered with overuse. And, when I say "patient", I mean . . .'

Silence.

'I've heard some people use the word "client", but . . .'

'Person?'

'Of course. Of course.'

Silence.

'Of course. I feel a bit weird asking and I totally understand if you're not allowed to say. I guess I just wanted to be honest because I have been wondering quite a bit, like, roughly when people start to break. I know there'll be a lot of me I can't see, hints of fracture, fractures, like that's why I'm here of course. I'd just—. I'd like to be prepared.'

Silence.

'Sorry. Sorry.'

'Are you afraid of breaking down?'

'No.'

Silence.

'I guess I'm not sure what that means, you know, "nervous breakdown". I just think of Almódovar.'

Silence.

'You know? *Women on the Verge*—. Sorry.'

Silence.

'Sometimes I'm under the Westway and I think a car will fly over the barrier, off the edge, hover in the air, Ford Fiesta, I think, yeah, a Ford Fiesta. Crush me to death, and I do sort of will that sometimes.'

Silence.

'This death drive stuff is common, I know. I don't take my Westway episodes too seriously.' Boots. Shins. Thoughts of Carmen's legs in her tights, three-quarter-sleeve blazer in red, Carmen's red nails chopping tomatoes sharp knife, necking gazpacho out the blender red kimono. 'That's not a coded message.'

'Yes. Thoughts of obliteration are not uncommon.'

'Yeah, definitely.'

Silence.

'Ugh.'

Silence.

'Sorry. I hate being like this.'

'Like this.'

'Yeah, like, "learned". So try-y.'

'Try-y?'

'Yeah. Like, conscientious.'

Silence.

'I hate the conscientious.'

'You hate the conscientious.'

'I *despise* them.'

'You despise them?'

'I *despise* them.'

*

Six weeks in I decided to leave. It wasn't for me. I just needed to leave. Leave analysis, leave London. I would move somewhere reasonable, bury my face in the flanks of a greyhound and walk the Otley Road in Mum's Sprayway fleece, walk and walk until I found myself unabridged. Rachel was expensive.

*

I made some arrangements, told a few people. Michelle first. We went for dinner in Angel and she went wild, had the prawns then complained there weren't enough for the money. She explained it all in numbers and asked for a partial refund. I wouldn't have treated myself to such an extravagant disappointment, but Michelle was a precise and forthcoming person. She was my friend.

I waited until we were heading out to tell her. 'I'm leaving,' I said and she was silent, stroking her mouth with her left hand, Citymapping with the other.

'I might have the menopause.' Pause. 'I'm rethinking everything.'

'What? What is this trash?' She put her phone in her pocket, grabbed my forearms. 'This is your home.'

'I know!' I said. 'I know, but it's time I think. I'm leaving.'

'There's nowhere to go,' she said, extending her arm for the bus, then she got on the back and leant out with her hand on the pole, Gene Kelly lamp post lean. *Mwah.*

I put my hands to my chest, palms heart centre, then tilted forward with the right leg bent, slow-mo, right arm flourish, big extension, fluttery fingers, chest pulled, little skip.

'LOVE YOU!' she called.

'LOVE YOU!' Air kissed my public, air kiss air kiss air kiss, alternate hands.

'Byeeeeeeeee!'

'Bye.'

I told Charlie. They wore their hoody with the super-sized picture of Rose and Jack from *Titanic*. We sat by an open window on the second floor of the Southbank Centre, sat with our yellow-stickered salads from M&S Waterloo. Refrigerated, calculated. Disgusting. The London Eye was looming out behind Charlie's head. The sky was thick and morbid.

Charlie was quiet, a thing they reserved for special occasions.

'Speak!' I said, peeling at my face with the flesh of my fingertips, makeupless and tenuous and desiccated.

'Darling,' said Charlie. 'I love your work but you're full of shit.'

I told Abi.

I don't have any money. I find men difficult. London is difficult. Women are also difficult

Well I forgive them.

The ticks went blue though she didn't reply. It was a Tuesday. She was at work.

When I told Matthew he winced. He winced the way he winced at Adam's jumpers. Adam had these four cream jumpers with different cables and cuts and on Saturdays he did a hot wash and hung them out to dry on the curtain pole.

I told Matthew I didn't like his wince and he denied the wince, then later that night he revived the group chat, the same one he'd made for his quarter-centenary, and arranged me some leaving drinks, something like that, something we could all be drunk at.

*

Jessica was first at the leaving drinks. Jessica was the love of Matthew's life now. They were *together* now, Jessica and Matthew. He was still trying to keep her to himself a bit but she was able just about to be Jessica, just coming into herself, in it but not wholly of it. The more I knew of her she was impeccable. Impeccable Jessica. She drained me of my sarcasm, I hoped. That's what I wanted for her, for me, for us when she was here. She looked like Holly Willoughby and that scared the shit out of me actually because I loved it. I fucking loved it. So Jessica was glam and she was engaged and she was engaging without being needy, would just talk to people at parties, small talk, because that was a nice thing to do. She didn't have that terrible drive to take captives, be memorable, favourable, she could be beautiful and glamorous and she didn't give a shit, actually, she'd retouch her forehead or her chin and she didn't give a shit and it was a shame she couldn't be more of herself, what with Matthew here, with

41

me here grasping for the mic, flapping. She had a deep ability to talk and depths she'd withhold quite happily, and happily she'd get high or else drunk. She sank gin like a trooper. She was great at getting drunk.

We had a few gins and soon I was full of it, awful: blah, blah, blah; me, me, me; let's go deep. But somehow I stopped myself and I went to the toilet and I wrote it down, right there in my mini fawn Moleskine I kept for excursions – *chill the fuck out*, and, *sometimes you are wrong!* Then I went to the bar and bought another gin for Jessica. I put her drink down in front of her and she looked up at me with a lovely warm *Grace* and I put my palms in the air and I hunched my shoulders and I cocked my head, a Sim from *The Sims* with eight orange bars. Dark orange, but not yet red.

At last orders Michelle went for a pre-leaving wee and a minute or so later I followed. I saw her matte navy raincoat poking out of one of the cubicles and went into mine in silence, weed and wiped and flushed, took a bit of oil from my brow, stuck a bit of tissue down my sleeve.

'Grace?'
'Hi Michelle.'
She flushed.
I came out.
Michelle came out.
I held her coat.
She saw to her hands.

Another girl was trying herself on in the mirror, raising and lowering her cheeks, wiping errant mascara from the tips of her eyelids. Michelle smiled at her and she smiled too so it wasn't trying on anymore, just a hi, hi between two people, and then it was a bit glitchy the way it gets when the mask pops off for a sec and it's safe because the right people are looking but then the mask's off, fourth wall, bit icky retrieving the flow. She smiled, this girl, lowered her eyes. I smiled. She turned towards the paper dispenser. I looked at the coat. We walked outside.

Abi was there, eating a bag of cool Doritos. She saw us and put them away.

'Sharing's caring,' said Michelle.

'Give the woman what she wants,' said Abi, taking them back out.

'Just a handful,' said Michelle.

We walked to the Tube.

'Oops,' said Michelle, flapping the empty packet in the breeze. 'She's eaten them all. I've eaten them all.'

'YES Michelle!' said Abi.

I clapped.

*

I took the hangover shopping, to Oxford Street. I got the bus. I felt a new-found energy watching those men in white coats swinging carcasses down the Seven Sisters Road. *We're all here trading flesh*, I wrote in my phone. *Be intentional. Be strategic.* Clickbait thinking though mine, vapid yes but energetic. I'll bookmark that, I thought, but then I saw a pug in a duck-egg plastic mac with ducks on it and I forgot. I went to Uniqlo. I bought some damson cocoon pants and a bottle-green baggy T-shirt. In the queue I caught my reflection in the Perspex-lined posters behind the till, giant flawless people with sloping shoulders making shapes, foreshortened. *We're good, Grace. We're good.*

My bladder started to catastrophise. Toilet. Coffee. 'Can I get a big long black, please? Great. Thanks.' I sat with my

£3.40 long black that wasn't very long and far too strong, treacly, but I didn't back down and dilute it. *Drugs! Fun!* The table legs were skinny copper pipes in an Airbnb curve and the tabletops were chipboard coated in varnish and the menus had the same texture for their background, a photograph of that texture, or maybe the photo that had inspired it, and there were two-day-old pastries under plastic at the till and grey mesh roller blinds, a mesh to match our Nikes. We were wearing Nikes. Everything was a gist, an invitation. I felt invited.

I finished my coffee and I did not walk my bags back up and I did not get my money back because I was a Londoner. I had a psychoanalyst. I was Diane Keaton.

I messaged Holly.
Drink?
Come to my office?

I went to 'Holly's' office in Marylebone. Holly worked in Marylebone and was a Senior Product Strategist. Holly was Adam's big sister.

'She'll be back soon,' said Beth the PA as I sat on the chair by the window. Holly's handbag was there, under her desk, so she must have just nipped to the loo. There was a black tray of Tenderstem broccoli poking out of her handbag, and up on the desk a stack of books and an apple tart. Beth was wearing a tweed jumpsuit and glasses with tangerine stems. She had a pair of moccasins on her feet. On her right foot she had a trainer sock.

'I like your tweed jumpsuit.'

'The tart's been there for like twenty minutes. We don't have tart every day.'

I liked her shoes too, and the sock. Determined.

A woman in a wrap dress and bolero cardigan and mothering shoulders came in then, began to use the photocopier. She stood while the rollers in the machine made their empty little gasps, putting her in speech marks.

'So slow,' said Beth.

The woman nodded.

'It's judging your print job,' I said.

Beth turned back to her computer, control-alt-delete, and the woman redid the tie on her dress and I unzipped the front pocket of my bag, checked my essentials.

Holly came back in with a laptop tucked under her arm.

'Hi!'

'Hi!'

We went to the place across the way and she bought a glass of wine and for me a black filter. I was braless in Marylebone and she noticed. She looked at me, her eyebrows parting, a smooth space opening out in the centre of her forehead. She was a thirty-six-year-old woman with a tray of Tenderstem in her handbag.

She looked at me.

'Are you OK?'

*

Rachel.

'Holly's very—. Well. She's very intense, the way she looks. Aggressive, almost.'

'She was looking intently.'

'Kind of. I'd say seeing actually. Seeing.'

'What do you think she was seeing?'

'Herself.'

45

Silence.

'Yeah. Herself, I think. Herself in me.'

Silence.

'Like, projection.'

'It made you uncomfortable, her seeing you.'

'I don't know. I find all this "being seen" stuff—. Well, I think it's a bit—. Isn't it a bit clichéd?'

'Clichés have a basis in truth.'

'Maybe. Well. Yes. Of course. Maybe.'

Silence.

'I don't think she saw "me".'

Silence.

'I mean—. I'm not disagreeing conceptually here, at the conceptual level.'

Silence.

'I mean—.'

Silence.

'What is there to see?'

*

Holly wanted a follow-up. A 'follow up', that's what she called it. I waited for her outside Russell Square, standing with the *Standard*s as they washed up on the pavement – drizzly, mizzly, but not too cold and perfect for Bloomsbury – then there she was: olive suede coat, patent winkle pickers, gentleman's umbrella to mark her advance. Everywhere was rammed and we wanted a table so she led us down Holborn to the Shakespeare's Head, me fiddling in my pocket for my ID for the bouncer.

'OK?' I said, flashing it.

Eyebrow raise. Nod.

*

We sat on bar stools, bar-height table, among a lot of nice tourist faces that were yet to find their angles plus young people who'd just finished work, all pink with the night and the vinegar. Puffy faces. Owl glasses. Suits, cheeks and owl glasses. I'd pep-talked myself while waiting out there for her with those *Standards*: *Grace, mate, try not to seem like a person falling off her own radar.*

I hunched, keeping my centre of gravity as low as I could, feet curled round the bars. I leant forward with my chin in the heel of my hands.

'I think—. Well, I think I'm going to stay. I'm staying, Hol. I'm staying. But I'm going to quit my job,' I said once she'd ordered us a bottle on the app. She was pulling her arm from her coat.

'Right,' she said, stopping for a moment, mid-movement, before pulling her stool in and draping the coat round the back.

'It's messy, I know, but, yeah.'

'Right. OK.' She looked at me with a frown, then over her shoulder at a man with a heaving tray, then at the Wetherspoon app on her phone.

'Maybe I should go and order at the bar, Hol?'

'No, it went through.'

A man came by with the bottle.

'Wine o'clock!'

We had our wine then she went to the bar to get us some water and a packet of salt and vinegar, didn't want to risk the app this time. She came back over and spread the packet out into a shiny oily foil platter and pushed it towards me but I declined, so she ate the crisps, wiping her fingers not licking, wiping them on a napkin she'd picked up from the bar. I assured her this wasn't melancholic self-destruction,

47

no, and the era for abjection was gone, we were life-building now, Holly. Lots of self-care. She wouldn't have to worry. *It's spiritual, Hol, I promise.* Though once the wine kicked in I couldn't seem to stop myself from using her full name: Holly Barrett, Holly Barrett. Holly Barrett. Holly Barrett.

*

Dream. I fly to Rachel's again. On the stairs I meet a woman in a bruised cotton hoody reigniting a spliff. Her lighter splutters. I lend her mine. I walk to the top of the stairs, across the landing and into the anteroom. There are more women. It's a doctor's waiting room now: copies of *People's Friend* strewn about, plastic dogs for the children. Half an hour passes then we all go through, into the *Consulting Room.* It says that on the door, this flashy gold plaque. It's massive in there, with sprung floors and big mirrors, a studio. We all fall down and spread out, fingertips touching. Starfishes.

*

I quit the job.

Caroline was cool about it; she worked from home most days anyway now, so our thing, whatever we were, I to her and she to me – I mean, really it was nothing. I'd go in and her Trebor mints would be sat there, paper spirals of varying lengths, there against her wrist rest. I'd tuck them in so the top one stayed fresh then I'd mute the phones and sit on her work-assessed chair with one of Adam's mum's second-hand *New Yorkers*, my legs dangling a touch, Caroline's curve in my spine. I kept the light natural, resting the mag between the keyboard and the riser, a nice neat arm's length away. There were contraband PDFs of Freud from time to time, though those I printed off and took home, reserved for the propelling pencil. When the phones started flashing I'd shut it all down, reload the strip lights, don her headset and there I'd be, taking the calls, six rings in. Six rings in because we were in demand; we were the Association for Office Stationers. But that was it. That was the peak. It was over now.

I told her and she went out for a fag and a text, paced around a bit on the forecourt. Then she came back in and put the job ad up, then and there, reading aloud the card details to the recruiters. It was perfect. I was so fantastically replaceable. I kind of wanted the job back. But she'd just spent £300 or something so I swapped my Clarks for my Airs and opened a new Word doc. *Speculations.doc.*

I thought first of all I'd be a primary school teacher, but then no, all those little Saras blowing my tiny mind, wouldn't survive it. Maybe I was an intellectual, then, maybe I should be an academic. Oh. No. Ugh. No way. I hated academics. Everything had to be filtered through our big heaving leaking sexy bodies and no one was allowed to say it. Everyone just said 'sort of' and 'it seems to me'. All those blue worker jackets and the brogue DMs and stuff, I bloody loved it, all of it, and I burned with envy and it broke my heart. So, no. No. Maybe I could be an art-adjacent intern . . . Erm, no. Back*space*. Or maybe some low-level jeans-and-Converse type thing, charity comms, good for the soul, good for people, citizen-ish, or a nurse, or, or a social worker. Oh god. No. No way. I used to think I'd be a psychoanalyst, but that would mean holding my tongue.

I closed my Word document.

I didn't want a career. I didn't want to transact. I didn't want to master a vocabulary. I wanted mystical communion.

*

49

'You quit your job.'

'I hate my job. I hate work. I hate it. I hate all of it, for all of us, like, everybody, like, I don't believe in it and I don't want to have to . . . I don't want anyone to have to work. Ever.'

Silence.

'And I *can* quit.'

Silence.

'Well.'

Silence.

'I mean, I can go a few weeks.'

Silence.

'I should say, I mean, I will get another job by the way.'

Silence.

'I don't want you to worry.'

'You worry about me.'

'I still have a bit of money, so. Yeah. I'm not going to ghost you. And I'll save a bit when we have the Easter break, so.'

Silence.

'Sorry, I should say I know some people do actually like their work and this is all a bit gross and Oxbridge of me this, toys out the pram, and I know—. I have a lot of cultural capital now and I can't disown that, no, but, yeah, and I'm not a communist. I get it. I get how things work. I just—. I don't know.'

Silence.

'Sometimes I think you just need to fall on your face.'

'To fail.'

'*Yes.* I want to fail. This meaning of "failure", like how it's been appropriated to make us "succeed", you know like that job-interview-boilerplate-know-thyself-but-just-enough . . .'

Silence.

My heart was going now. Sweat on the brow.

'Are you afraid of failure?'

50

'No. No, definitely not. No. I was talking about the system, actually.'

Silence. A nod, I think, some movement in the shadow.

'I wonder if you're afraid of success. I—.'

'No.'

Silence.

'What would it matter either way?'

I preferred her old house. She'd hung some Hockney iPad trees there. I liked to see the coats on a stand and her Hockney iPad trees. Now there was just this cobalt cloud and a weeping woman and her mastery.

Silence.

'Sorry. I don't know where that came from. I—.'

This 'I' was a tired child's. A bottom-lipped one, the kind that staggers into more of the same, I begets I. I, I, I. I should have kept my mouth shut but my hubris kept me talking and now she could hear it, she could hear it on me, she could smell it on me.

'I'm so—. I'm so—. Fuck. *Fuck.* Shit.'

Silence.

'So—.' Sob.

Silence, I thought, but then a box of Kleenex appeared by my side.

A minute passed. Probably less.

'Thanks.'

Mansize.

Phlegm, but I didn't expose her to a full blow. I folded one over and over, felt the nice firm wad in my palm and popped it up my sleeve.

'God. Sorry. This is so embarrassing.'

Silence.

More silence.

'I'm not embarrassed.'

I brought my palms up to my ribcage, diaphragm, cradled my fingers. Silent tears now. Strays.

'We have to finish.'

I stood up slowly and walked to the door for my coat. She gave me her bill and this was the Easter break, now, this was it for the next few weeks. I nodded.

'Can I just use the loo?'

'Of course. The light's broken, but there's a candle in there.'

I walked down the landing and there through the open door was the toilet. A Waverley toilet with a proper chain, pine seat. Aglow.

I pulled down the seat and put my head in my hands. Then I picked up the nice cold Neal's Yard bottle from the sink, wet with condensation, Geranium & Orange, rolled the bottle across my forehead, dispensed a little blob. Another. I rubbed it in and sniffed. I put my head back in my hands.

APRIL 2015

I didn't tell Mum I was coming, knew she'd like the rom-com surprise, but I could tell from right up the top of the cobbles that no one was home, hadn't been for a while. Maybe she'd forgotten what I'd said at the funeral, I thought, then no, no, she never forgot a promise; that was me.

There was a note on the door, *NOT THIS WEEK STEVE! XXX*, and I could smell the Iams through the flap. Always more pungent, somehow, when left to someone else to dole out, or maybe it was just the dead air.

Outhouse key. *Oof.*

'*Mabel*! Fucking *stinks* babe.'

I heard her stir, dumped my stuff. Mum hadn't left any instructions on the side for Sue or Hannah or Sally Bray so I went down to the cellar and yes, she'd just tipped the big bag on its side, carvery style.

'Miaow.'

I looked up. Two reflective circles.

'Hi Mabel.'

I came back up. She'd really had a field day, left big white moulty clumps of herself all over the carpet. It looked kind of nice if you squinted, kind of marbled, but that and the

Hobnob crumbs and the L&Bs crowding out their ashtrays and the stale old echoes of primetime canned laughter, it was all a bit much. I opened the back door, pulled my sleeves up and got Mum's Marigolds out. My pores went mad. I took them off.

I did the fridge first, rinsing it of mould-licked packets of low-fat no-fat cheese, old teabags in little tumblers she'd saved for a second dip, half-finished bottles of strawberry Ribena gone cloudy. I swept the kitchen, ran the Hoover round a bit, opened some windows. Then I boiled a kettle, standing for a second and eyeing the fridge door while the tannins crept in a bit – liked it good and strong. *A precious few have a daughter like you; I'm not over the hill, I'm on the back nine; I'm so clever, I don't understand a word of what I'm saying.*

I locked up as she liked us to and took the tea up to Mum's room, got her old photo box out from under her bed, the one with the pastel magnolias on it. Emotional slot machine. I had a flick through found that one of Mum in her late twenties, sun-kissed in a stripy little jumpsuit, perm pushed back with Wayfarers, two flaxen tots at her feet. Another, one of me at nine or ten or eleven with pappish little flabs of tit, fattened on Nana puddings, sweating in a rubber ring on the Gower. Another, Rebecca on a Southport donkey from behind. And the school ones, greying shirts with cockeyed collars, pimples pimples pimples clear.

There were none of Michael, but she had some stuff we'd made for him when we were tiny: coloured-in mermaid me with Dad as Poseidon (sugar paper, Crayola); collage of dolphins with me and Rebecca and Dad riding the dolphins (card, PVA, glitter, papier-mâché). Cute, consistent with the nautical theme, nice sense of composition and mood, I thought, but they'd made their way back to Mum's so it seemed he hadn't been taken. He'd been around a bit at the start, Mum said, then she heard he was out in Ireland, labouring, good at it, brick shithouse back in the day, before he wound up back in Harehills with Alison, and we did once go down there for Micro Chips, Micro Chips and *tonight Matthew I'm going to be*. I think. But then the crash came and that's when things went bad. That's when he went yellow.

I shoved this all away bar the photo of Mum and sat up on the bed, waited for the feeling. Nope. To her wardrobe. It was always meticulous in there and sometimes that felt like a tragedy. Sniffed the lavender Ariel. Nope, still a no. I gave up, started working through the shoulder pads and dangly bits of sleeve, culottes, waist belts, looking for the jumpsuit. She'd bought several sets of clear plastic coat hangers, the sort that click against one another and have clips to push down over trousers to secure the fabric, so it felt like one of those nineties boutiques with the white tiled floors and the free-form silver rails, or perhaps that was just any clothes shop ever, yes, maybe that was timeless. I found it, took it, and from her nail drawer I nicked some berry Barry M and a tube of liquid eyeliner. I had hairs on my legs half an inch long and my skin was coarse and angry but I felt I'd be a girl, so I ran a bath, deloused, blast of Elnett, headed out.

It was chilly now the night had drawn in so I brought along my coat and my rucksack to stash it in and a middling banana and a bottle of vodka-laced strawberry Ribena.

I couldn't bring myself to wait at the bus station. The smell of the cooling concrete gave me the creeps, and the sausage and pastry and the pigeons, and the closed-up cash machines, and the sweating leather from Club Energy, wafting across the road. Plus there'd be a busload dressed for town this time of

56

night. They wouldn't be people I knew, to be fair. Our year stayed in the Otley pubs now, had started to colonise tables and nooks. Peacefully, except maybe at the Junction. I hadn't dared look in there. Anyway there was an ecosystem; you could find who you wanted to find at Spoons or the Crown or the Bull or the Manor. Fleece, Woolpack, Black Horse. Old Cock if you wanted it fancy. It all worked out and it worked out cheaper with an Otley surname, and me and Rebecca, we had one, though maybe I'd got that wrong, maybe it really was just £1.25 for half a mild.

Some of our year were managing these pubs now, serving at least. Tiring work, and Otley's cosy, charms you when you're ready to settle, Leeds gets long, though the younger ones, the kid sisters and such, they'd still be at it on the regular, yes, I should have thought, yes. Out-out from the off, some of them, straight to Leeds with the big guns and the lashes. Or there was the Headingley semi – Skyrack, Box, Oak. Or there was a Headers-turns-into-Leeds yeah come on lads, out-out, quid each for a taxi to the club, aka messy.

I didn't know any of these new ones but they had the genes of the people I did. Couple of seconds and you clocked it, all in a nose or a jawline, and that made me feel a bit sick. Gen Z they'd started calling them so they were different, raised with the Internet from scratch where we'd known Eden. But six, seven years' difference was nothing, not really, and I knew that. And yes I knew it mattered that I cared to point it out (Rachel). I didn't do lashes now, had learnt not to want to, but I was criminally shy still and in need of transportation, so we were just the same, the same, and I wasn't standing there at that bus station for love nor money, not now, not now I was paying Rachel to cry in her Waverley loo, so I waited for the bus up Leeds Road.

It was always deserted, this stop.

I chugged my Ribena, holding my seal, praying I hadn't missed it – on the hour every hour and it was still ten to, but. I kept my gaze on the garage opposite, equally deserted, pondering the dismantled coconut shy shoved between the counter and the window. When I saw Jackie pull in to fill up I shoved my Oyster holder down my pants and turned around, faced that spooky white house. Cannabis factory, that, once, and a woman was murdered here too, just up from here, Grandad said 1908. A grocer in his trap had found her body in a field. There were tiny little crosses still etched into the wall.

The bus came. I got on and sat downstairs, in front of two young boys.

'Suzanne Proctor.'

'Urgh. No way. Butters. Three.'

'She's not that bad. Six.'

'Nah. Every class she says what's the difference between a simile and a metaphor she is SO annoying.'

'That's so easy.'

'Simile similar, metaphor is.'

I arrived at Oceana at eleven. PRYZM, not Oceana, PRYZM now, though nobody cared for the change. There was a little queue getting in and a fair few people there already, eligible people with phone numbers, but the space wasn't dark enough yet, just that booze-inducing, queasy light they always put out at the beginning and the end. I made my way to the edge of the floor and stood with my coat in my rucksack at my feet, big between my legs. That was a problem but the cloakroom was a racket.

Some minutes passed and a couple of boys came into my peripheral, somewhere to my right, then behind me, then in front, the way things are in a crowd. I didn't see them coming and I didn't feel in need of it now, not with this weight between my legs. I was actually just a semi-sober connoisseur. I was actually just trying out my mother's eighties jumpsuit.

One of them roped me in, Joe, and he introduced his friend Tom and I gave them both some light entertainment, had a few jelly shots from the woman with the tray, tried to give her eye contact, tried to give her the wink and I think maybe I got one but then I had to know about it, feel that ripple, then I had to buy more. I let the EDM loosen me up. Tom had a Burberry shirt, short sleeves, and a clean-on pair of Reeboks, white. Joe had a cream beanie hat with a milk-bottle nipple up top. I was after some skin-to-skin and I thought they were maybe students. That was what I wanted, a southern student, Oxbridge dropout, North London would have been the jackpot – more masochistic for me, more confusing. But then I remembered this was PRYZM. And probably not even term time. Anyway, Tom had this bouffant hair I found charming, well waxed, and his naked sockless ankles had a femme feel I could go with and Joe made way.

'Smokes?' Tom asked with his fingers.

Nod.

We went out.

He was Bulgarian he said, half-Bulgarian, and he'd served and I asked where and he shook his head, Afghan he said, sic, but now he worked at Bella Italia. I lied and said I was twenty-seven. Then his hand was on my leg. The shots must have been duds though because now I was fucking cold and I wanted my banana and I wanted to go home.

That was easy enough. He said, 'I don't meet many like you, you're so—', and I said go on and he said confident he guessed. 'Yeah, confident.' 'Well I live in London,' I said.

His eyes glazed over. He said he was off for a leak. I peeled my bruised banana and waited for my Uber.

Rashid liked working for Uber. No, nobody had given birth in the Uber. Yes, people were often sick. He turned up the Modjo.

*

I woke up at six, raring, took the duvet down and tried to slam this pointless hangover with oats but oats there were none, so: Cinnamon Grahams. Fistfuls. I took the box through to the lounge and they were heaven.

Mum thought porridge was weird, especially my stuff, pan on the hob, Taste the Difference chunky at the start of the month. If you were taking your time you might as well do a butty she said. Egg, bacon, egg and bacon, sausage, sausage and egg or, for lunch, spicy chicken nuggets and Bisto in a barm with the bottom gone spongy with the gravy. Knife and fork for those. She'd still tried to make them for me when I first left home, at Christmas or if I popped back in the holidays, though I sofa-surfed down south pretty well, stayed with Adam's mum properly in the end, got myself a zero-hours at Nando's Finsbury Park. I'd tell her I was a veggie but it didn't really work.

I'm a vegetarian Mum.

Right. Right. Still? Do you eat the meat part, the Quorn?

No Mum.

We'd do this exchange then she'd go into town for a mooch and end up back with a big shop. *Eggs, Bunny! Happy yellow eggs for my big fat veggie!* She'd place three packs of twelve eggs on the worktop, side by side, and I'd pick them back up and stack them for efficiency and she'd beam like a toddler presenting on the potty.

60

I've got these nice yellow ones, top of the range.

Mum.

You'll eat these.

What? Thirty-six?

She'd go sit with the Sky Plus and the *Radio Times* then, and I'd put the eggs at the back of the shelf and leave them be. She'd forget about them in the week. Then on the weekends she'd come back in with a new big shop and pull them out again and go to town, looking up ways to use them up on the iPad.

Look Bun! Eggy bread! Here, or shoulders, got your classic shoulders there.

Soldiers?

Yes, love. Ooh look! Egg and gammon Quorn.

She'd start on something for me, put something on but the pan would get too hot or Mabel would distract her or we'd run out of sauce and she'd fuck it. This woman knew how to feed people. She fed a school a day. No, twice a day, three times, breakfast club she did too. With me she lost her nerve.

I had my Grahams, bathed, napped, watched back-to-back *Come Dine with Me* with a tray of ranch-dressed wedges, then I went up the road for a pot of sweetcorn soup and some noodles from Wok Away. *Obscene*, I thought for a minute, but only a minute, eating my noodles with a knife and fork, refusing to give in and ask Sunny for chopsticks because, well, *he didn't give you chopsticks Grace so don't be a dick*. I didn't ask about Deliveroo, if Deliveroo was taking off here, or was it here yet. *No of course it's not here yet you tool*. I sat on the little plastic chair in the window, wolfed my way through, though my stomach was beyond me by this time, all tight and truculent. *Just be* Otley *Grace, this is your home, don't pretend you don't know how*. That's how the thoughts ran, though this little moment wasn't Otley at all, this sexy fluorescent vignette. Hopper, this, almost a cliché. I downed my soup, still too hot, held on to my heartburn and made my way back to the house, loitering a bit this time, edging myself towards the bus station. No. Still a no.

I put the TV back on, found some old *Hairy Bikers* and watched them eat, now – oil, groin and meat in Transylvania – but eventually the noodles caught me out and I felt ill. The credits rolled and I pressed pause, breathing through that watery pre-vom in the mouth, rolled my head back. One of the bikers, the small one, he was intolerable. Si I liked.
    'Miaow.'
    'Hi Mabel.'
    Why are you here?
    'Shut up.'

*

Another day passed. Mum was still gone and I didn't want to tell her I was here. She'd tell Sue or Hannah or Sally Bray and I couldn't handle it. There could be a few days before she got back, it could be tomorrow, though I knew at heart it would be Friday or Sat; she always did her weeks off as weeks.

I got into a routine. Half-hearted morning sessions on her bike machine then when I was properly pumped I dared some hoodied visits to big Sains, big bug sunglasses for the street. Then I'd walk some circuits, perimeters, take some nice glam nature wees, squatting and spraying great volumes of myself in this place like it was my territory. Then I'd sit in Mum's bed listening to the bypass – nodding off from time to time, masturbating inefficiently. Dreaming.

Dream. A Saturday morning at home – here, Otley, Mum's. The three of us are hanging around in an air of unrelaxation. Me, Mum and Rebecca. I'm hot with the too-hot heating, pink-cheeked, wrapped in my Dorothy Perkins leopard-print dressing gown. The door goes and it's Sarah, Sarah the American. *Bloody hell! It's only Sarah the American! Mum! Rebecca! Look who it isn't!* Hi we all say. She's older now. She wears this shirt and sports shorts with the thighs, tanned and marked and downy and butch and she asks me to go upstairs. She asks me to go upstairs with her, so I do, and as we walk she takes my arm and says she has something to tell me. No, I say with my hand on her mouth then my hands on my ears and I sit on the ground. I curl into a ball. I fall asleep.

Dream. I'm in a warehouse, me and the girls I went to school with. We're wearing beige bodysuits with crystals, that BHS flesh and the faux-Swarovski. Tit tape, gauze, fingers. There are all ten of us, showgirls, suspended, flying on trapezes, crawling on the ceiling.

Dream. We're driving in Mum's Ford Fiesta, it's 1995, Mum's at the wheel. It's icy and I'm shouting to be careful but it's too late. We slam into black amorphous space, just like Grand Theft Auto. I curl, again, into a ball, and I spin.

*

Mum was in Corfu with Jackie, darling! I'd given in and sent her a WhatsApp, selfie with Mabel from the chair in her window.
  Oh my GOD! Bunny!
  Haha surprise!

Can't believe it!
I'll come get you what airport
Bunny!
Yes! What airport
Mabel's litter tray REBECCA room
Thanks
If there's a pong I use nappy sack straight outside black bin
and pouch a day half morning half teatime, five-ish she likes I
don't keep her in now no need!
Thanks what airport?
Manchester!
[Thumbs up, palest skin emoji] Get off the plane get a train
to Leeds I'll come get you
Yay!

*

I went for a final walk before I got her, one last lap in the blue Sprayway fleece, my fave, the one she took to work sometimes so it smelt of fine white pepper, the powder they weighed out from those industrial plastic pots. It was raining heavily and oddly humid and when I was done the fleece was steaming, distinctly parsnip now. That smell. I don't know. I don't know what it did to me but I had to stop and crouch down, there opposite Stephen Smith's Garden Centre, touch the floor with both palms, watch the rain melt into the tarmac for a minute. I got in, had a bath, ran a bit of serum through my hair, did my face. I went to get her.

She was on the concourse, sat in a cordoned-off bit of Subway, rolling a cookie into little balls with her left hand and scrolling with her right. I walked up behind her new peroxide head and hovered for a second. It looked good, suited her, and she looked thinner, too, and wired with the change, sly forward slash proud in the shoulders.

'Nice hair, Mum.'

'Bunny!'

There was a pause and a strain and she let out a laugh then I picked up her stuff and she talked us to the car. Germans, she didn't like Germans but she liked the kittens, rabid little sods but she loved them kittens. Jackie went off with some bloke but she'd met Steve and Janet and Ian and Christine and they did on-demand omelettes with ham, bits of ham in the egg, and salami, weird sheets of iceberg laid out with salami. 'For breakfast, Bunny!' On day two she'd stood on a bee and she'd had to go to A&E so her tanning wasn't quite where she wanted it.

'You look great Mum.'

'Really?'

'Yes.'

'Do you want the rest of this cookie?'

We got in the car, flew up past the university, Hyde Park, then sat for half an hour or so as Headingley set in, edging our way past St Columba Church.

'Have you ever seen anything like it?'

'It's always like this, Mum.' It was school-run time.

'Shocking.'

'It's Headingley, Mum.'

'I can't bear it.'

'It's fine. Here,' I reached over to the glove compartment with my spare hand and pulled out *Hopes and Fears*. 'Do the honours.'

She let out a little *ahh* and put it on and there was that song about strangers that was on the nose and we liked it. Blaring.

We might as well

We might as well
We might as well
BE STRAAAAAAAAAANNNGEEEEERRS
BE STRAAAAAAAAANNNGEEEEERRS

But *Hopes and Fears* was brief. All the bangers were done by the time we got to Adel and I always turned it off before 'Bedshaped'. We went funny with that one.

'What's next? Robbie, Mum? George?'

'Well actually I have a confession Bunny.'

'What?'

'I have a confession.'

'Yes, I heard. What?'

'I did something naughty.'

'Mum.'

'Don't be cross.'

'I'm not cross.'

'When you told me you were moving back I went a bit mad and I booked us a cottage. Northumberland! Just like old times. Do you remember?'

'Right. I'm not—. I'm not mov—.'

'You're not pleased.'

'How much was it?'

She waved her hand.

'No. Tell me.'

'Don't worry about *that*, love. Goodness me.'

'Mum.'

'Don't you remember?'

'Of course I remember. Of course.' She was looking at me now. I looked out the front of the windscreen, her side. She followed my gaze back. 'I remember, Mum.'

'Don't you want to come?'

'I do. I do, I just—'

'Oh dear.'

'They're really expensive those cottages. Especially if you're not doing Sunday to Sunday.'

'Last minute dotcom. Bargain. I promise.'

'Right.'

'Come on, Grace. Chill. YOLO!'

I smiled. 'Oh god. Where'd you pick that up?'

'All change at work, love. Angela's the panini queen again and I'm back where I belong, serving. That's how it should be. I know them kids, I *know* my kids and I don't make a fuss at the till you know, showing up the free school mealers and Julie was a right old B I T C H with that and I love them kids. I love it. I hear it all now. Anyway Julie's gone thank god, RIP Ginger Whinger. Ginger Whinger we used to call her, did I tell you that?'

'Yes, Mum.'

'We have a right laugh. It's great. We listen to music now and Jamie's out you know, RIP, byeee, so we can give them chips like they want and if they ask for a second spoon of cheese on their jacket I give 'em three. Growing. Those lads especially. They need it. All wrong, all that. All wrong. It's great now. Whole new world.'

'Hmm. Sounds it.'

Her bottom lip went. 'You're not pleased.'

'How much have you spent, Mum?'

'You're not pleased.'

'No. No, I am pleased. I'm pleased. I am.'

'Don't get weird, love.'

'I'm not.'

'I'm on it.'

67

'Right.'

'I am.'

'OK. Have you asked Rebecca?'

'Will you?'

I side-eyed her, adjusted my feet.

'You will won't you, Grace? She'll come if you ask her.'

'I—'

'You'll ask her,' she said to her wing mirror, re-bobbling her hair.

*

'I'm doing a Davina now, love,' she said as we got in. 'I'm dead stiff.'

'Have fun.'

'Will you go do Nana and Grandad? They'll love that.'

I walked up to Weston, dropping in at big Sains on the way for the shop plus a special tea on me, a nice fish pie and some crisps and dips. Nana and Grandad lived right at the top of Weston in a pebbledashed semi, Coral windows with mock-Tudor diamonds. There was a permanently upturned Little Tikes car on the drive, a stack of concrete paving slabs leaning on the porch (2006 patio tombstones) and a crop of early dandelions.

I knocked. No matter how long I waited at their door it always felt longer than it should. Partly it was the PVC on PVC, crappy acoustics, though in truth I came home so rarely they would always be older, there'd always be a lapse, a pain, and that was my doing. I could hear *The Chase* through the curtains. I looked at my watch. Bit late for *The Chase*. Must have been on plus one.

I knocked again. Nothing. Rang the landline. Still nothing, though as I made to go round the side the rubber unclutched.

'Look who it isn't!'

'Hiya!' I turned. There he was, gazing with his head slightly bowed and his big dark eyes, two front teeth clenching his bottom lip like a little boy, one hand on the door frame. He was paler, his skin on the same spectrum as his favourite jumper, Cotton Traders fern. Yes, definitely a base tone of fern there, though with the wine in his cheeks he was alive. And he might have been pale but he'd never not been big. That wouldn't change. He was big in the bones. Enveloping. Safe.

I put my hands to my head and ducked. Then I stepped to one side and did his Marilyn thing, his big-band-bring-the-cake-out thing, our greeting. Kiss kiss flutter flutter. Grandad was Marilyn mad. He had her calendar every year and her postcard taped on the inside of the bathroom medicine cabinet. Tiger had been there, too, at one stage, Tiger Woods for Nana, but then he was a bad lad so she snipped him up with the kitchen scissors.

'Come 'ere.'

I pouted, knocking the knees again and blowing another kiss.

'Ooh she's a one.'

I laughed. We went inside.

'Never comes these parts this one,' he said to himself.

'I—'

'Well, shows well for it, whatever it is she's scheming.'

We moved into the kitchen, his hand firm but gentle at the nape of my neck.

Grandad was born in Armley, a Waddington's lad, his dad too, though he had some enterprise that came good in the eighties and they moved up to Pudsey. I'd never worked out what it was. They had enough cash for Otley, eventually. His fingers were still thick and jet-black with hair and when he touched things they moved. He made stuff. He made stuff happen. I felt such a sharp pang of shame just there it took my breath away.

I tucked my shoes under the radiator in the hall, kissed him on the lips and unpacked their tea from a fading Daunt tote.

'Close your eyes, Grandad.'

He did, immediately, wriggling in anticipation.

'Open.'

'Ooh! My favourite!' He held the fish pie aloft. 'Charlie Brigham's.'

'Bigham's,' I said, opening the cupboard for that little plastic bowl designated for crisps, the picnic one with the faded midget gem print.

'That's his name. Now, let's have a look at 'er.' He left off the fish pie and held me by the shoulders, arms outstretched. 'If I were ten years younger,' he said. He let me go and gestured a drink with his hand. 'What yer havin'?'

'I'm OK.'

'She'll have some white,' he said, opening the fridge for a foil bag disembowelled from its box. He took a glass from the sink, turned it upways and started squeezing the foil with his fist. I eyed the little white circle on the metal.

'Grandad.'

'No child of mine looks a gift horse in the mouth. Yer havin' it.'

'I'm your grandchild, Grandad.'

'My favourite. Here.' He reached into his back pocket for a crumpled twenty.

'No, Grandad.'

'Take it. For your keep.'

'Grandad.'

He put the note on the counter, taking my hand and pressing it on top. Then he walked past me with the wine, stopping at the door. I folded the money into my pocket and emptied the crisps.

'Courting yet?'

'No.'

'Bonny lass like you.' He shook his head. 'Come and say hello to your nana.'

I followed him into the lounge. He sank into the three-seater along the back wall, brown faux-velvet with shapely piping, and put his feet on the pouffe, always draped with a waffle tea towel, another behind his head, for best. There was a stack of little tables for the crisps and dips and on occasion honey cashews, a cream plastic landline resting on a knackered *Yellow Pages*, and a jaunty little statue of a red setter. The rest was the TV, Nana and Nana's new chair. Bradley was cranked up to eighty. I knelt down next to her, kissed her on the cheek and took her hand. I turned him down and she looked at me, formidably dazed.

'I got you some tea, Nana. Fish pie.'

'Don't like fish pie.'

'That's the first I've 'eard,' said Grandad.

She frowned.

'We're always learnin' 'ere you know.'

She looked at him.

'It's Charlie Bigham's, Nana.'

'Don't like him.'

'Oh dear.'

'Full of carrots.'

'Never mind. You'll have some crisps, though?'

I put the crisps and the cheese and chive on the sideboard next to her. There was a bunch of daffodils and the Virgin Mary, a candle, an ashtray, a bottle of Chanel No. 5 and a standing ovation of strawberry Complan bottles, mostly full though all punctured with transparent straws. Behind all this was a photo of the three of them nestled at the back – Mum in the middle and showing, white linen, Portuguese sun. Nana had her palm to Mum's stomach and was leant towards the camera with her mouth slightly open, sparkle in the eyes. Grandad had his arm round Mum. She was smiling.

'I love your new chair, Nana.'

'Only the best for yer nana,' said Grandad, standing now, taking the controller from the pouch on the side and pressing a button. The chair began reclining. He pressed until it was almost horizontal. Nana stayed upright with little effort, just the smallest hint of it, opening a fresh packet of Silk Cut with a sharp pearl-peach nail. He pressed the other button while she took her inaugural drag and the chair caught her back up.

'Top of the range, Nana!'

'You don't get that with your communism,' said Grandad, waving the controller at me, giggling. 'Got her chair, got her fags. Wants for nothing.'

I put my hand to my brow to cover my face, paparazzi-shy.

'You look well, Grace. Going steady?'

'No, Nana.'

'Don't go getting in trouble.'

'Ha. Don't worry. No extra cash for that kind of thing.'

'Skin's better.'

Blush. 'Thanks.'

A pause. A drag.

'I had to have a hysterectomy after your mother.'

'Oh, I—'

Grandad's iPhone chimed in then, from the gap between the cushion and the armrest. I pulled it out and gave it to him. He gave it a jab.

'Hello? HELLO? Susan? Susan who? Right. Right. Hello Susan.' He took her into the hall.

'Who's Susan?'

Nana shrugged, slowly shaking her head at Bradley with a long fluent drag. 'You be careful.'

'I will.'

'There was a thing in the *Post* you'd to send off for,' she said, eyes still on Bradley.

'Hmm?'

'You don't remember that. Aunty May did it.'

'Who?'

'Clubbed together half a crown with the girls.'

'Aunty May?'

'Aunty May.'

'Who's Aunty May?'

Grandad came back in. 'Mrs Woman from British Gas,' he said, throwing me the phone. I hung him up. '"Susan" she calls herself. I know 'er sort.'

'Grandad, I—'

'Keep Toby out,' said Nana, eyes on the screen.

'What?'

'That's what it said. Big letters. *KEEP TOBY OUT.*'

I turned the TV back up and put the fish pie on. When it was done I served it with peas and ketchup, plates on the trays with the beanbag bottoms. Nana had eaten her crisps and most of her cheese and chive by now, abandoned her fag in the pot. She sat transfixed on Paul O'Grady, Charlie Bigham slumping on her tray.

'Not eating, Grace?' Grandad.

'I'm a vegetarian.'

'That's what you think.'

'*Grandad.*'

Wink.

Tongue out.

I cleared up, fished some buttery goodbye kisses and walked back over the river. The roads were dry though the air was close and the walls smelt of ale. My heart was racing.

*

Mabel was scratting about when I got in. Her claws needed doing but we'd lost the little clippers. She'd pulled her mat and bowl out from the wall and into the middle of the kitchen and her biscuits were now in her water, bloated into little weightless floating chunks, variously scattered and stuck. I picked up the outliers with a slice of towel and Dettol, put her bowl on to soak and laid her down half a fresh sachet.

'*Mabel.* Tuna!'

'Bunny?' Mum called from the lounge.

'HIYA.' I said through the sound of the tap before walking through. Mum was sat on her Pilates ball in the dark. I put the light on and she turned to face me.

'I rang.'

'Oh.'

'Your sister's not coming.'

'I thou—'

'I knew you wouldn't ask her.' She reached for her glass.

'Oh. I—'

She sliced her neck with her hand.

'I—'

74

'Turn the light off please.'

I turned off the light.

*

Mum had her legs wrapped in Veet when I came down, catching a bit of *Saturday Kitchen* with a semolina submarine and cold sausage.

'What are you bringing?' she said, making her way past me and back up to the bathroom, phone timer buzzing.

'I'm just bringing what I brought, Mum.'

'What?'

'What I brought.'

'I can't hear you, love. Come up.'

I followed her up.

'Hold my sausage.'

'Give it here.'

She scraped off the cream with the little plastic scraper like a pro, took the showerhead then rinsed and towelled down. It was rank, that stuff, but her hairs had come on a fair amount since her last wax, all that Greek sun, and it worked a treat on your mid-length growth, great little stopgap. She asked if I wanted a go, too. I lifted my leg out and showed her – already done.

'Fab!'

'Little treat,' I said, holding out her sausage.

'No. You have it,' she said, moving towards her room. 'Come through.' She pulled on a pair of pants and a bra and lit up while her deodorant dried, her Corfu stuff strewn on the bed, suitcase emptied out and now a den for Mabel. 'Help me.'

'Let's just put some old T-shirts in there?'

'They're old, love.'

'Doesn't matter.'

'It matters to me.'

'It's only Northumberland.'

'Don't say that.'

'You know what I mean. It's only me.'

She turned around. 'Mabel! Get OUT! OUT! Bloody *hell*.' She slammed the case and started rifling through the pile of Corfu dirties. 'I wonder if I can't just—. There'll be a machine there and a dryer I think. Go get my phone, love.'

'Nah! What a faff. What about these?' I picked up a pair of shorts. 'You haven't even taken the label off these.'

'No, no I don't like them.'

'Right. Well. Hmm . . . Right. I know. I've got a plan. I've got a plan.'

She tapped her ash into an old teacup. 'Ooh!'

I went into her bottom drawer, the dodgy one with the false front, tiny dowelling sticks hanging out the back. That was for her exes. I pulled out one of those early noughties flowing skirts, the ones Siena Miller wore. It was soft and clean and ready to wear though gone a bit at the bottom – little sprays of bleach from the odd Mabel poo-gate clean-up, a few trailing snatches of cotton here and there.

'Let's do a repair job on a couple of these shall we? Vintage, Mum.'

'Mmm!' She exhaled, popped her half-finished butt in the cup. 'Let me find the Wundaweb.'

'Can I?' I pointed at the butt.

'Oh. Yes, love.'

We pottered for another hour or so then I went for a parting wee, door open. Mum came in to do her teeth.

'So Sally's put her head in on the new family.'

'Oh yes.'

'Yeah. Fresh meat! Where Jumpy Dave used to live. He's gone AWOL. He's gone to live in the States. Strange man. Strange, strange man. Anyway. Young family in there now. Number nine. You know? You remember Jumpy Dave?'

'Yes. Jumpy Dave.'

'One of these from the university, India's her name.' Wide eyes. She lowered her voice. 'Gay.'

'Mu—'

'No, now ah ah ah, you know I've nothing against that, love, but she does have kids. I guess they're sweet things, really. Bonny. But. Well. Well! Anyway they're ruined. And she's stripped the carpets. Bare floors. Ridiculous. All you can hear's toys now, clattering all over the shop, toys here, toys there, "that makes Mummy feel sad, sweetheart," this that and the third. It's terrible. Poor Sally.'

'Mum.'

'It's awful, love.'

'Hmm.'

'And the names!'

'Oh yeah. What's she called them?'

'You'll love this, you. "Betty and Clarice."'

'Amazing.'

'Anyway, I've forgotten the best bit! I've forgotten the best bit. So our Sally goes in and she's offered a coffee and you'll never guess. Wait for it. There's a load of them reusable nappies in the sink, Bun. Can you imagine!' She put her toothbrush in her mouth. 'In the *sink*.' She started laughing through the foam.

'Gross,' I said, pulling up my knickers.

*

77

Mum drove, stopping us briefly for a late Scotch Corner lunch.

'Why do they sell scarecrows?' I said from behind her, walking over from the M&S. She was in Smith's.

'Do they love?' She peeled back the flap of a Kinder Bueno.

'Yeah.' I pointed at the scarecrows. She looked over briefly, looked without looking then put the Bueno back and picked up a mini tray of edamame peas, giving them a shake.

'Don't you want anything, Mum?'

'I'm not really hungry.'

'Are you sure?'

'I don't really eat in the day.'

In the queue to get back on the motorway we saw a hitch-hiker stood on the verge and when we went past he smiled.

'He liked you, Grace. I saw that. Did you see that? He liked the look of you.'

'Eyes on you I'd say, Mum.'

'Me? Do you think? Really?'

I nodded, cranked up the Texas.

We were too early to pick up the keys to the place so we went into Alnwick for some bits, to Morrisons. By the door there was a yellow bin cage full of cut-price Fudco pistachios, shell-on.

'Bloody hell,' I whispered, dipping my hand in, picking some out.

'Put them in if you want.'

'It's OK.'

'Go on.'

'*Go on go on go on.*'

She giggled. 'No expense spared, love!'

'No they're still a bit much, Mum.'

'Go on!'

'No, no it's fine.'

'Go on, love.'

'I don't want them, Mum. I'm just surprised to see them here.' I faded out. I was thinking of Ottolenghi, iced baby loaf cakes with the rosewater.

She retrieved the bag I'd dropped, gave them a shake then let them go. 'Faffy, these.'

'Since when have you—'

'Ah! Look! Strawberries!'

The conveyer belt stopper said *THANK YOU FOR SHOPPING AT MORRISONS*. Pineapple in plastic; strawberry mousse; Cookie Dough; mini trifles; fresh cream muffins; tin of pimento olives; Babybels. *THANK YOU FOR SHOPPING AT MORRISONS*. Comté; oatcakes; avocado; cucumber; Maldon. *THANK YOU FOR SHOPPING AT MORRISONS*.

'This is my daughter,' Mum said to *Irene, Happy to Help*. 'We're mother and daughter.'

'Well yous have a nice time sweethearts.'

'What's this?' Mum picked up the Maldon, showed it to Irene.

'It's for the cucumber, Mum.'

'Right.'

Irene looked down.

'I'm just going to nip to Wilkos,' I said, pointing over the road.

'We've only got two free hours!'

'It's fine. Won't be a sec.' I vaulted the car park wall, bought two fine china mugs and a cafetière.

'I'd have got you coffee out, love. We're not that hard up.'

'Nah. All they have are pubs up here, filter stuff. It's shit.'

79

'Language.'

'Sorry.'

'It's nice here, actually, thank you! Dead posh these days. Especially down Alnmouth.'

'Yes Mum,' I smiled, tinkling the mugs. 'You can have these when we're done. Bone china!'

'Aw! Thanks, babe.'

I noticed then I was missing my ring, the garnet one, Nana's old engagement. Inner pockets, outer pockets, trouser legs, shoes, glove compartment, sleeves, *shit*.

'What's wrong now?'

'Nothing.' Drink holder, glove compartment for a second try, little snickety hole for the window control. No, just a fossilising apple core. 'Let me just check something.' I opened the door.

'What have you done?'

'One sec.'

'*Grace.*'

'Let me just—.' Tarmac scan. Nope.

'What have you lost?'

'I—. Let me just go back a sec. I just want to check something.'

'What have you lost?'

'Chill! Chill, Mum. I just need to check something.'

'Let me just—.' I shut the door on her, not a slam but not the well-run, look-here-Dad's-in-charge situation I'd hoped for. I'd have to re-enter with care.

There was a queue at the Morrisons' kiosk. Katie Price had some new beef. Cheryl Cole was Cheryl Cole but by another name. In front of me a little boy was eating a rotisserie chicken while his mum got a refund for her platinum Fairy. 'I wanted original love! I wanted the original!'

Just as she was slotting her receipt into her purse, turning away, I remembered I hadn't even brought the ring along, none of that stuff, not even a toiletry bag. I knew exactly where it was, right where Mum left hers to wash up, above the kitchen sink. *Idiot. Moron.* I couldn't leave the queue. I told *Janine* I'd lost it anyway, turned my blush into a panicky blush again and she smiled at me kindly, said she'd have a look in the back.

'Nothing love. Sorry.'

'Oh well. Worth a try.'

'Always worth a try, love.'

'Actually . . . Can I get one of these?'

'Which one, love?'

'Erm. Ah. Erm. OK Cash Millions?'

'Right you are.'

'Let's go mad. Oh. And. Erm. Can I get one of these please, too?' I picked up a Caramel Freddo.

I caught Mum's eye as I approached the car, opened the door nice and slow and edged her Cash Millions and Freddo in before me.

'You forgot me.' (Pretend Freddo voice.)

'Oh love!'

*

We picked up the keys and unpacked the car. Embleton. Crest of a hill. It was snazzy, a set of barn conversions with a little on-site office.

'Mum. This must have cost a bom—'

She took my wrist. 'Listen now. I don't want to hear it. I'm serious, love. *Don't.*'

We dumped the bags and I smoothed things off with some eight-year-old enthusiasm, removing the nets from my bedroom window, reading her out the more exotic names and locations from the guestbook. Doug and Wendy from Toronto! Chris and Toni from Barnes! Then we made our way down to the beach, down through a field, the sky as vast as a sky can get, impervious to my iPhone 5, to description. The rain-spattered pattern in the path was an expensive steak, a worktop, the moon.

'Look Bunny! A caterpillar!'

'Hey little man.' I crouched for a greeting. 'What's your name?'

She took out her phone. We paused for a moment while she filtered.

'Done?'

'Done.'

We walked on. When we got to the beach she held my sleeve and took off her shoes and socks. I watched her walk towards the water and dip her toe in then I took off my shoes and socks and did the same. We paddled for a bit then I broke away, back to the firmer stuff, strode out, almost a jog, just going to get my heart up a bit. Mum ran for me after a bit, bag flapping on her thigh, tugged at my T-shirt.

'Hmm?' I stopped, turned.

Her hair was stuck to her forehead. She was pointing at the Fitbit. 'Guess, love!'

I turned back.

Tug.

'Go on. We've been walking an hour Bun. Guess.'

'Mum.'

'Guess.'

Turn.

Tug.

'*No*. No.'

'It's just a bit of fun love. Take a flippin' chill pill.'

'Please Mum.'

She was silent. I looked back at her. She gestured for me to look out to sea, at the shore. There was a woman paddling in Breton stripes, funky quartz glasses and Breton stripes. 'Told you it was posh.'

I showered off the salt then rummaged in her case for something spoilable and old that I wouldn't have to add to my wash when I got back. She'd packed an old T-shirt of Rebecca's. Perfect.

Downstairs she'd drained the olives, topped us up with wine and taken it all into the lounge, laying out two Kleenex on the arm rests for fingers.

'God. Oh my god, oh my god.'

'What's up?' I called through from the kitchen, checking to see if she'd changed my fridge arrangement.

'GODSAKE.'

I walked in. 'What is it?'

'I paid for Sky. I paid for Sky, love. I did. I paid for it. I can't *believe* this.'

'Give me it here.'

'Argh.' She was shaking her hands in front of her, the zapper discarded on the coffee table. 'Ahhhh. What are we going to do?'

'Give me the zapper.'

'ERROR.' She picked it back up. 'Look. I press this and it's just E R R O R. ERROR.'

'Give me it.'

She threw it on the cushion next to her, reached under for the coffee table shelf and pulled out the ring binder. 'They won't hear the last of this. They won't. How dare they. Bastards.'

'It's fine, Mum. Look.'

'*Bastards.*'

I left her to rifle the paper, oft-fingered and soft with it, a different consistency, marked on the edges with foundation. I took the other remote from under the set and turned it on.

'Oh. Oh.'

'There you go.' I handed her it and she started scrolling. *Taken 2* was on 4.

'Liam, Mum?'

'Liam!'

'Pause it a sec. I need a wee.'

'Again?'

'Yes, Mum.'

I weed, paused on the bowl to make sure I was empty, washed my hands, no, bit more, had another little wee, took a bit of Nivea from her room for my hands, came back down.

'I will put it on Facebook, Bun, their Facebook page. It's not intuitive.' She slouched back. 'Phew. What a day!' She pointed at her glass. I handed her it.

Ads.

'I'm enjoying this Bun. Int he gorgeous.'

'Wouldn't kick him out of bed.'

'Ah! Cover my ears! So sad about his wife.'

'That was *Love Actually*.'

'No, his actual wife died, Bun. Didn't you know? Died. Flew off a cliff, love.' She googled it and showed me.

'Shit. That's well bad.'

'Tragic. So, so tragic. Wonderful man. *Wonderful* man.'

'God.'

'Don't you ever go skiing, love.'

I topped us up again. 'God these ads are loud.'

'I don't think so, love.'

'Listen.'

'OK.'

'Hear it?'

'No, love.'

'It's deliberate. They make them loud deliberately to get in your face. Companies pay for it.'

'That's nice.'

'They do.' I took her phone. 'What's your password?'

'2005.' She stood up. 'Right. Cookie Dough.'

'Are we not having tea?'

'I don't really do a big tea, love, not now it's just me and Mabes.'

She went into the kitchen for the tub and two mugs and teaspoons, always mugs and teaspoons so you could get away with more, put them on the coffee table.

I reached to squeeze the tub for the give, see how long we should rest it.

'Bun! No! Wait.' She got back up, moving the olive debris to one side and nipping back into the kitchen to replenish our glasses, rearranging it all into a flat lay. 'Give me that.'

I handed her the phone.

Click.

'Nice.'

'Rebecca *loves* Cookie Dough,' she said, moving her glasses down from her head, waiting for the Internet.

'Mum. Maybe don't—'

'Well!'

85

'Don't, Mum. It'll wind her up.'

'Right. *Done.*' She threw the phone back on the sofa.

'Mum!' She shrugged. She giggled. 'Liam's back. Look.'

*

She came into my room that night. It must have been two, half two, just as I was finishing a REM cycle. There was a 'Bunny' in a whisper then a 'BUNNY', still in whisper territory but more urgent. The door was ajar but she opened it wide, the bottom plane making that frictionny noise over the too-thick new pile – this place must have set her back hundreds, though to me that sound was symphonic. I thought I was a varnished floorboards person and I wasn't. Pile. Any room you could get away with. Bathroom. Loo. Thick cream pile.

'Hmm,' I said as she got under the duvet.

'I had a freaky dream.'

'Hmm.' I turned to face her, eyes still closed.

'*Bun.*'

I frowned, eyes still closed.

'*Bun.*'

'What.'

'Are you awake?'

'Mm-hmm.'

'Rebecca came. She came in the middle of the night Bun! The DPD man dropped her off. She was wearing a water-proof poncho with her arms out for me and the safety light was shining through the back of her, through the poncho. It was so *freaky.*'

'Oh dear.'

She was silent for a moment.

'Bun?'

'Yeah.'

'I believe in angels, you know.'

Silence.

'*Bunny.*'

'Yeah.'

She went dead again. I started to drift.

She tapped my shoulder.

I opened my eyes and turned to her properly. She was shivering.

'Come on. It's OK. She'll be OK. She's not dead, Mum.'

'Well it *feels* like it.' She staggered into high-pitched sound, and sort of jowly, chewy, like she was biting on a cube of jelly.

'Oh Mum.' I tried to pull her snugger with the cover.

'No, love. You just have to let it go. You don't know that but you do.'

'Mum.' I reached out for her.

'No, love. I've let it go. The both of you. Good. Bye. Bye. See ya. Bye.'

Silence.

She got back out and pulled the duvet back to where she found it, corner to corner to corner.

I took a deep breath.

She paused at the door.

'Is it me? Please don't blame me. Do you blame me?' A whisper, still facing the door, hand on the handle.

I got out, reopened the duvet, and she walked back over and she got back in. I tucked it flush around her and wiped her hair back from her face. 'Shh,' I said, over and over, waiting for the breaths to form strong firm peaks. I didn't have an answer.

*

We got up early the next day and headed to Lindisfarne. There was a bank holiday heave and on the path out from the car park an impromptu industry to meet it – stalls selling mini eggs and bundles of miniature shells and plastic fishermen in yellow macs, a few empty yards then a lone ranger with the Barbara Cartland backlist in a blue catering crate. It was busy but still there was a feeling of holiness I felt, a severe, bracing one, Jesus in the temple. I liked it. Mum went spooky, glassy-eyed, dazed and bored and on her phone, so I bought her a little glass worm with goggle eyes and I bought myself some crab – something needed treating. We made our way to the car.

She drove us back to Alnwick, to Barter Books. It was raining now, heavy, and she liked it there, she liked the form if not the content. We'd come here last just before uni started, five years now, with a list of classic books I'd googled to stock up on, greedy, bushy-tailed, though none of them had been good enough. Wrong editions. Wrong apparatus. And we started with medieval anyhow.

Inside it smelt acrid now, not as I'd remembered, gross – neglected coffee and raincoat, untreated flagstones, anxious paper. Mum sat down by the self-service percolator and ate a packet of honesty-box Walkers shortbread and I tried to browse. If Rebecca had been there and not too hung-over to cope with Mum I'd have taken myself off for a bit. Maybe I would have hammed up the dickhead thing, those wilful, semi-wilful pretensions I could use to get under Rebecca's skin, then Mum could calm her down, then they could tut and bitch a bit and bond and I'd feel worthy, beaten and replenished in the corner with my book, one maternal eye half-trained on the two of them, the words on the page a mush but the symbols crystal clear. That's how we worked. Triangular. Today was a three-legged stool with two legs.

I didn't want anything. I wanted to lie down. I wanted to be stretchered out. I picked up a hardback *Birthday Letters*. *You've heard of this, Grace, it's problematic; it'll be good for you.*

I stood in the queue while the man in front went through and at that point I had a look at the blurb and realised *Birthday Letters* represented a dead and othered woman being othered all over and to buy it and to read it was another kind of beating and I was supposedly Sylvia but undoubtedly Ted.

'Yes, love?'

I held it with both hands, alien, like I'd never held a book in my life. 'Sorry. Sorry. I can't. Sorry.'

'That's fine love, ne problem.'

'Don't you want anything?'

'No.'

'Not in this whole shop, nothing?'

'It's OK, Mum.'

'Right.'

'Brightening up,' I said, pointing out the window.

She looked out. 'Yes.'

We got in the car. I drove now, drove us back to Embleton Bay, pausing on the way at the Londis to get her a ham and cheese sarnie and some Dairy Milk. We parked and made our way to the sand. I had my crab in its plastic and in the cold bag I'd put the Comté and half an avocado wrapped in cling film. We set up our chairs. It started to spit again. It started to plop. I dropped my avocado in the sand.

I watched it for a moment. 'Fuck.'

'Language.'

'Sorry.'

'Pick it up,' she sighed, holding out the little Londis bag she'd repurposed for our rubbish. She'd rolled the edges down the way you would with a bin and was holding it there, glaring at me, agitated. Suddenly she was the mum.

'No.'

'Come on.'

'*No.*' I crossed my arms. How could I pick it up? I'd get crap all over my hands, grains. She could. She should. I was losing my shit. I put my hood up.

'Grace.'

'Fine.' I stood up, kicking a new shower of sand over it, shoved my nails right in there, curling my hand into the flesh. Filthy. I over-armed it into the dunes.

'Right. What have you done that for?'

Shrug.

'For god's sake.'

I pulled my hood further down my face.

'What's wrong now?'

'It's *raining.*' I kicked another whiff of sand. '*God.*'

'Right.' She stood up and shoved her open sandwich in the cold bag.

'No. No, no I didn't mea—.'

'Stay here being a madam if you like. I'm off.'

'I didn't mean—.'

'I know you want to go. You hate it. *Hate* it. You're going. We're going. GONE.' She was off.

I followed her in silence to the car park – back to the Michael steeple fingers so it looked like a ritual, cinematic at the least. The rain helped with that. She was bustling, her camping chair bringing up a cloud in her wake. She dropped it when we reached the top of the dunes, dropped it with a tiny little 'FUCKSAKE', capitals though tiny, breathless, left it for dead. I picked it up and put it on my shoulder and she charged on.

At the car she opened the boot gently, a gesture so tender it seemed to surprise her and she went hard again on the driver's door, flinging it wide, slamming it shut and sitting still behind the wheel, hands at ten and two, inch between her back and the seat, staring straight ahead. I took my time with the chair, wiping it off, packing it in, then I smoothed off the cover shelf and closed the boot, hand on the handle, all the way to the seal. There.

'Mum.'

'Belt.'

'Mum.'

'I'm a mug.'

'Mum—'

'No.'

We got back to the cottage. We packed up. She put the untouched food in a pile on the counter.

'Can't we bring these back and put them on the compost or something?'

'What?'

'I don't know. Isn't there a compost heap somewhere we can dump them?' I felt bad about the avocado.

'Do you have to be so bloody weird?'

Back, back through Otley and straight into Leeds, straight to the station. I didn't mention the stuff I'd left at hers, the toiletries and stuff. It would mean I'd have to go back. And maybe she was thinking the same because she didn't say to take off the Sprayway fleece. She didn't have to say it; she wouldn't have me on a train without a proper coat. We didn't speak, but she drove like a learner just learned and I listened. I listened to that worn-out clutch. Tried to.

On the train, yogic flying (shopping). *BODY SHOP . . . Olive Pumas . . . 501s . . . ~~black,~~ ~~grey,~~ <u>acid</u> . . . Socks . . . ochre, charcoal, umber, rose quartz, CADMIUM. CADMIUM! CADMIUM! Cadmium red.*

I went to Oxford Street. And then I went home. Nobody was in. Matthew was out at a party, an exhibition launch.

Can I come?

Come, yeaaahhh [yellow thumbs up]

So off I went to Clapton, little silk scarf wrapped round my head like the Mother Mary, second-hand 501s, cadmium ankles. It was fashionably dusk, and there was a lot of concrete, low ceilings. There was a table dressed in tiger loaves and pots and pots of houmous and tzatziki – plundered already by the time I got there though there were plenty of cherry tomatoes, plenty of those. On the walls there were paintings of angular girlish nudes with waifish blank white faces. It was gross. I wanted to tell Matthew. They couldn't have all these girls on the walls, Matthew. I'd say something devastating, political, then, *don't like it Matthew.* Bottom lip. *No like.* Then Matthew would laugh and relieve me of my insight. But every time I looked over, every time I looked it was just Matthew, there, Matthew talking to other people. Well, women. Irony Don Draper hair this evening.

I gave up and went to the bar.

'G&T please.'

'Wine's free.'

'Sorry?'

'WINE'S FREE.'

'Oh. Wine please.'

I took the glass and then, behind my left ear: 'Grace? Grace? Is tha—'

'*No*, Freddie. Shh. No I don't thi—'

'GRACE! GRACE!'

I turned round.

It was Freddie. Freddie with the blazing cheeks from Magdalene (*maudlin, Grace, maudlin*), Freddie and his partner Flo.

'Grace! It is. How are *you*?'

I took the end of my scarf. It was dangling down in front of me now. I swished it back over my shoulder and pushed my glasses down my nose, peering over, peering up. 'Oh hel-lo. It's only bloody Freddie from maudlin! Freddie and Flo!'

'Grace! What are you doing here?'

'Oh. You know.' I swigged. 'Dissociating.'

'Ahh. Excellent. Taken anything?'

'No. Are you offering?'

'Ha.'

'Give me Flo, please, Freddie. Stop keeping me from Flo. Flo! How are *you*?'

'Delightful.'

'Excellent.'

'I'm in recovery. Did Michelle say?'

I pulled the scarf off now, shoved it in my bag and put the bag between my knees. Eyes closed, glasses up on the head. 'No. She didn't. You look—. You look radiant.'

'Thanks! I've been baking bread.'

'We have French toast, now.' Freddie squeezed her hand.

'I've made a lot of French toast,' said Flo.

'Amazing. I love French toast.'

94

Someone tapped Freddie on the back, a woman in a long leather coat that seemed indeed to be bona fide leather plus Charlotte Gainsbourg hair plus popper-sided trackies plus Kickers. She had deep bags beneath her eyes and a thin silver chain round her neck. Her pupils were gone.

'Cressida. Darling,' said Freddie.

Something distracted me in the other direction and I cricked my neck to look and 'veritable' I heard Freddie say behind me, 'ostensible', 'if you will', and then I turned round and he had his back to me proper now, his left hand cupped just above his sacrum. He looked back at me for just a sec, *on me*, he mouthed, then back at Cressie. He opened his fingers. I took it to the toilet.

It turned into a cellar in Dalston. There was a bath with lion's claws and poison ivy crawling out of it and all these fallen statues and then Michelle, Michelle arrived in the 2-a.m. haze, high in high-collared lace, burnt plum. I was there too and I think I did another bomb then, I had something else in my palm and I dropped, god knows what, hell knows what but it wasn't ecstatic. I moved and moved in any case, head curled into myself, a little comma on her own, smoke machine ripping all the moisture out my throat. There was a stage thing I think, too, a little promontory. A tall svelte person danced topless to Prince.

*

I woke up with no clothes on. No clothes, also duvetless, though I still had my watch. My body knew this light but I had a look to check. Yes, three in the afternoon. There was a man here and this was his room. He had his mouth open. He was creaking with the in-breaths then pausing, smooth exhalations. His teeth clambered on top of one another, furry at the roots. That felt kind of Norse, somehow, Germanic. And I was moved by it. It was cute. I was glad he was asleep and sleeping with abandon.

I swung to one side and sat for a moment on the edge of the bed, palms flat on the mattress. I could feel a track of dribble down my chin and my muscles were thriving now. Every orifice hurt, properly and thoroughly. *Ahh.*

I bundled my stuff out to the loo. My face was hot and dry and crusty and for once, for once my bladder was dry as a pip, though when I splashed the skin round my mouth it turned pink, angry, my calm just slightly slipping there, a slight pressure, just lodging there in my face.

I looked in the medicine cabinet to see if a woman lived here. No. Bare face it was. Fine, as long as I kept off the glasses. *No woman no soap*, I hummed, *no woman no soap*. No toilet roll, no toothpaste etcetera and the loo bowl was its destined brown. I'd left my knickers in there. I went back in.

He kept his eyes closed as I pulled the door a crack but his hand moved, a little wave. I started looking for the knickers and he made a gentle moaning noise, self-directed, the one you do when your alarm goes off and you're knackered and alone.

'I'm looking for my knickers.'

'Zhhhhhh. Fack.'

I turned my back to him, got on all fours. The knickers were under the radiator, scrunched in a ball and they were damp; the radiator was on but chronically unbled. I opened them out. Well, I'd had a bit of fun. Enough. Not much. I stood back up and put them on, inside out, back still turned. He was looking now, his quiet was a looking quiet, but I stayed there assessing the radiator.

'Have you got a key?'

'Hmm.' One eye opened. 'Hi.'

'Hi. Have you got a radiator key?'

He pulled his fingers at his face. 'What you say?'

'For the radiator.' I pointed at the radiator.

He shut his eyes and groaned.

I looked up at the ceiling. There were lots of blobs of Blu Tack there. Ex-glow-in-the-dark stars. I thought of the child they'd have belonged to and the mother taking them down and moving out so this man could fail to bleed this radiator. I thought of my orifices.

He opened his eyes.

'What's the Blu Tack?'

'Oh, it's a piece. I'm an artist.'

I got weird pins and needles on the bus back, blacked out for a bit then I must have dozed because I found myself in Seven Sisters, and at Seven Sisters I sat down and vommed, a discreet spot round the corner from the Colombian place with the temporary gazebo/veranda thing, always packed and funky. A man came out and gave me some water and I told him I spoke Spanish once, *hablo español,* I probably said, *Jesus,* and he nodded, a firm warm Grandad hand on my shoulder. I cried the automatic cry of the sick.

*

Nobody was home when I got in and I was hungry, now. I was fucking starving. I wanted a bagel, a slightly dry, maybe second-day plain white New York Bakery bagel, maybe two, but there was nothing in the bread bin and the fridge was empty bar a plastic bag of ex-coriander and a Tesco mango sticker was blocking up the sink and Adam's jumpers were

97

vegetating in the wash and there was a cascade of brown down the kitchen drawers. I thought it was coffee and licked it. It was bacon.

I went through, chucked my bag on the bedroom floor and sat with the Velcro strap. I undid it. I redid it. I undid it. I redid it. I undid it.

I couldn't go to bed. *There is too much anxiety.* That's what Rachel would say. It must have happened, though.

I woke up. It was six a.m. I went through for some water and Matthew was there. Matthew was there in the kitchen, face illuminated behind his Mac, pair of black earphones round his neck, one in one out.

'What are you doing?' A whisper.

'Working.'

I furrowed my brow.

'Got any downers?'

'Erm. Tins?'

I put my thumb up.

'Grace. You OK, mate?'

I hung my head.

'Come here.' He squeezed me. Tight.

We got kind of pissed, then. Mellow shallows then a little bit pissed, played some iPlayer roulette. We watched a doc on problem boozers and there was this man with gorgeous tousled blonde-brown hair and a brown sheepskin coat and a browning pink jumper and brown skin and brown nails and he was an alcoholic and his ex was ignoring him. He cried like a baby. I took off my glasses. Fuck.

'No. No I can't do this, Matthew——.' I did a time-out with my forearms.

He stilled my hand, leapt up to spacebar it. 'OK. Next.'

We watched a Howard Hodgkin *Imagine*. Howard Hodgkin was sitting in India, an open peaceful shaking void.

'Shit.'

'You OK?'

'I want to be Howard Hodgkin in India for the rest of my life.'

'Shh.'

'Can we go terrestrial?'

He nodded.

We watched Lorraine's transition wardrobe for all sizes and then we did a bit of the Smirnoff he kept in the freezer, next to Adam's jeans – *they self-clean!* – and then we did a line or two and then we ran it off. We went posh. Right up Muswell Hill – *ARGH, ARGH, ARGH* (Matthew), *WAH* (me) – until our heads and thighs were damp and volatile. We stopped by the Mossy Well and Matthew stood tall, breathing heavily, his hand resting on a tree. He bent over and started comedy-thrusting, tongue out.

'That's horrible, Matthew. Stop that please.'

'Feels GOOD!' He pushed his chest out, sort of roared. 'Does Rachel make you feel like this?'

'Make it stop.'

'Does she?'

'No.'

We walked back via Crouch End Waitrose, picked up a couple of bananas to claim our free coffees with.

'Wait.'

'What?'

'Grace!'

'Matthew!'

'Grace!'
'What!'
Vom.

I took us home and put him to bed, in his boxers and his faded Chang vest with the low-hanging armpits, that fuzz of dark hair speaking well to the yellowed cotton. He smelt but it wasn't allium yet, sicky. It was nice. I pulled the duvet off him, quartered it then laid it on his chair. Matthew curled up foetal on the sheet and I lay next to him for a while, facing the opposite wall. This one was straining now, this sheet. It was beginning to shine – silk mix once – and it was dusty at the edges but it smelt of Jessica. It smelt safe and well. I must have dozed for a while. Then I got up, opened his windows, pulled down the blinds, laid back and thought of Jessica. Stroke. Stroke. Still so tender but *AHH*.

Matthew worked from home the next day. He sorted the Wi-Fi then he made me a CV and we put Excel as a competency and he taught me Excel. He was a great consultant. He was kind. He never stepped in and touched the keypad himself. And when I finally got the AutoSum thing he was so proud. He held me on the shoulder, squeezed. I said I'd pay him in tins and Tangfastics, made to go to Tesco Express. I slapped on some trackies and some red lipstick, too. Chic. Not a big old mess. Louche. I walked past Stanley of *STANLEY'S* caff. He was slicing a sharp knife through a block of corned beef on a plate, cling film rolled back. I waved. He did an air kiss.

In Tesco there was a man in the aisle with a can of baked beans and a weather-worn black fleece and a shifty expression. I held on to my bottle of red and reached for the honey-roasted cashews. He walked on by with four fillets of salmon and right out the shop. The till person rolled his eyes.

'Red lipstick!' said a schoolgirl on the forecourt, clinging to her friend with a schoolgirl cling-fall.

I stopped. I took the tissue from my sleeve and wiped it off.

*

Matthew printed off some CVs for me at work and I took them down to the Portobello Road.

I was down to my last few quid now, really skint, unfeasible, but when this happened, and it happened quite a bit, I'd get aggressively consumptive, all this aggression pointing at Cressida, the meaning of Cressida. I'd get deep into my overdraft, why the fuck not, she could, deep in, but then I'd get so close to this all falling down, to bussing back to Otley for real, a shrivelled bitter wreck, that I'd freak right out and find myself a job quick-smart.

So I bought a set of seventies short silk shirts and a turquoise beret, non-refundable, the real deal, and then I started throwing CVs about, right on down to Holland Park. I couldn't say quite why I'd come west. It still wasn't time for Rachel again, still the Easter break, and in part I was *yeah, I'm well over that Rachel, Matthew, you're right*, but I thought I'd come back down here, be here, see, just in case.

This is where Ferdinand popped up. He was out on the street with a bottle of disinfectant and a cloth, a note for staff in the window behind him. 'Still looking?' I asked with my post-spend halo and he said, 'Yes, come on in!' He was Ferdinand he said. He was Australian. Melbourne.

He asked if I could make a decent coffee and I said yes and he said go for it, dude, gesturing at the machine, and I made one for him with a running commentary: tamp the grounds with a bit of air to spare, too tight and it burns, too long and it burns.

Milk? Same again: wipe the creamy scudge from the wand with the blue roll before it dries. If it dries you're fucked.

He clapped his hands together. 'Ah, beaut! When can you start?'

'Now.'

*

Ferdinand taught me to make things with love. *Make sure you add a few herbs there, Grace. Grace, get this, see these raspberry teabags? See this? You put the water in there first and then the bag. See? Water first, then the bag. Water. Bag. Pretty. Tastes like shit but it gets the people going. See?* I loved those swirling raspberry teabags, I really did. Before long I'd progressed to spinning blades and cheese wire and I was keeping my top buttons open like Lola the chef, braless Lola with the tanned forearms and the blue hair, silver hoops. Lola had dainty teeth with a lovely little overbite and feline eyes and hair that conspired to fall from her bobble. No lippy, no mascara. Big matte red lips sometimes, if some customer was a massive dick and she just needed a bit of something, just a little lift, but Lola had it down.

Soon enough Ferdinand was calling me dude and telling me about his future wife. I managed. I managed it all, though sometimes the intention of it gave me the shivers.

He wanted her freedom most of all, he said. And sometimes he'd give snippets from a romantic past that felt encapsulated. Really, genuinely, as though such an achievement was possible. I couldn't tell if it was or wasn't and that made me feel a racing energy in his presence, a sort of sexual feeling, though the caffeine was bottomless and the fridges vibrated at the waist and downstairs, Lola.

102

Ferdinand was tall and lean and on a twelve-month visa. He had a sleek inky man bun, black DMs and a line in those long slubby fishtail T-shirts, the ones with the All Saints feel. I watched him very closely. That's what you had to do with a person like this. Whatever your birth or configuration you had to watch it.

He's a dickhead, I'd tell myself often, or *GRACELESS MAN* when I heard him baptise a new dude or saw him close in on a new mother. He loved new mothers, rushing to lift their wheels for them before I got the chance. *OUTRAGEOUS.* I'd think it all up into Caps Lock because that really made him a dickhead. He wasn't a dickhead. He was an excellent flirt in fact, Lola loved him, and he made us all racy and was giving and kind.

There were a few weeks of this and then I settled down and he was Ferdinand, simply Ferdinand and there were as many weeks more. May passed, most of it. I put him on a shelf and worked towards some good thoughts again, edifying, decent, thought-through thoughts.

I started making plans for a hustle. I needed a thing, some 'thing' I could talk about, some tangled attachment or dynamic or set of ideas for Rachel – Rachel-Rachel or the inner Rachel I'd probably imbibed by now – to get her teeth into. Underemployment was too universal a topic for her, I felt, too concrete.

The café was quiet in the mid-afternoons. Ferdinand was mostly downstairs with Lola and Lola was Lola and Ferdinand was Ferdinand, and Ferdinand was on a twelve-month visa so I tried to be less pissy and be present for my thoughts and win some mental freedom.

You could do a course Grace! Bookbinding? Climbing? Rollerblading? Though by the end of each shift it felt grubby to keep on imagining like that, yearning away at such slim and withering pickings. Yearning wasn't really what it was. I hoped not. I hoped this wasn't yearning. Whatever it was it was too much and my neck would start going, spreading its discontent right down my back.

At first the problem was my neck, and then the fear of it. Sometimes I'd have a walk and a smoke on my break and try to soothe it, go watch the carp in Holland Park, or I'd stand in the whiteness on Abbotsbury Road, this stretch of eight-foot wall and its silent misery. There was often a security guard/driver there too, out in the sun with me. Sometimes I'd catch a bit of that sun, or a deep regard for my flailing neck, my sacred body in space and time, dying and thriving and moving about all at once, such a nice sense of absurdity, and I'd be absolutely fine. But a fag break was a fag break however prolonged.

In the end I was convinced it was my hair. Sometimes you just needed a cut. Sometimes you just needed a look. So I went to Mr Toppers on the Tottenham Court Road and I paid the man a tenner for a back and sides. A pixie cut. That worked. I could feel every which wind and I felt punctuated, had a real face to speak of, out there in front of me. I was a sexless floating hairless thing, skint and scared and emulating, keeping them all off the scent. That's when I met Patrick.

JUNE 2015

A lot of men like Patrick came in the café. Patricks, Jacobs, Nicks, Olivers. Blur-era stoops, natural cotton tote bags with ochre handles. Cultured men in early middle age. When they walked in my heart would start, that racing Ferdinand feeling in the stomach, and I'd find I had all this wit, hair, jazz, this whole vibe to play around with, smooth off the transactional edge. This was culture.

I wasn't lean and tall and Australian but I had my Leeds accent and I could bring that out slow and supple, deliver it derivative, out the side of the mouth, dimples, big words to take the edge off. Big, but not too big. A cloud could be tumultuous, a dirty spoon perverse, and we'd be warm and safe in this space we'd opened up, safe though sometimes squeamish, watching the coffee drip through its filter.

Patrick was a property developer. He had a Roman nose and he liked slate cashmere and his voice was mellow and fatherly and his two-year-old was called Rose. She didn't live with him or here but sometimes she came in. 'I like your earrings,' was the first thing he said to me. 'I like your Roman nose,' I said, caffeine-bold and I meant it. He should have a little earring too, I thought, and I told him, one of those tiny gold ones. He said he lived in Royal Oak, just off Westbourne Gardens. A townhouse. We didn't bother with a courtship.

*

The first time I went over I said I'd make us dinner while he went for a run. He'd been stuck in Reading all day and Paddington was messy and his energy was off. Go run, I told him, go sweat, smiling with my mouth closed, forehead spacious. Our boiler was on the brink so he should run while I got warm. I'd have a go in this waterfall shower he'd advertised so well. He always smelt good when he came in for his morning espresso, sort of green and a little bit bitter. I'd say so and he'd say 'waterfall shower'. Then 'cologne', he'd add, a little rearrangement of his hat. It was June but the mornings were still a bit nippy. Also he was losing his hair. Double espresso in porcelain. Gone.

He ran and I went to find the bedroom. There were four and I couldn't tell the guests from the master. All of them had bare varnished floorboards and were laundered and aired. There were a few miniature Farrow & Ball tins around the place, lots of scuffless cardboard storage boxes and empty chests of drawers. Solid antique stuff, lined. Wicker laundry baskets. I couldn't find any photographs, though in one room there was a stack of vacuum-packed baby clothes and Rose's old Silver Cross pram.

Patrick was still married to Jane, Rose's mum. They were estranged but consciously uncoupling. He told me that early on, with one of his Saturday lattes. Consciously uncoupling, he said, though in air quotes. I'd seen his ring and asked and he'd said yes, they were married, and then came the air quotes. I guessed they were there to indicate some superior feeling we were both supposed to have towards the personnel involved in this arrangement. He called it that, 'personnel'.

There was hate here, but not for his wife. That's how I thought this worked. No, he didn't hate his wife, it was just the personnel. 'That's really healthy,' I said to the conscious uncoupling. 'That's great.' I'd meant it. Still, when I saw the pram I had to pause, sit on the edge of the bed. I looked at my phone. It was 7.45 p.m. I was sat on a set of strong white sheets with buttons in a big white room, and they were creased, creased evenly and all over. They'd been dried in an A+ dryer, dryer balls, quick and hard, and then left for a bit and then hung but not ironed. I took off my shoes. I searched along the edge of the duvet for a label. Yes. *THE WHITE COMPANY.*

I left off the shower and went downstairs, back to the kitchen-come-dining room. In the centre was an Ercol table lit by a low-hanging lamp. The lamp had a cord of cornflower blue connecting it up to the ceiling. There were fairy lights around the window, a seasonality chart on the fridge and the Collins *Companion to Dreams* on the dresser.

I opened the fridge. It opened slowly. Winsome, nonchalant. It had its own set of tiny little fairy lights marking the rim and shelves and there were several deli pots in there, the low, wide ones, flanked by some form of whole smoked fish, salmon or trout. I pulled at one, the foil gleaming. Trout. I put the fish and the pots on the side. Artichokes, tapenade, cream cheese Peppadews, set it all out like a picnic. Poor curation, but each of the elements was so worthy of itself it didn't matter.

I had a look in the living room. Stack of *Monocles* on the coffee table, bouquet of apricot lilies. Someone had snipped out the stamens. I went over to the bookcase. Teak I think. I ran a finger. Not a speck. There was a lot of *Lonely Planet* and a small selection of literary fiction, all your Bookers etcetera. Jane's I think. I hadn't read *On Beauty* yet. I put it in my rucksack.

Patrick came back and had a shower while I set up the TV, then we ate plus Sauvignon Blanc plus more, Netflix menu crowning the hearth. We talked, a bit, a little bit, a little bit of politics, drugs, parents. He liked Ed Miliband. He'd had a pill problem in the nineties. He always kept some coke on him for special occasions. His dad was Scottish originally, couple of generations back, hence the surname, MacAskill, and a barrister. His mum was French. That was Patrick. I'd sketch me out later, after the fucking. Better that way. Vague early outlines with the promise of fucking, then the fucking and the staying and the morning fuck – immediate, vertiginous depth. I found it wearing to put off the act too long. It seemed he did too, but he was politer, he had his power to contend with.

When I did add something he'd recline and move his fingers towards the bottom of his jaw, or else stretch his arms up behind him, stretching his body out of the frame.

After eating we watched *Breathless*.

'You haven't seen *Breathless*,' he said, a hand slapped down in shock, there on the knee, and once it was there it was there to stay. 'You have to watch it!'

We watched *Breathless*. There was no mould and no Matthew and no Adam and no Blu Tack blobs on the ceiling and I was fucking Jean Seberg. *Grace. Grace. You are not Jean Seberg. You know how that turned out for her. Don't be a dick. Shh, you shut up.* I was Jean Seberg. I was drunk and he was drunk and we were fucking Jean Seberg.

I followed him upstairs. He put on *I Love You, Honeybear*. I undressed. I knew where my nerve endings were and I was proud of that but I was drunk. I was drunk and it really wouldn't do to instruct him, use my power so early on, not when he'd been so thoughtful with his. So I watched him watch me, saw what he saw and mirrored it back and it wasn't that bad, actually, method acting, kind of slyly powerful too. I was a director. I was an au*teur*.

'Look at you,' he said, over and over – affirmative, like we'd just taken my stabilisers off – and I liked that. And it was sweet when he collapsed on top of me that first time. It was lovely, all the sweat and the grassy-flavoured stuff and coagulated hair. He got off and laid on his back and then, body completely still, he turned his neck to face me, right in the eye, heady and replete and absorbed and mine – a toddler with an iPad, a baby just unlatched. He was my son.

Patrick was forty-two of course and had a little girl. That would need explaining. The immediate explanation, the sex/Oedipus/Rachel one, that was pretty sexy but I didn't want it hackneyed. It would need a while, this one, a bit of marination. For now it was still too abstract, a concept and a crappy one at that, like an old white bed sheet standing for a ghost at a teenage Halloween party.

*

There was someone downstairs in the morning. It was Ines the cleaner, he said. He got out of bed, came over to my side and looked at me like I'd been here forever and this was our routine and he was off to work, and I remembered again though I wouldn't have forgotten that he wasn't long married, and that was how a married body got up out of bed – a dry quick kiss on the lips, a peck, then a girlish waffle dressing gown and slippers. He paused for a second at the door. *Don't move. Don't move and don't speak* was the feeling, but not in an aggressive way. He just wanted things as they were.

I considered bolting, but I wasn't convinced I could carry my stomach. I didn't want to take it through King's Cross and I wouldn't have him offering to pay for a cab, though that, I knew, was exactly what he'd do, not even an Uber but a proper Bridget rain-soaked cab. He'd insist upon it. Ines would go then we'd have melted fat on seven-seed carbs and honey and then he'd put me in a cab. I wanted that so much I couldn't be bothered to think about it so I closed my eyes. I was hanging. And when he came back upstairs, half an hour later, forty minutes, I liked that, all very fort-da.

I started again on the justification. I didn't want this, no, no way, not about that domestic life, but I could shelter in someone else's for a bit, feed off its comforts as it imploded in slow motion. It was symbiotic anyway. I was some kind of pollinator. Personnel at least. He needed someone to make him feel less bad about this stuff, his house and his dick and the world being his mirror, and this little thing was good for me because I was a masochist and, yeah, masochism, and rattling the system, infiltration, Trotsky stuff plus irony. Charlie had been into that, back in the day. Yeah, that sounded cool, Michelle and Charlie and Abi would be up for that, sat round some future sticky table, beer mat pyramids and quote-unquote world revolution, that would do. So I slid back down into the sheets, into his white, white company and his White Company bed and his White Company house and I closed my eyes and I taught him how my clitoris worked and I stopped thinking. I didn't want to think so I didn't. I didn't log in to my online banking, either, but that didn't mean I wasn't in debt.

*

111

That first morning we fucked four times. We fucked. We dozed. We fucked. Eventually I made it to the waterfall shower: Yes, yes, YES! And when I'd dried off I went snooping in the vanity cupboard, found his scent. L'Eau de Néroli.

'Patrick!' I called through to him, giddy, dousing myself till I felt a bit sick.

Silence.

'Patrick?'

I put my head in.

He was holding *On Beauty*, shaking his head. *Oh. Here we go. Little breath. Right. Placeholder coy. Ahem. Shake your head. You are seven. You're holding a copy of* The Queen's Nose *at your chest, gap-toothed, in a second-hand Benetton jumper and brown velvet leggings and white plastic trainers with Velcro straps. Now, place your hand across your mouth. Raise your eyebrows. No, not like that. Forlorn, Grace, forlorn. That's it. That's it! Got it. Great.*

'It's OK,' he said, smiling. 'Have it.' He threw it behind him.

Nod. Bite your bottom lip.

'You're a little thief.'

Lower the chin. Keep the head down. Raise the eyes.

'You're a fucking lout! I love it.' He laughed. He stopped. He pursed his lips. He came over to me, sniffed my neck. 'I like it.'

Patrick woke up before me, the first time and always. It was an age thing I think, though it was kindness too. I'd open my eyes and I never had to lie there with my cortisol raging, wondering what to do, never had to check my phone or creep downstairs and get his teabag ritual wrong. I woke instead to hear his thoughts on the coalition government. Or, more often, better, I woke up and he was pretty much on top of me already, hard. They really helped with the dread, those morning fucks. He'd hop downstairs for bananas straight after then go back down to plunge the cafetière, return with the seven-seed sourdough and Président (blue), fulfiller of dreams. Sometimes we had porridge, whole milk with grated apple and cinnamon and walnuts. Greek yoghurt on top, honey. I'd bless each feed with my tongue in my cheek like haha, jokes, we're infidels really and then I'd say *MARRY ME, GOOD LORD! MAKE ME AN HONEST WOMAN!* And then he'd do the anti-vampire crucifix and we'd laugh and then we'd fuck.

So the breakfasts were cracking though I had to sit before eating, sit for a minute, wait a bit longer for the throbbings and dislodgings to subside. He could blast right through and, *yes, yes Patrick, your end might be a bit sore, Patrick, yes, but no one's been inside* you, *you're not the one making the room.* I tried that talk with him but then he pointed at the trays of food, mouth still full, and then he pointed round the room in a big wide circle, and then he pointed at the *On Beauty* on the bedside table. *Room enough?* Damn. Scowl. Eat. Slide back down. Belly stroke. Hands in pants.

We'd spend days on end at his. Michelle took my shifts at the café and I sacked off Rachel, sacked her off proper. I did not think. I did not read or write or text or connect my phone to the Wi-Fi. I played with the fridge and watched *Murder, She Wrote* while he did a bit of work and then we fucked, and in between the fucks I stroked the skin beneath his eyes, just beginning to loosen. Back and forth, back and forth. Data.

*

'This is like John and Yoko,' he said one morning. 'The bed-in.'
  'Ha. And that poem, *Lamia.*'
  'Lamia?'
  'Yeah. It's a poem.'

'Sorry, no.'

'It's a poem by Keats.'

'What's it about?'

'Oh. Never mind.'

'What?'

'Doesn't matter.'

'Tell me.'

'Forget it.'

'Read it to me.'

'No.'

'Read it.'

'No.'

'Read it.'

'Patrick. I'm not going to sit here reading fucking Keats to you. Fuck off.'

'You fuck off.'

I threw Rose's bug-eyed monkey at his head and he ducked and snorted, then he gripped my forearm and down I went and I looked back up at him, stared, eyes wide, bottom lip again. I was Rose. I was Rose then I was Jean again for the thing itself then Rose again, grabbing his chest for a nestle. He liked that. I'd concentrate on the nipples, watch them coarsen and release, or a stray goose feather. Nice close focus. Plenty of blind spots. Good, yes. Nothing good could come of a natural confusion, the kind that arrived without you planning, no, so yeah, here I was, my head stuffed into his armpit, sniffing and blinking, double bluff.

Patrick wasn't confused. He knew what he was doing. He was middle-aged and middle-class, upper middle-class, and middle-class people lost themselves with calculation, with relish, with an overarching plan to find themselves. That's what I decided.

114

I liked the sound of that. And I could do that too. Fuck, he was my little newborn son and I was Rose and he was Daddy and I was Jane and Jean and John and Keats and fucking Yoko.

*

Dream. I'm walking up flights and flights of stairs. I don't know the number of the flat I'm visiting, but after seven or eight floors I get an intuition I've done one too many, and when I come back down the door's ajar. I push it open and walk inside. There are floor-to-ceiling bookcases in beech wood, aching with broken-spined books. I feel a presence the next room, turn and see the back of a head on a green chaise longue. It seems to be Patrick in some Wizard of Oz moment, Patrick transformed into the Forbidding Father manifesting as the Wizard of Oz. But when I get closer the pressure drops and the dream dissolves and I wonder if it's god.

*

I found out about Jane at an angle, as though there'd been some briefing I'd accidentally slept through. There hadn't been. I'd have nabbed a front-row seat for that. He'd just forgotten to lay it all out. That was an age thing. Age plus Sauvignon Blanc, though latterly we'd moved along to Chablis.

She was with a guy called Rob now. She lived with Rose in the marital home in Woodingdean, a place they'd been doing up when they split. That was the base, he said, but Jane was in and out of town with Rose. Town, they called it, town was W11, W8 and a little bit of Bayswater, and sometimes he'd be on the phone and he'd say 'London or country?'

I often thought Jane was downstairs. Once I swore I heard her making a shake. That was her Queen's English, unmistakable, that was her Queen's English amid the NutriBullet pulses.

115

'Oh my god! It's *Jane*,' I whisper-shouted, flopping the weight of my hand on the down. Deathly sink.

'It's Ines.'

'Ines doesn't do the NutriBullet.'

'She can use it if she wants.'

'She can?'

'Yes. She can help herself to whatever.'

'OK.'

'Yes.' A pat on the head.

'Patrick.'

'What.'

'How much do you pay her?'

'Shush.'

'How much do you pay her?'

'Why, are you offering?' Another pat.

'You could help a woman out.'

'Is that a joke? You shouldn't joke about that.'

'No, "Patrick," I don't joke about stuff like that. As if. I'm being obtuse.'

'Right.'

'Relax!'

He took a long breath.

'How much, though?'

'Leave it.'

I did my own long breath. I cleared my throat and took a vocal intake of breath, high-pitched.

'*No.*' He grabbed my shoulder, oops, felt the force, release.

'Chill! God. I wasn't going to scream.'

'Yes you were.'

'No. I wouldn't do something like that.'

'Yes you bloody would.'

Damn, I thought, and then I thought again and he was wrong, actually, yeah, he was – but that he'd think like that of me meant I was winning.

Along with her Queen's English, I gave Jane long chestnut hair in gentle waves with honey-blonde ends, a crew-neck cable-knit cashmere jumper, pedal pushers and Tod's, and despite being hauntingly thin – a lollipop head, a spoon, Mum called it that, spoons – *all head and nowt else, love, she needs a hot meal that Kimberley Walsh* – Jane paid handsomely for keratin, collagen and water, gliding around in that nice big Woodingdean house by the sea. I didn't share this image with Patrick. Something felt off. Rob, though, Rob was fair game. We'd dress him up in his Patagonia vest and then we'd do a Rob-off, which looked a bit like this:

'Going forward!'

'Move the needle!'

'Raise the bar!'

'Get in the weeds!'

'Deep-deep dive!' (Race to dive deep under the cover, bonus point.)

'Ducks in a row!'

'CAPACITY!'

'BANDWIDTH!'

'RESOURCE!'

'SYNERGISE!'

'360!'

'CLEAAAAAAAANSSSSSSE! *Cleanse cleanse cleanse cleanse cleanse cleanse cleanse.* Cleanse.'

'Going forward.'

'OUT!'

'Damn.'

117

Eventually he showed me her.

'Want to see her?'

'*Yes!*'

There she was, real, I thought, widening my thumb and forefinger. Here's Jane! Luminous and real! Indescribable, though actually when you looked she had a look of Rachel Cusk, late thirties Rachel Cusk.

I didn't flinch, which I tried to take as meaningful, though non-flinches came in time and when they came they *came*. Rachel had built a whole livelihood on it.

'Is she younger than you?'

'Yes.'

Silence.

'Don't worry.'

'I'm not.'

'She likes you.'

'How could she?'

'I talk to her.'

'Bit harsh.'

'She's fine about it.'

'How do you know?'

'We were married for five years, Grace. She's fine about it.'

'Right.'

'Don't be a child.'

'Oh, really? You love it, mate.'

'Grace.'

'I'm joking!'

'Good.'

'I am, mate. I'm joking.'

Those *mates* stayed there for a bit, off but unspoken, broken wind that could have been funny but left too long to make light of.

And then he was in his phone and I was ringing up Roxy from Specsavers.

'Is that Roxy? I'm just calling about my new glasses, Roxy. I came in last week?'

'Oh? Oh yeah! You're the one with them Elton ones. I remember. Alright are they?'

'They're a bit loose, love.'

'I'll tighten them, not a problem. I'll tighten those for you. They want tightening.'

'Thanks!'

'Oh, and erm, hang on.' She put her hand over the receiver. *What? What Paul? Customer? Oh yeah soz, hang on.* 'Sorry. Sorry I meant sorry for any convenience caused.'

'Oh no, no don't worry, love, not at all. Not at all.'

'What's your name again?

Here I spelt my surname with Alpha Bravo Charlie, did up the accent too, right out of *Emmerdale,* and I called her love and love again, and then I went for a full-on Huddersfield love because no one here would find it weird for Leeds to start talking Huddersfield. So she's northern then? She's that northern one? *What are you* doing *Grace? How embarrassing. Leave her alone and let her sell you your glasses. Stop trying to be her fucking pal. Weirdo. Fuck off Rebecca. You fuck off. Fuck off. Grace! Grace!* Patrick.

Patrick. Patrick. He was smiling. 'Ee bah gum!'

'Ha.'

'Ee, there were a hundred and sixty of us living in a small shoebox in the middle of the road.'

'Cardboard box?'

'Aye.'

'Luxury. We had to LICK the road clean with our tongues.'

He chucked his phone to the end of the bed and pinned me down. 'Lick? Is that right?'

'LICK. And when we got home Dad would thrash us to sleep with his belt.'

'Mmm.'

'Patrick.' A whisper.

Little nod.

'So in Huddersfield they say love like a totally different love, it's like, it's like a "lov", you slam the brakes on the V so it's almost an F, an F like a FUCK, as in fuck off, as in *fuck* you.'

'Fuck you?' He stroked his Roman nose with his middle finger.

'*Fuck* you.'

'Fuck *you.*'

We fucked. Once more for luck then I went to the loo. I used Rose's flannel with the cows on it. I plunged on in, great big panda crescents, red plumes of lip. I returned it to the rail. Then I paused, walked back, rinsed it over and over until it was mint and hung it back on the rail.

*

He had to go to Margate for a bit, urgent site visit he said, so I went back to the flat.

On the Tube there was a petite woman with wide thin finger-nails. She had on a pair of desert boots and socks the colour of grapefruit flesh, cycling shorts and a pale grey T-shirt. It was busy and I stood behind her, too close, wet with sweat, lactic from that sprint to beat the doors. She had ashy hair, fine, and her skin was hardy, makeupless, and she was older. I was struggling to stack up my twenties and here she was, thirty, maybe even thirty-five. Her hair began to soften with her sweat. I watched her type in the names of foods into her phone – MyFitnessPal. She had 1900 calories programmed in at the top of her screen. She added houmous and it said 190. She flitted, she hovered, she added. She added three crackers at 30 each. Then the Wi-Fi went and she couldn't figure out what a vine leaf was.

The doors opened, a lot of people alighted, we reconfigured. I caught her eye and smiled.

'I like your glasses,' she said, barely audible.

'They're a bit old now. Spares,' I said, joining her down in her just-above-whisper, barely believing we were here. I put them in my hand to take my face out of focus.

'It doesn't show. They suit you.' She leant down and pulled her bag between her legs.

I put the glasses on my head, stared the emergency handle into a blur.

I alighted early and bought a Pret from KX, heart racing – avo and herb wrap and a little pot of Bircher muesli with the cinnamon mixed in and a little slab of sea-salted chocolate and a little bag of plain mixed nuts – and when I got in I put those on the side for a moment while I got my TV sorted, block-booking the evening with *This Is England* on repeat, out for the. Lol and Woody stuff.

I pinched my face, I tried to cry. Nope.

I ate my four-step Pret.

I slept.

Time to go back to Rachel.

*

We started up again the next day. I went for dungarees this time. Flaky calves, piggy eyes, dungarees and battered blue Gazelles from 2008. I was back in 2008 now, 2008 at best. The era of Danish cigarette pants was behind us.

I knocked.

'Come in.'

There was no *oh, oh it's you*, nothing like that, she just wanted me to come in and she said it, and we went on through and I got on the couch and we continued. She'd put away her ankle boots. Red Mary Janes, today, and three-quarter-length black trousers. This fine black material that sat close to the skin. Leggings but sophisticated. In the weeks to come there'd be fewer cowl necks, fewer cowls and more crews, and more of those necks that cut across in a line. Boat necks, that was it, boat necks. She managed all this with aplomb, the weather, though she said she was going away for August. *We'll have just a few weeks now then we'll have our summer break. OK.* It was high time she got outside, donned a vest and shorts and took the air. She summered in France I think. She liked lavender in there, the consulting room, bergamot at first but now lavender, lavender pretty much exclusively, actually, and lavender soap in the loo. And a Courbet, there was a Courbet in the toilet.

'I don't not like him, Rachel. I think you'd like him. He's an OK person. He's on the side of progress.'

A pause. 'You like him.'

'I like most people, really, when you really drill down.'

Silence.

'I'm seeing it as an opportunity.'

'An opportunity.'

'I mean, I guess—. Yeah, an opportunity. The longer I'm with him the less I'm alone and—. That helps me to want it.'

'You want to be alone.'

'It's not that I never want to see him again. I'd quite like to see him, actually. Maybe every few weeks, every four weeks . . . Maybe every few months.'

'Every few months.'

'God. That's bad isn't it?'

'That's how you feel.'

'Erm. Yeah.'

Silence.

'Maybe.'

Silence.

'I mean, well, lots of people sit in things they know won't last, don't they? Try to learn something?'

Silence.

'Is that weird?'

'Would you like it to be?'

'Erm.'

Silence.

'I mean . . . I'm keeping my eyes wide open. I'm awake.'

Silence.

'I think so.'

Silence.

'God.'

Silence.

'I don't want to sound—. I . . . Well, yeah . . . I definitely—. I definitely think there's something immoral about it. Definitely.'

'Immoral. Something immoral.'

'Mmhmm.'

'What do you think that is?'

Silence. 'Maybe it's me.'

'You?'

'I'm bad . . . It's bad. I know it's bad.'

Silence.

'God. I don't know . . . No. Yeah . . . God, sorry. This is exhausting. Sorry. Ugh.'

'It sounds like he has a lot of his own to work through.'

'Oh god, absolutely.'

'But we're not here to talk about him.'

'Oh.'

Silence.

'Sorry.'

'Patrick is an adult.'

'Yeah, he thinks I'm one too. That's the problem.'

'Is it?'

A significant chunk of silence. Mine, now. Thirty seconds. Mine.

'I'll definitely die alone.'

'You'll die alone.'

'Definitely. When I think about it, the future, the "future", like in my mind's eye, I'm just old. Oldish, maybe I'm not even thirty but whatever, I'm older than I am now and I've got my hairy hairy down on my upper lip and I don't give a fuck and some silent benefactor's seen me right and I'm living in no man's land. I don't know. I'm not here. I'm—. I'm in fucking California.'

Silence.

'Sorry.'

Silence.

'Sorry I didn't mean to swear.'

'You can swear.'

'I'm just.'

Silence.

'I'm jus—. Well, I'm David Hockney. I've gone. I'm in LA and it's the sixties, or is it the seventies, sixties I think and it's all very primary-coloured and exquisite and the light is perfection but tragic, really sad, but I'm fine because there's the *sun*. I'm spraying my garden – Radio 4, I've managed to get Radio 4 out there so it's Sunday afternoon, *GQT*, socks and sandals – and I'm *alone*, and maybe I'm out of my mind like I've lost it, I've lost my mind a bit but I should think that's for the better. Being in it is—. It's—. It's—. I'm alone.' A silent and single tear, no correspondent emotion. 'I'm tired. I'm tired of this shit.'

Silence, hers.

Silence, mine.

'Even the most minimal life is an implicated life.'

Silence.

'I know, but there are ways to be minimally implicated.'

'Is that what you want?'

'I don't know. Probably not.'

*

A week passed. Dungarees take two.

'I—. I—. I do want to end it.'

'End it.'

'Patrick, I mean. Not my life.' Nasal *ha*.

Silence.

'I don't even like him. He's actually not that nice.'

Silence.

'I just want to be wanted and that's ethically . . .'

Silence.

'Don't you think that's bad?'

'You're being very hard on yourself.'

I fiddled with my strap. 'I want to be.'

Silence.

'I hate him, actually.'

Silence.

'I hate him. I hate men.'

'You hate men.'

'Well, him.' I dropped the dungaree strap, a little clang. 'No. No, I don't mean that. I mean men.'

Silence.

'I don't know what they are. I don't get it.'

Silence.

'I mean, obviously there is some sexual compatibility there but with, with someone like Patrick, Patrick as MAN – white, cis, able, southern, all that – well you're just never having the same conversation, are you?'

'Can you say some more?'

'Well he just hits all the categories doesn't he.'

Silence.

'Privilege.'

Silence.

'He doesn't understand himself.'

'You don't think he knows himself.'

'I mean . . . I'm not saying that. I'm. I—. He kind of does, yeah, I mean, he definitely does . . . A bit . . . I don't think you can get to that age without some of that, that's got to be inevitable, I can go with that, and he's definitely—. He's definitely put me in my place a few times. But that kind of structural, political self-knowledge, I mean, how could he have that, really? Like, not to extrapolate or generalise . . . Well, I don't want to, but, well, I do think . . . I think when you think about *Everyday Feminism* and that sort of thing and domestic violence stats and what have you I mean it's obviously

. . . It's obvious that men like this, I mean . . . Men like this, they kill women don't they and they kill themselves so, yes, I mean . . . I know it's overdone and I guess I actually hate this kind of thing, I hate shit like this but—. But yeah, I do feel quite strongly about it, that the world's made in their image.'

'*Everyday Sexism.*'

'Oh. Oh yes that's it. Sorry.'

Silence.

'It is all about sex, isn't it?'

'Is it?'

'Yes.'

Silence.

Her iPhone went here.

'I'm not going to answer that.'

I nodded up at the ceiling.

She didn't answer it but she let it ring. I wanted to tell her about the button on the top, how to mute it, but then I kind of got into the swing, started tapping my right fingers to the rhythm. We needed a bit of entertainment here, a change in the tone, some local colour, a turn.

'There's this dream I keep having.'

Silence.

'Shall I—'

'What do you dream?'

'I'm the dreamer and I'm watching the action with the sweeping drone's eye view. It's not always like that. Sometimes I'm the main character but here I'm god but the main character is also me. I'm walking through the big car park in Otley, there's this one main car park, and then I'm making my way up this long street, it's a terrace, can't remember what that street's called actually but it's a main through-road with terraced houses either side so the front step is straight on the pavement, iron grilles on the floor for the cellar vents I think and it's really narrow.'

She coughed. The iPhone had freaked her.

'It leads up to the building on the corner where Argos is and the gym, Club Energy. I'm walking then I notice someone's behind me, really close, hovering, just behind my back and I just have this hunch that it's Patrick. I think it's probably the Forbidding Father but it's this great feeling of Patrick manifesting.'

Another cough from Rachel. *Good work*, I thought. *Works nicely, Rach. Nice.*

'Anyway it gets all Vic and Bob. I stop, he stops. I cross, he crosses. I cross again, he crosses again. You can tell from these antics even before me-as-the-main-character turns that my shadow is smiling and then there's this super-cinematic slow-mo turn and she turns, I turn, with all my hair flapping in the wind. I can feel its gloss whipping my face. I have hair in this dream. I always have hair when I dream.'

Silence.

'I turn with all my hair and it's Patrick, I'm right, and he's smiling, and the feeling, I think the major strain of feeling here was that I wanted him to say I understand you perfectly and I wanted for us to be actually right in step, in a routine, choreographed, that's what I think the vaudeville was, Vic and Bob. But when I focus on his gaze, Patrick's gaze, I see he isn't quite smiling at me. He's looking out over my shoulder and his smile's the smile of a Disney princess on a helium balloon.'

Silence. A long, long silence. And then I put my fingers on the sternum and I started to drum them. Slow then quick then quick quick slow.

128

'Sorry. This is ridiculous.'

'Ridiculous.'

'Yeah! Ridiculous. God. I don't know what the hell I'm . . .'

Silence.

A little laugh here, and another *ridiculous*, whispered, whispered and emphatic, a Mum one.

'You're using the word "ridiculous". You're not laughing.'

I watched my Gazelles on the end of the couch, lolling. I would never see her feet like that.

*

I skipped the next week. She'd need some space after all that. And the next. And in fact altogether, at least for now. We'd had a little booster but frankly I was skint. And Patrick was playing it cool now so my psyche was robust. He was out in *Margate*, which I'd taken to thinking of in italics, *Margate*, a chuckle. I was enjoying that, the space. It was kind. I was much more comfortable. Fine. Supple. Light, even, though I guessed I was alone and dungareed and therefore chaste and that was why. I started doing sun salutations, six in the morning and six at night. I'd take the mirror off the wall and lean it at an angle on the long edge of my yoga mat so I could see my sagittal plane. I'd finish off with some spinal twists, but when I looked in the mirror, looked properly, held the pose, held the gaze, I knew I shouldn't be left alone with this person – me, her. I shouldn't belong to her.

Matthew and Adam were both away.

I had Patrick over.

*

I watched him approach from the kitchen window, watched as he paused at the corner to pull his phone out of his satchel and check his Maps. *Interesting he keeps it in his satchel*, I thought. *Why not a pocket? Who can say! He's a real person.* It was good to see him there with that happy congregation of peach polystyrene, stray chips, a couple of leftover boys in blazers. I liked walking there myself at the end of the school day, nice thick haze of hormones and fried chicken and wit, ready to be roped in, willing. I watched him nod at the boys as he approached the flat. He looked up. Saw me. Blushed, I thought, though I didn't have my glasses.

'Is this where you *live*?'

'Shut up.'

'What a hole.'

'It's charming.'

'It's tiny.'

'It's bohemian.'

'It's tiny.'

'Look. Do you want to fuck or not?'

This one was hot. Violent and immediate. Ah, ah, AYEEEE. Fifteen minutes after losing his Nikes he was flush against the wall in my headboardless bed, wiping his hands with the loo roll on the floor. He reached into his satchel for his Amber Leaf, humming a little and a tenor. He was a new person.

'Grace.'

'What.'

'Let's have a dirty weekend.'

'Fun. Where?'

'Paris.'

'Oh. No. No I don't want to go to Paris. God. How soulless.'

'This is basically Paris.' He pointed at his cock. 'No complaints so far.'

'You're a dick.'

'Where do you want to go?'

'Berlin. I want to go to Berlin.'

We went to Woodingdean.

*

The Woodingdean house was detached and single-storey, almost LA if you mentally Photoshopped some bougainvillea up the side: white stuccoed outer, floor-to-ceiling windows, sexy long corridors with skylights. White floor tiles inside, a corner bath, Jacuzzi. Jane and Rob and Rose had gone away and the deeds were his said Patrick, this house was his.

We opened up. Patrick breathed in, buckled his nose. It was a bit damp. Not terrible, but right away he was on one, khaki windcheater flapping all over the shop. He bustled about from room to room, slamming out the windows to the edges of their hinges, dragging the dehumidifier out the garage.

I followed him into the laundry room.

'Patrick.'

'Grace,' he said from deep in his dehumidifier wipe-down. It was filthy.

'I don't think it works to do both, Patrick, like, isn't it windows or machine, either/or?'

'Don't start.'

'Just a thought.' I drummed my fingers lightly, lightly and slowly on the side.

'Christ. She does this to spite me.'

131

'OK.'

'Look at the fucking windows.'

'They've been away a few days already. It's normal. It's fine. It's those sheets. It'll just be the residual stuff off them. There's washing out. Look.'

'What?'

'Look.'

He looked up. I pointed at the clothes horse.

'What the fuck. Who *does* that?'

'What?'

'You don't leave a load just out like that.'

'You don't leave dirty sheets vegetating, Patrick.'

He huffed. He puffed.

'Come on. It's fine. Rose will have wet the bed or something. It's nice of them if anything. They knew we were coming.'

'Leave it.'

'Right.'

'Bitch,' he whispered. 'These are *my* sheets. They've had fucking sex on my fucking sheets.'

'Oof.'

He threw his cloth down, took the container out and poured the rotting water down the sink, banging the plastic on the edge. 'Jesus.' He wrinkled his nose. 'They haven't used this in months.'

I put my hand over my mouth.

'*Bitch.*'

'Patrick.'

He swilled it off with the tap in the corner, banging it again to shake the water.

'Yeah, fine, gross, but there's twelve months in a year. It'll even out.'

'Nope. Not how it works. Sorry!'

132

'Come on.'

He was hunching again now, interfacing, container and machine. He couldn't get it back in.

'Patrick. Let me—'

'Fucking *hell*,' he said and he flung his thing in the sink and slammed the door. I watched him through the frosted glass. Completely still, hint of a slump in the shoulder blades.

I opened the door.

He had his head bowed now and was exhaling.

'Patrick.' I put my arm out, moving it up to the nape of the neck, placing my index finger and thumb there, across the width, spreadeagled.

'Mmm.'

I took his right ear. 'I like your khaki windcheater Patrick,' I said. 'I like your house in Woodingdean.' I put his little hood up, held the ropes and toggles on each side of his face. I pulled them, didn't yank them, no, a gentle pull.

'That's friendly.'

'Patrick.' I was whispering now, hand down in the boxers. Yep.

'Mmm.'

'Go run.'

He left and I mooched. There were miniature shoeboxes in the hall and Disney cereal bowls in the cupboards and, on the walls, Rose, though I looked at her with a squint, pixelated. I tried that, but actually that was even weirder – I felt like a plain-clothes police officer in the first place, here, here in this house in my shoes, so I took them off, borrowed Jane's slippers from the porch and a dustpan and brush for the floor. It was getting cold now, colder than the chill from the windows warranted. My fingers were going. I gave the place a freshen-up to get the blood pumping. Worktops. Sink. Closed the windows. Still cold. Freezing. I put the kettle on and pulled a mug from the back of the cupboard, right at the back, kind of dusty in fact, biggest I could find. Poured. The water hit the china and the china started cheeping and then there was a puddle. *Shit.* I rushed it to the sink. *Fuck.* Fuck, though the china didn't break thank god. I gave it a wipe with some kitchen towel, put it back.

*

That night we went for dinner in Hove at Dasha and Julian's. Julian was Patrick's older brother. They had a portico. Like Rachel's, though this one had pillars.

Julian came out to greet us, portly and in sun-bleached Ralph Lauren – pink polo. *Of course*, I thought, rolling my eyes, though as soon as we opened the taxi door and the full fact of his energy made itself known it was clear it wasn't a state-ment that polo. It wasn't an accident but it wasn't a statement, and Julian lived on that side of the difference. He was sound.

'Come in! This must be Grace! Pat, hi. Come in!'

The house was a blend of Issey Miyake, unevaporated shower and tiny chorizo bites.

'Miniature turd?' Julian offered me the plate.

'Oh, thanks,' I said, swallowing my pescatarian thing. Patrick put his palm in the small of my back.

'Thanks, Ju,' said Patrick, taking two, and then there were two gins, cut glass and lemon.

'Cheers!'

'Cheers.'

We went through to the conservatory. Dasha was in the garden, back turned. She sensed us, waving with a flick of her hand.

When she turned around I saw she had a Marlboro hanging on her bottom lip and a fistful of rosemary. She brought the grass in with her Crocs, gave her feet a cursory wipe but the floor was tiled and the stray blades didn't halt her. She pushed her photochromic specs into her hair, an ashy blonde, killed the cigarette, handed the rosemary to Julian and moved the pack and ashtray from the dresser to the coffee table. Then she brought the weight of herself down next to me, all of it, glorious. She owned her body and she owned this chair, a love seat with calamine stripes.

'Abigail. Heard a lot about you. Pleasure,' she said.

'You too,' I said. 'Cheers,' I said, handing her her gin.

'Sweet girl. Cheers.'

'She's called Grace, Dash,' said Patrick from across the room.

'Grace! Yes. Yes. Grace. Sorry sweetheart. Cigarette?'

'Oh. Yes please. Let me.'

'You're a peach. Now.' She looked me up and down. 'You're arty. You look arty. Seen the McQueen?'

'No—'

'Did it last weekend. The light was *appalling* but the scarves were *marvellous*. I bought six – one for myself, a few for the girls. I'm a sucker for a scarf, aren't I, Ju?'

Julian had taken the rosemary through and was showing Patrick his treadmill. He'd set it right next to the glass so he could watch the sea.

Dasha rolled her eyes and reached down for the lighter. I'd gone out.

'Oh, thanks.'

She tossed it back on the table. I dragged deep.

'You'll suffer long with a MacAskill, darling. Selective hearing. I believe it's genetic. Isn't that right, Ju?'

Julian was walking on the treadmill, side-eyed her but played along.

135

I let a little laugh out of my nose, mouth still shut but smiling, took another drag.

'I do like a scarf of an evening. I have a collection. Reminds me we've lived, you know. Julian's intrepid. Drags me all over. Borneo! Borneo, last year. But we summer in Europe and in Easter we Rome. Every year. Sicily, last month. We stayed on a while and the *lemons*. I always bring some back. But we're diabetic now. Pat! Hear that, Pat? Diabetic! Diabetic, the both of us. Pre-diabetic.'

'Syllabubs are out then.'

'Quite.'

'No, no sweet tonight. I said to Ju we just can't, I can't because I'll stuff my face and I don't know what the hell they think I'll do, explode, I don't know what but the doctor's very mean, very pimply and severe. All of you, you young ones. So severe!'

'Ugh. Hate it, Dasha. Hate it. May I apologise on behalf of us all.'

'Well, there's strawbs for you and Patrick.'

'Oh *yes*.'

'And choccy. That doesn't count.' Wink. Drag. 'What a hoot!'

I pulled the ashtray in.

'Thanks, sweetheart. It is a *shame*. I love tropical fruit. Papaya. Do you like papaya? Papaya I love. Papaya, lime juice and salt. MMM.'

'Sounds delightful.'

'I must say, I like garlic. Garlic I like very much so I can do garlic for my first course, I can do something garlicky on a prix fixe and cheese, cheese. Gosh. No, no I don't feel too cheated.'

'Oh *yes*,' I said. 'Love it.'

She nodded deeply, floating her cigarette towards the garden then pausing for a moment, contemplating. Her gums were receding a little.

'All my life I've had a connection to this house, Grace. My mother's widowed sister's, my "aunt". Long story there. Long story.'

'It's lovely.'

'It is rather winning, isn't it? I'm leaving the deeds to my sons.' Another drag. 'You're from Yorkshire.'

'Yes. West. Leeds.'

'I like it, Yorkshire. Do you know something – I love it. Such authentic people, something of the *campesino* about them don't you think?' She paused. I blinked. 'HA! Look at your face! I'm joking with you, darling.'

Smile. Gin-mitigated blush.

'No, in all honesty though, I find it charming. I've sat in that mill, Titus Salt's Mill, that mill with the Hockneys.'

'Salt's Mill.'

'Not much culture though, is there. I couldn't live like that. I like things.'

'Ye—'

'Ju!'

This time he turned.

'Olives!'

We had our olives and went through for dinner. Orange Le Creuset. Ta-dah! A swamp of olive oil and crème fraîche and little slivers of red pepper and black pepper and basil, yes, basil I think, and chicken thighs on the bone. Mash, half a pack of butter sitting waiting on the top, never fully melting. Pyrex of leeks, sweated off and fattened in a gratin. Sprouts and bacon, cheese on the sideboard.

I sat next to Julian.

'You see these sprouts?'

'Yes! So green!'

'Bicarb.' He winked.

'Hmm?'

'Bicarb in the water keeps the colour.'

'Oh! Fab.'

'Don't tell her I told you.'

I winked.

'A Cambridge girl,' he put his palm on the table – not the fingers but the heel, a little firm landing. English. Correct choice. 'Excellent. College?'

'Oh, I—.' I glared at Patrick.

'No, no. In fact don't tell me, Grace. Don't let me get on that topic.'

'I—'

'What are you reading? This is exceptional.' He leant back and took *Straw Dogs* off the bookcase behind him. 'Take it.'

'Oh, no, that's fine.'

Patrick side-eyed me and smiled.

Julian put the book back and I turned with him.

'Lots of Terry Eagleton there, Julian.'

'Know thy enemy, Grace!'

I smiled.

'No, he's a fine thinker. This one, this was fine, fine, this is a *fine* piece of work.' *Hope Without Optimism.*

I dropped my fork on the floor. The gin was working.

'Excuse me one moment Julian while I retrieve my implement.'

He guffawed.

I went under. His heels were bulging out the back of his shoes and sockless. Black Converse. Hmm. Curious. Sockless yes, but Converse? I came back up and looked at Patrick, brows knitted. He smiled and nodded.

'Favourite novel,' Julian said as I emerged.

'I—'

Patrick winced.

'Pat! I'm sorry old boy. Good grief I'm a bore. Do excuse me Grace.'

I smiled, eyebrows raised, draining the gin.

'WINE! Dasha!'

'Ju!' she called through from the kitchen.

'Relieve this woman of her gin!'

'Wine, Pat?'

'Wine, Grace?'

Nod nod nod.

'What a hoot!'

Toilet. *Don't be sick. You're fine. You're fine.* Mirror. Wipe.

Strawberries.

'Strawbs Pat.'

'Oh, thanks Dash!'

'Cracking strawberries Dash. They're not wooden at all.'

'Liar, Ju. They're wooden and tasteless.'

'Let me,' I said to her, little jug of cream poised.

'Oh she's a *peach* Pat,' Dasha said to Patrick, palm flat on her placemat. 'Isn't she a peach!'

She looked at Julian.

Julian nodded.

We had our cheese and our choc and our port, port wine, port wine from Porto, and there were some photos, old eighties photos of the port wine in Porto, this giant glass you put your whole head in and passed round, *squiffy with the fumes*

139

alone, young Grace! It started blurring up around there. Julian called for a taxi.

*

Taxi.

'They loved you. Well done.' He took my hand.

I pulled away.

'Grace?'

Window stare.

He exhaled. 'Grace.'

'What.'

'What is it?'

'What? Hmm? What's that? Hmm?' I perked my head up, looked out over the headrest and the dashboard, tiny little movements side to side. Like a meercat, I thought, though on reflection it was cruel, a cardboard-cutout Dasha. 'Hmm? Hmm?'

He sighed. 'Go on.'

'No, no. No, I'm fine! I'm *fine!*'

'Spit it out.'

'No! No, I'm fine. I'll send my invoice on. What's your email again?'

'Funny.'

'I don't do cash in hand. We did cover this.'

He brought his elbow to rest in the groove at the bottom of the window, stroked his chin, pursed his lips and looked out at the road. 'Again?' he said, still staring out. 'Are we doing this again?'

'Doing what? What are we doing?' Meercat head.

'Look. All I was saying was they liked you. They liked you. Good job.'

'Urgh.' I flopped back.

'"*Urgh.*"' He mirrored me.

'Fuck off.'

'You're drunk.'

'You're a dick.'

'Come on.' He tapped his little finger on my knee – the inside, the tender side – and let it rest there.

'You picked me. Well done you.' I said and I picked up his finger like a snail off a path and dropped it back where it belonged.

'I'm bored of this.'

'Great package, right? Great choice. Easy clit AND Cambridge AND a bit of northern soul! So cool. So relevant.'

'You're making a tit of yourself.'

'*Great* ROI.'

Silence.

I did a cotton-fresh laundry advert sigh, vocals from the top to the bottom of the breath, five, six seconds, then a hot sharp splice into abrupt silence then a cross of the legs then back to my window.

'Yeah me too, mate. You and me both.'

'Mate. Mate mate mate. Mate mate mate mate mate mate mate.'

'Fuck off,' he said.

'YOU fuck off.'

'*Shh.*'

'I don't give a shit. You don't have a clue. You don't have a fucking clue.'

He started playing a mock violin, Eeyore eyes.

'Fuck off.'

'We are what we are, Grace.'

Silence.

'You like nice things and nice things cost money. That's how it works. We are what we are.'

'Oh my god.'

'You got out, Grace. You got out of there. You're here. You made the fucking sandwich. Eat it. Eat the fucking sandwich.'

'What the *fuck*.'

He shoved his head back. Yawned. Sighed. Opened the window a crack. 'I did *not* sign up for this.'

'FINE. Have your fucking money back. Have it back. Here.' I took a pack of fags out my bag, threw them at him. 'Here you go.' I turned to my window. 'What the *fuck* am I doing in this *fucking* car with this FUCKING DICKHEAD.' I turned to look at him. 'I *fucking* hate you.'

The driver slowed down. 'Everything OK, love?'

'Sorry about this,' said Patrick. 'You can—. We can stop here. Here's fine. Just—. Yes. Here's great. Thanks.' He paid him double, cash.

I charged off. 'You're a *dick*, Grace,' I thumped myself on the temple. 'You're a *dick*. FUCK.'

'Grace.'

I turned back and put my hands in the air, turned to mock stone, tongue lolling out, stared him straight in the eye.

'It's this way, Grace.'

＊

We got back to the house, undressed in silence and got into bed. He turned out the light.

'I'm sorry Patrick.' Whisper.

'Shh. I know what you're like. I know you. I know how it is.'

I turned and looked at him, voice normal now. 'Thanks,' I paused. 'You're a twat, though.'

'I'm a twat?'

'You're a twat.'

'I'm a twat?'

'Yeah. Actually yeah, you're a twat. You don't "know" me.'

Silence.

'I *hate* you. I hate you.'

'Fine. I don't know you. I don't. I don't fucking want to.'

'Correct. I'm scum. I'm a dickhead. I'm a fucking D I C K
H E A D. Card-carrying. Traitor. Scab. But *you*.'

'Me.' He reached over for a fag, shimmied up a bit to rest
on his elbows then his bum, lit up.

I watched the smoke plume in the light from the window,
the curtains set adrift to ward off the damp. 'You're a—'

'I'm a?' He was smiling now.

'You're a *KNOB*.'

'Knob?'

'KNOB.' I threw the cover off me and stood up, put
the bedside light on and my glasses and started unbutton-
ing Jane's silk pyjama shirt. I wanted my knickers back. I
went over to the chair, bent over and then, 'Jesus. Oh fuck.
Nhhhhhhhh. Nhh I feel sick. I'm—. I'm going to—. Nnnh.
Nnnnnnh.'

'No you're not. Come on.'

I flopped back in bed, put my head in his lap.

He stroked my head.

'Who am I?' I buried this question in the duvet. This one
was for the duvet.

'Shh.'

'Nhh.'

'Shh.'

'Who *am* I?'

'You're Grace. Shh.'

'I'm not asking *you*.'

*

143

We stayed like that for a while. I must have drifted for a bit and then I turned and looked up and he was still sat up, headphones in, seeing to his emails.

I pulled at his buds.

'Scamp.' He smiled.

'Wah.' I flopped the head back down.

'Grace.'

'What.'

'Grace.'

'*What.*'

'Is it weird that I love this. I fucking love this. I do, actually. I love it. I love you.'

'Fuck off.'

'I do.'

'Lol.'

'You know what I mean. This has probably been my favourite kind of arrangement I've had, you know, of all my arrangements. It's so—'

I put my fingers to his lips. 'Don't. God. How gauche.'

'I'll say what I like. It's . . . Being with you . . . It's very freeing.'

'Well, obviously.'

'See, there. I like that reaction. I like that. It's cute.'

'Fuck off.'

'I'm having fun.'

Grimace.

'I feel. I don't know. I feel—. Well. You're a nightmare and I don't even mind. This is new for me.'

Pretend vomit.

'Look. It's fine Grace. I want to feel like this. I really don't care if you don't. I really don't mind.'

'I do. *I* mind.'

'You're upset because you don't want to hurt me. I'm not hurt. Look at me.'

Erm. What, I thought and then the little tin-eared happy voice inside my head said, *he's a man!* I screwed up my face at her.

He shimmied back down now and I turned out the light and he turned on his side to face me. 'Am I hurt?'

'You stink of fucking garlic.'

'Stop being so defensive.'

'Stop talking so confidently about your inner life . . . About *my* inner life. It's—'

'Go on. What is it?'

'It's so *gauche*.'

'Christ. Everything's gauche now, isn't it. Let's try this.'

'What?'

He went down to a whisper. 'I'd like to see you pregnant.'

'What the *fuck*.' Head back in the duvet.

'It'd be hot.'

Silence, then a little *wah* from me (concessionary, and, well, knackered).

'You need to chill Grace.'

Silence.

'You need to relax Grace.'

I nodded into my duvet.

He tapped me on the back of the neck.

I looked over my shoulder and let the back of my head fall so I was gazing up. I bit my lip.

He smiled and put his fingers on his lips, the index in his mouth, down to my left nipple, started stroking.

It hardened. 'Get off my nipple.'

He smiled and began to slowly massage it. Tiny little circles, just at the very outer edges of the areola. I stifled a moan.

'Now.'

He removed his finger and reached over to the bedside table. I saw now there was a new bottle of red there, half empty, and a tumbler. He poured more wine and handed it to me.

'Why am I here, Patrick?'

'You tell me.'

He put his finger back.

I downed my wine.

We fucked.

*

3 a.m.

I woke up with an empty bladder and a raging throat, put his Nikes on and went through to the kitchen.

Fridge door.

Brita.

Fridge door.

I stood there for a second, eyeing my reflection in the chrome. *Have his baby*, it mouthed. *I give up.*

I stared back for a while. Frowned. Stuck out my tongue. Frowned.

Do it. Mum'll lose her shit. Have a kid and send them up – send a whole little flock on the train, King's Cross, do the nine-and-three-quarters thing with them, wands and a scarf or a hoody or whatever they want, all of it, merch them up and send them off. Here, Mum. For you.

She looked away.

I looked back up.

Mum can give them their mini packs of Coco Pops and their culture, and that's what it'll be for them. 'Culture.' She can give them an ear for an accent and school them in eye contact, gratitude to bus drivers, morning love, morning love. She can teach

146

*them when it's worth being afraid, who to fear, when, what to
do with it – they'll know it just to know her. And Grace, Grace,
listen, you can hear all about it from their happy little mouths,
second-hand, hand-me-down, and maybe then you'll forgive her.*

She looked away.

I looked back up.

She looked away.

I looked back up.

She'd gone.

I bought my hands to my clammy little brow then scraped
them down, cradled the cheeks, the dimples.

No, yes, they were here.

*

5 a.m.

Patrick was stood at the foot of the bed, tying a lace.

'What are you doing?'

'I'm getting dressed.'

'Patrick. What. Are you leaving? What are you doing? Get
in bed. Please.'

I rose up onto my knees and shuffled across with my hand
outstretched.

He took a step away from the bed.

'What are you doing?'

Silence.

'Patrick.'

'What are you doing?' My heart was in my mouth.

'I'm hungry. I'm going to get some food.'

'It's 5a.m.'

'There'll be somewhere.'

'Wait for me.'

'I need to be on my own.'

147

'Oh.'

'I want to be.'

Boot in the stomach. 'Please. Please, don't leave me.'

'I'll be back in a bit.'

'Please.'

'Do you want anything?' Back turned, hand on the door handle.

'Erm.'

'Do you want a banana?'

'Yes. Erm, please can I have banana please?'

He nodded, back turned still. He left.

I couldn't sleep. I stole a Barbour and some deck shoes – massive, men's, but it was a look with the cadmium ankles; semi-deranged was a look. I walked for a bit, to this park they called *HAPPY VALLEY*. The day would be spotless but for now it was moody, low-hanging fog, salty mist. There were a couple of dog walkers in the far distance and here, in the foreground, this gleaming white couple with blankets and triplets. The mum was flat on her back and the kids were doing some jigsaw or other on this enormous family tray, straight from the kitchen so they must have lived just across. The dad had this hair in a knot on the top of his head. Everyone was silent. A relationship.

I went back to the house, back to the bedroom, tried to stay dressed, stripped the sheets and left them in a pile by the door. When he returned he took off his trousers and socks and sat down next to me and I tossed him a fifty pence piece for my Texaco banana – evens, peace. I took off my trousers, also evens, and we sat together in our undies and socks with the backs of our legs on sheetless bedding, one final go at a temporary den. He wriggled his toes. I peeled my banana. I ate it. Then I blew him and he blew me, the best we'd ever had and then we dozed.

We woke, we packed, we left.

*

I got out the car at Royal Oak. *Are you OK to take it from here? Yes. Yes, that's fine.* Peck. Peck. Wave. I got off at Finsbury Park and walked it from there. Shona was under the arches, Shona and Maureen and Maureen's shopping trolley.

'I used to light a cigarette with a match and turn around for the ashtray and it would've gone,' said Maureen.

'He was a compulsive hoarder, Maureen,' said Shona.

'Right from the start,' said Maureen.

A few metres up a bathroom bin bag had split on the kerb and there were all these balls of hair ripped from the brush and there were sanitary towels, one unfurling with a late-stage bleed.

I let myself into the flat, dropping my bags in the hall and standing for thirty seconds or so before going through. Matthew was in the kitchen making a carbonara, his two raw eggs in my cereal bowl. He turned around and saw my face then he stopped, turned properly and gave me a cuddle with his eggy hands, rocking us to and fro. Then he turned back to salt his water. I watched him beat his eggs in my bowl. I watched him eat. Then I took the bowl back, washed it twice and hid it in my bedroom drawer.

*

That was it. We hadn't goodbyed and we wouldn't. I got to work forgetting.

I deleted the photos and I worked double shifts for days on end and in between I walked, walked and made lists: calories, acronyms, street names, calories. At night I did super-easy sudoku with *Fish Tank* on repeat, trying to inoculate myself with that bit where Michael Fassbender catches a fish, gives Mia the piggyback. I'd freeze her face resting on his shoulder with her little tuft of ironed fringe, hoops, kohl, that learnt amount of foundation – enough to make it visible so people know don't mess. I'd stop it there then I'd stare into space then I'd get up and dance to 'U Don't Know Me', belting the lyrics to my nasty little superego there in the mirror, middle finger shoves, hood up, sweat sweat sweat, dry empty scream, Edvard Munch, gasp, laugh, growl, sleep.

Sometimes Matthew and Adam knocked and asked if I wanted to come to the pub, I didn't, and later they'd come back in with their voices down. That was the worst part. I wanted to hear them. I wanted a bit of life to listen to. Good to keep a hand in. I often caught Adam saying *girls* because he was Tindering, Adam was Tindering hard. He said his *girls* in a mock Essex accent.

I came out once or twice a day for form and they were nice if they were there. Kind. One morning I spilt a bit of coffee on the carpet in the hall and Adam came up behind me as I knelt, granules of Vanish in hand, a big ledge of Blue Harbour slipper at my eyeline. 'Thanks,' I said.

The calories went down well. I thought of myself at twelve in unelected Matalan Lycra and down they went. I didn't want to be smaller, or take up less space, and I wasn't clean

150

or virtuous or good and I didn't want to look like Tess Daly being a Well Gal on the Tube and I didn't believe in hair removal and I'd read my Chimamanda and my Caitlin. I did it for the arithmetic.

Bagel 230, butter 75, beans 145.

Nectarine 70.

PB spoons at 90, 90, 90. (120 for that last one, 120.)

Two Petits Filous 90, 90, cup of tea, milky, 25? 30?

I kept the feeds small so they were harder to trace and did my counting every spare moment. I'd get a total then try and keep it in my head while I started from scratch, replicating my result, then I'd doubt I'd included some portion of milk or an extra almond or something and I'd have to start again. I'd think of Rachel. *Retarding the growth of a body by depriving it of food is connected to sexuality.* That's what she'd say. Sometimes I thought about why she was a psychoanalyst. Perhaps it was just something she wanted to do.

Small feeds, big outputs. This went on for weeks. Sometimes there were days where I couldn't get a shift and I'd take a photo of a patch of land out my *A to Z*, write a list of street names or a little memory prompt down my left wrist, stuff my phone in my pillowcase and walk. When I'd seen every street in the postcode I went linear. I'd go out four or five Tube stops from home and follow them back on foot until I needed a wee too much. Maida Vale and back through Kilburn. Euston, Chalk Farm, Gospel Oak, Archway. Stratford, marshes, Tottenham Hale.

Matthew said I should start running but I wasn't *running,* Matthew. *Darling, please. I'm not 'escaping' Matthew. I'm earthing.* I'd walk at a pretty ploddy pace and try to think, and if thinking was naming and counting and listing these days then so be it. I'd name my streets and I'd count my calories thank you very much and my brain would sit astray somewhere north of the noise and I'd watch it in meaningful silence. Stun-gunned selfhood.

Once I saw a tall thin woman on Inderwick Road, up near the summit where you can see Ally Pally, her chestnut hair just turning grey, worn in a bun at the nape of her neck. I'd seen her round here before. She always wore fisherman's jumpers in earthy tones and a silk neckerchief and bare ankles and copper pumps, Superga. She had two greyhounds. Not whippets. Greyhounds. Today she walked in front of me then she stopped while one of them sprayed a tree. I overtook her. Then I heard her upping her pace from behind me. I thought she was running to catch me up, maybe I'd dropped a tissue or something, so I turned back, and then I saw the dogs were gone and she'd started to run. She really went for it. She galloped. She galloped into the spinney by the side of the road and then on, into the thicket, the branches and leaves cracking behind her.

Once I went to Hackney Wick. A couple of students with a camera, women, stopped me just by the station. They were wearing silver rings on their fourth and fifth fingers and thumbs and noses and had expensively untamed hair in tendrils, expensively unkempt. They were doing a short course at UAL and could I tell them about a time I'd experienced prejudice? I was in the Sprayway fleece, overcast that day, though for now I delved into my head and mentally donned my damson cocoon pants and a short silk shirt and I did my accent up too and I was straight out the blocks, astute and syllabic and silky with wit, Barbara feat. Bette feat. Alan Bennett. *Oh, darling, can you be my* northern *friend she asked? Cambridge with this accent? Can you imagine!*

Someone please come in here and help, I thought as they walked away, save me from the self-evaluation. Tell me what a delight it was in fact to be lights-camera-action ready like that, drop of a hat, what a skill it was, an achievement, a USP, a necessary defence, and wasn't it inspiring they were making art and stopping people on the street, out on the street working their nifty little camera like pros? YES GIRLS. *Calm down, Grace. A tendril is a tendril, Grace. Leave their tendrils be.*

I went on, on to Victoria Park. I saw a woman with a big elastic band round her shins, taking side steps with this giant elastic band. Ripped to the point where there was nothing left to rip. I turned from her. I hung my head and turned around and here came a woman on wheely overground skis.

I walked on. Far, on and up to Lidl. Here was a woman in a Coach backpack and a riding hat in Lidl. A high-fashion riding hat in Lidl. *OMG Rebecca will love this omg fucking whaaaaat* but where was Rebecca? Who was Rebecca?

It wasn't safe here. It wasn't safe, such a high saturation and quantity of people like this, identikit and rich and sad and most sinister of all in *Lidl*, what that *meant*. Everyone was so young and recently disgorged and subsumed by something that couldn't be named, working, banking a wage, losing the wage, having sex and perhaps in a gradual, healthy, articulated way or else not, filling their leisure with smashed avocado and glazed edgy chipboard and coffee and UAL camerawork and boulders and giant elastic bands and big cut flowers off Columbia Road, full in the knowledge of the cliché, fine with it, opting in, opting out, opting in, opting out. *These people are lovely!* They were, they were lovely. They were reckless. It was reckless. Would someone please intervene? But hey, who wouldn't want to wear a riding hat? Who wouldn't want to own a Coach backpack? Was that not fabulous? No. Yes. I liked for it to exist. I did. I did. I did. I did. I think I did. I lived here. This was my life. I was working on myself. I was working to be satisfied with working on myself.

Then the thinking stopped altogether. I was a stone. I couldn't get through the catchment area. Rubbishy dashes and brackets, clauses, caveats, turncoat ellipses. I stopped. I couldn't get up.

I liked difficult things, as a rule. As a rule I liked to fill my head with the difficult elegant things other more difficult elegant people said about life. None of that now. Now it was just difficulty. Now it was just off-white light and Matthew being out with his door wide open and Adam fucking *girls* and bottles of Innocent waiting in the fridge for the come-down. I was losing time when I could have been awake and it wasn't even agonising.

*

Rebecca.
  Can I come to Sheff for a bit?
  ?
  Please?
  OK
  Please
  U OK?
  Yeh, yeh just . . . Can I then?
  Yeh that's fine

*

I left a note for Matthew. *Had to go. Sublet me? I'm* <u>sorry</u>. *Jess said her mate Oliver's looking? I'll pay the difference. I'll be back. Love you, will explain, ~~soory~~ sorry. Sorry. XXX*

SEPTEMBER 2015

She was wearing headphones, the woman on the train. She got on at Chesterfield, rush hour, and gestured to the empty window seat next to me. 'Of course,' I said, nodding but not daring to smile, and in an officious, halting, fearful tone that made me wince to hear it, as though this was a job interview, a mini ritual shaming. I was still in London mode.

With an East Mids or East Coast train, a northbound one, you were generally safe to switch back, assume a mode of northernness that was, well, I didn't really have the words to say. Older. Less a mode, less a choice, less prone to your machinations, your intentions. No bow ties, no tap shoes. Yes, you were safe to switch back and emphatically once you hit Donny, Wakefield, Meadowhall, Chesterfield and merged with the local commute, but I hadn't spoken to anyone for a long time.

I got up for her, and as she sat I refocused and tried to rebrand, repair the damage. I took a leisurely drink of water from Aunty Jan's flask (I am green, I am friendly). I tipped the last of that tiny plastic package of trail mix straight into my mouth (less green but friendly still – and loose, and fun, and available, interruptible, with appetite).

She was in her late thirties I'd have said and she was wearing an aubergine fleece. Fleece, soft grey trackies and a red plastic arch on her head. She was listening to Rihanna (*Loud*-era), and

I was circling unknown and familiar words from Matthew's *LRB*. Some for looking up. Some for rehabilitating. I added *sangfroid* to the back of the Moleskine: *sibilant, avuncular, bewildered, soluble, indolent, armistice, sangfroid.*

The ticket person entered and the woman removed her headphones, the cushions falling on her collarbones with a little click. She started rummaging in her fleece pockets, piling her fags and keys and loose change out on her lap and then up on the tray table. Then she seemed to want something from her bag down below so she shoved everything back in her pockets and folded the tray away again. She unzipped the bag and a yellow pac-a-mac came tumbling out and under that there was a hammer with a blue rubber handle and a bottle of paint-stained turps wrapped to prevent leaks and empty Tupperware of various sizes. One was ribbed and cylindrical and still had some milk in it. Blue-top, I guessed from the viscosity. She took a swig then applied a film of apple Vaseline. Then she sighed, loud, soft, and stroked the edge of my paper with her pinky.

'Sorry,' she said. 'I'm feral.'

'No, no,' I said, bundling my stuff up now and clicking the tray shut, cheeks alight.

She offered the Vaseline silently, gently, and I shook my head and smiled, looking past her at the bright white crack in the edge of the window.

The ticket person did the tickets.

I put my glasses on my head.

'Worth a read?'

'Oh,' I said. 'I—. Do you mean—?' I stared at my closed tray, the *LRB* lurking there behind it.

She nodded.

'Oh. Erm. Yeah. It's not—. They're second-hand. I have complex thoughts.'

She paused, considered, smiled. 'Yeah.'

'Mmm.' There was a silence here, a thoughtful, chosen one she didn't rush to break, and then I said, 'Best off with Rihanna.'

She held tight to each side of her headphones and gave a deep *mmm.*

'I don't know why I do it to myself,' I said.

She raised her eyebrows knowingly. 'Yeah. My—. Yeah. Vicky gets them,' she said, smiling and laughing silently, tiny breaths through the nose, mouth shut, little bobs of her head back and forth. 'Beautiful art, though, beautiful covers.'

'True.' I wanted to ask her if she made art too, about the turps and the hammer and the packed lunch. I was trying to think of a way to ask without it being a me thing disguised as a question. Not: *I know about oil paint.* Not: *I see you drink whole milk, yes, I know about that too (like me, like me, love me, love me).* But: *tell me who you are.* I knew deep down she'd hear the latter; that was what stopped me.

'What's your name?'

'Oh. Grace.'

'Ginger. Nice to meet you, Grace.'

'You're Ginger.'

'That's me.'

She put her hands out and turned the palms up, one by one. 'I'm actually a Jen, but.' She pointed at her pulse points. There were little grazes of fake tan on her inner wrist bones. 'I used to be pale as fuck and then I got hard into my Fake Bakes and now . . .' She winked. 'Complex thoughts.'

'Ah,' I said, then she lowered her chin towards her chest and looked up at me with a flare in her nose and her lips big, bottom jaw protruding, turned her hands back over and started playing an imaginary organ, the opening bars to 'A Whiter Shade of Pale'.

I stayed static for a second, stuck on the side of the dance floor, and then somehow I'd started clicking, clicking my fingers, giving her a beat. I closed my eyes.

'*And so it WAAASSSS that later . . .*' She sang with soul and purpose, unembarrassed and not just that, unembarrassable, and I was with her. Beatbeat CLICK. Beatbeat CLICK.

She did the killer line then stopped, fingers still in the air, closed her organ and shook my hand. My adrenals were going nuts. Then, 'AHH! Needed that,' she said, bringing her fingertips to the root of her fringe – very sleek like Carla off *Corrie* and otherwise undercut – and she tousled with vigour then swept it all back then paused. I was chuckling. She pushed her head back quick and let out a massive laugh.

'I feel like a right ghost now,' I said.

'Well, I didn't want to say, but.' She smiled, a wide smile and a tilt of the head and the elbow like they do in the ads. 'I can recommend Fake Bake. *I feel fantastic!*

'Ooh,' I said, releasing my tray table for my pen and I did a little action that meant *Fake Bake, Fake Bake, you hear that Angie? Fake Bake! I must write that down!*

She laughed. 'Jokes. This is a vibe,' she said, gesturing at my damson cocoon pants and the Gazelles. Her pinky was back to work now, grazing the outer edge of my leg. Then she caught her bottom lip with her two front teeth, looked ahead for a second, smiled to herself then looked again at me, the smallest fraction of a look and a smile that meant—. I didn't know. I only knew what I wanted it to mean. It pulsed right up my spine and softened me at the shoulders.

I looked down.

I wanted to look.

*

The train stalled, waiting for a signal to pull in to the station. We sat in a silence that wasn't a silence; we were doing something with it.

As we gathered our stuff she dropped her scarf on the floor.

'Now she's dropped her scarf on the floor . . . now the scarf's on the floor and she's going under, she's going under . . . aaah aahhhh aaahhhh she's in the box . . . she's in the box AYEEEEEEEE! AHHH IT'S A NO. It's a no. Aah. So close, great effort, great effort. Great effort.'

She came back up empty-handed.

'I'll get it,' I said, and I did just that.

*

I walked up from the station and stood by the pay and display in Dev Green car park. A guy in chefs' whites came out of Vodka Revs, lit up then Rebecca followed, gestured goodbye to him. She was on the phone. She waved at me, walked over and started fiddling in her pocket for something, eventually giving up and putting a give-me-a-sec index finger out. I nodded. *Tash*, she mouthed. I got my purse out.

'Yes . . . yeah, yeah she's here now.'

'Hi Tash,' I waved.

'She says hi. Yeah I'll come get you. Half an hour . . . OK. OK I'll drop her off first. OK love you . . . Love you.' She put her phone away and picked up my bag.

'Hi,' I said. 'Thanks.'

'Hi.'

'How much?' I shook my change.

'I've got a permit.'

'Oh right.'

The car was just across from us, pipping distance. She took her keys out. Rear lights. I watched her put the bag in the boot. 'Get in then.'

160

'Oh, thanks.'

*

Rebecca had a new flat. She was renting in Hillsborough now, on the main stretch, this bargain place in the back of an ex-office building with sage-green eighties cladding. She parked and led us up from the street, down into the belly of the building then back up the stairs then into a hall and a kitchen-come-lounge. Beyond that there was a bedroom and a bathroom, all in one narrow strip. The place had been carved up from the bird's-eye view of someone in a rush or else on drugs or else just mean, the bedroom tapering into this trippy narrow V. In the acute bit there was a shower curtain up and fairy lights and behind that curtain there was stuff.

I pointed at the curtain and the lights. 'You do this?'

There was no response – she'd walked back out to the lounge, was sorting the TV. 'NICE LIGHTS,' I said, still from where I was stood.

'THANKS.'

'DID YOU DO THEM?'

'TASH.'

'Nice work.' I came back through now. The *Countdown* clock was on and she was stood returning something to the fridge with a tinkle.

'Yeah.'

'What's that?'

'Don't start,' she said, handing me the remote and heading out for Tash.

I opened the fridge. Yellow Tail, white, and a still-sealed bottle of Bristol Cream. I closed the fridge. The night was coming on and a chill so I went to lean my shins on the storage heater by the front door. It was set on a four, about the temperature of an uncovered hot water bottle after thirty minutes. I went back to the corner of fairy-lit stuff to root around for a fan heater, torch on my phone to see better. Damn. Nothing. I put my coat back on and sat on the sofa with Susie Dent, checking the heater situation at Angel Street Argos. Nope. *It closes at five, Grace. Duh.* I made a cup of hot water and sat for a bit longer then I did some sit-ups and some of those movements where you sit on your bum and bend your knees and raise your heels and pass a weight from side to side, improvising with the bottle of My NY DKNY on the coffee table. Sweating now. Yes. Better.

I refilled my cup and moved to the other side of the sofa, better to look out the window. There was a silver heart frame on the sill; Tash and Rebecca selfie in matching grey winter bobble hats, Christmas lights behind them, pupils massive. I turned it round to face the toddler and the little papillon playing out back, out by the rubble of a derelict pub. There was a digger.

After half an hour her car returned. Rebecca walked round the back to the passenger door, dragging her left foot a bit as she went. Someone had probably stamped her with studs or, no, yeah it would be that shin splint thing. Rebecca opened the door and Tash got out, a single dainty pointed black work pump at a time, and they embraced. Well, they got out the car and hugged.

Tash opened the boot and handed Rebecca a sleeping bag and a pillow. The bag started unravelling and when she hitched her load a gap opened up between the waistband of her skinnies and her gilet, deep tan. I would have rested the load back in the boot and pulled my trousers up and tucked the undergarment into the trouser (can't handle a bladder chill, however brief). I would have gone further, giving myself a camel toe just to make sure the tuck would last the journey from the car to the flat. We were strangers. We were twins.

162

I watched Tash take out a bag for life, one of the freezer ones with the reinforced handle and the poppers at the top, slamming the boot with her free arm. Then the two of them stood for a second. Tash had her back to me. Rebecca had her mouth shut, mouth shut but a face on. It said *yeah, I know, it's a pain, bear with.*

I turned the photo frame back and took my coat off sharpish – height of rude to keep it on, bane of my life, then I sat back down and natural as they came in. They were having an exchange verging on a talk about the wok versus the big pan for frying up mixed peppers. Tash looked over at me and nodded. I nodded.

'Alright Grace?'

'Hi Tash. I'm good. You alright?'

'Yeah, good thanks.'

'How's Jill?'

'Yeah, sound.'

'Ronnie?'

'Cracking, tar.'

'Smudge?'

'Best life,' said Rebecca.

'Excellent.'

Jill and Ronnie were Tash's mum and dad. She was an only child and Jill had had her late so they were far into their sixties now, Ronnie turning seventy. They lived in a retirement bungalow in Scarborough.

Tash put the bag down on the floor and unpacked some bits. She'd bought bits: stuffed Peppadews, olives, coleslaw, own-brand Doritos (blue). And a fajita kit.

Rebecca had her bum on the counter and was sorting the Bluetooth on the mini speaker.

'B,' Tash looked up at her. Rebecca looked back, widened her eyes. 'Wok.'

'Can I help?' I got up.

'B!' Tash had paused now. Rebecca was scrolling. 'WOK.'

'*Yes*,' she said, opening the cupboard underneath her and handing me it.

Rebecca went down to the petrol station to get some beers and me and Tash got to work. We made guacamole in Rebecca's bullet juicer. We made microwaved nachos. Then we all ate the bits and the guac and the nachos and fajitas, and then we watched *Educating the East End* in a row, phones out.

We paused it to make a brew and I nipped for a wee and when I came back in something was up.

'Everything OK?' I said.

'There's two spaces come up tomorrow,' said Rebecca. 'For Chris and Josie's wedding.'

'We can't, B,' Tash said. 'It's tight on Grace.'

'Is it?' Rebecca looked at Tash.

'She's only just got here.'

'She doesn't mind.' Rebecca looked at me.

'It's tight, B.' Tash looked at Rebecca hard then back at the TV.

'You really wanted to go,' Rebecca said to Tash.

'Yeah,' Tash was still looking at the TV. 'But . . .'

'Come on,' Rebecca looked at Tash. 'They need the numbers.'

'Yeah, I guess.' Tash looked at the floor.

'You don't care, do you?' Rebecca looked at me.

'Who are Chris and Josie?' I said.

Rebecca cocked her head to the left and got me in the pupils, dead centre: *shut up*.

'I used to work with Josie at Tesco,' said Tash. 'Proper sound.'

'Absolute nutter.'

'You should go,' I said.

'Are you sure, Grace?' Tash.

'Go! Go! If you're going, go!'

'Lol. Are you though?'

'It's fine.'

'Aw cracking. Let's get on it!' said Tash, and she walked into the bathroom.

I looked at Rebecca. She handed me the last Peppadew. I shook my head.

'SAN TROPEZ?' Tash called back through.

'Bedside table.'

'WHAT?'

'BEDSIDE TABLE.'

They put me on the lilo that night. I'd had three tins and it'd gone to my cheeks and briefly to my toes, though by the time we were doing our teeth my feet were numb again and the bathroom was cold and I'd forgotten my toothbrush. I did my best with my finger and the paste and once they'd shut the bedroom door I put my coat over the end of the sleeping bag and my scarf on my head and my earphones in.

Rebecca came through for some water, looked at me, filled the kettle, then she went back into the bedroom and came through again with something shoved up her top, sliding it out jauntily. Hot water bottle.

'Oh! Thanks.'

She nodded.

*

They got up early, seven. Rebecca needed her gold wedges from Tash's but she needed to set off from here for some reason I hadn't managed to figure out and Tash wanted to get ready at hers so Rebecca drove Tash back to Tash's to get the gold wedges. Something like this. It was seven a.m. and I still had half a tin in my system. 'Back soon,' Rebecca said.

I stripped off and showered as soon as they'd gone and it was scalding. '*Thank god thank god thank god,*' I said aloud and then I briefly got out and put Rihanna on my Spotify and I let the water run and run, pushing my hands back through my hair. I couldn't stop wanting the feel of hot wet hair between my fingers. I rinsed off the Alberto Balsalm (coconut) then did another batch and then another. I did not want there to be no water falling on my head. I wanted—.

The heat started to go a bit eventually. I negotiated my release with the shower curtain, trying to get out without it wrapping itself all cold and clammy and real around my leg. Half-managed. Then I got dressed without moisturising, maximise that heat retention, made a milky Nescafé and watched *BBC Breakfast*. I made another. Rebecca came back an hour later with an almond croissant in a plastic bag and a couple of ready-mixed tins of gin. She'd bought me a box of red Alpen and some milk.

'Sorry,' she said. 'Rush hour. Got you some bird food.'
'Thanks, love.'
'"Love"?'
'Yes.'
'No.'
'I can still say love.'
'No you can't.'
'Yes I can.'
'It's weird on you now.'
'Why.'
'You know why.'

She got her magnifier out, started on her brows.

'Can I straighten your hair?'

A look, her look, a look at my look, which said *is that weird too then or do you want good hair?*

'Fuck off.'

'Can I?'

She nodded.

I sat on the sofa's edge with my legs apart and she shuffled into the middle. Rebecca had long hair, the same she'd had at fourteen and fifteen and sixteen. I picked up the giant claw and the irons, white GHDs. They peeped when they were ready, and then I took a small section at a time and zapped it with TRESemmé before pulling the irons through, cracking and steaming and fizzing a bit as they met the moisture. I pulled them through each section of hair two or three times, at a good speed and without gripping them too closely together or you got that telling kink at the part of the hair closest to the skull. I upped the grip at the ends to try to hide the split ends, stop the ends fluffing up. The ends needed discipline.

This was maybe twenty minutes, half an hour. Then she went through and came back out in a short body-con thing with armbands. I zipped her up but she'd forgotten to put her arms in the armbands so I zipped her back down and then up again. She put on her wedges and ate her pastry.

'I'll be back in the morning. It'll be cheaper to stay at Tash's.'

'Oh, OK.'

She took the key off the ring, handed me it and left.

I sat very still with the metal in my palm, waited for it to heat up.

*

I folded up the sleeping bag, trampled the lilo and ate a mound of Alpen in a high-sided bowl, wondering when it was I'd turned to blue when there was red. *Who* does *that*, I thought, and while I was on that vibe I thought fuck it and did a full face of make-up. I found an old Marc Jacobs Daisy tester and I put it on my wrists and neck and I painted my nails cherry blush and then I went out. I got off the tram at the Tesco Superstore for a paper then I walked across the A61 and over to that pub with the red velvet bar stools, Fat Cat – just opening now, fire on. I had half a pint of Pale Rider next to a pair of women playing cards and their big white dog who fell asleep on my feet. A staffie in a hot-pink harness joined us and a collie and a whippet in the care of a woman with spider-leg eyebrows that arched in and out the rims of her glasses and she had jet-black hair and a greatcoat browned by the light and I ordered a second half with my accent and I said love – love, I said, I called her love the lass behind the bar, *fuck you Rebecca*, I tried to think, had a go at thinking, feeling, but my gut wasn't playing. I couldn't say it now. I felt weird. I pulled myself back though, just about, returned to my big white dog and a round of silent rummy with the women. We finished, I had a wee, I left, and then I went to Division Street. I bought a leopard-print Bet Lynch coat from a woman in a Charlie Brown pinafore. 'It's reversible this,' she said.

*

They came back in the morning and Rebecca drove us out to this new boujie place up Walkley for eggs. They did eggs Benedict and eggs Florentine and eggs with smushy avo and slabs of brioche and sourdough, white, and crispy bacon and chilli jam and waffles and maple and French toast, and there were photos of kids in NHS specs on the walls. The menus were set in American Typewriter. I asked the waitress if these were local people and she said what's that love and I pointed at the walls and she shrugged. 'I'm not actually sure to be honest,' she said and Rebecca rolled her eyes. I ordered the Florentine and an Americano. 'Black?' 'Yes.'

After food Tash nipped to get some jellies from Asdas while Rebecca and I sat a bit longer, digesting. Rebecca was scoping a post-lunch drive in the Peaks with her Maps.

'Rebecca.'

'What.' Eyes on her phone. I peered again. WhatsApp now. She pulled it closer.

'What are you doing for Christmas?'

'Erm.' Eyes still down. 'Dunno.'

'I think I might volunteer, actually.'

'What, like, homeless stuff?' Eyes still down. Double home button, up up up. Home. Scroll.

'Yeah.'

'Bit tight on Mum.'

'Is it?'

'Yeah.'

'Won't you be at Tash's, though? I mean, you go to Tash's now so it's not like we have to be—. It's not like we can't mix it up a bit. Won't you be at Tash's?'

A speaking look: *And what?*

'I mean, I thought I might like to, maybe, maybe like do something different. I wondered if you were planning on—'

'You're not going to go home?'

'Well, I mean—.'

She turned the sound on her phone for a video. West Street 3 a.m. chanting.

'What's that?'

169

She showed me. Topless lads with capes on and a big fluffy lion and a traffic cone and that black and gold song. 'Dickheads,' she said.

'They're Uni, right?'

Silence.

'Rebecca.'

'What.'

'Black and gold is Uni right, not Hallam?'

'Yeah. Dunno.'

'It is, isn't it?'

'Yes, Grace.'

'I was just thinking I might volunteer. Do something different. Take the presh off. I was thinking it could be good for us.'

'Right.'

'I was thinking maybe you, or you and Tash, maybe you and Mum could do something without me, maybe, and maybe I could just, I don't know, maybe I could do something different.'

She kept her eyes on her phone. 'Don't you want to see her?'

'Yeah. I mean, yeah.'

'Bit tight.'

'I just thought you might like the chance to—. I don't know, I know you guys have been a bit—.' I pressed my knuckles together. 'Since Tash and stuff—. And—. I don't know.'

She pursed her lips. Her foot was tapping – the OK one, the right one.

'I'm just saying, carte blanche, is that the word?'

'You what?'

'I'm just saying, she's yours if you want to do Mum's this time. If I'm there too it'll be too much for her. She'll freak.'

'Right.'

'Won't she?'

'We always go to Jill and Ronnie's.'

'Yeah but even before that—.'

'Grace. Leave it yeah? I'm hanging. I'm knackered.'

'Sorry. I—. I just wanted to say it—. I want to help.'

'You're not a social worker. Godsake.' She pulled her bobble out, dragged her fingers back through her hair and tightened the retied bush with both hands. Extra tight. She sighed.

'Yeah obviously. Come on. I'm not trying to—. Please.' I looked at my mug. She unlocked her phone. I looked up at her.

'Shut up Grace.'

'What!'

'You know what.' She flipped her phone back over, started messing with the sugar cubes. 'I nearly got you a book the other day.'

'Right.'

'Yeah. It's this kids' book where the girl lives in a cold place and she won't play out and her friends knock for her but she's too scared and they say it's not cold when you're playing, you forget, you don't even feel it, and then after you just go back in and warm up, like.'

'Jesus.' My stomach flipped.

'That Matthew lad told me.'

THUD. 'What?'

'Facebook.'

'What?'

'Give him a ring, yeah?'

'What did he tell you?'

'Your counselling. Summat. I don't know. None of my business is it.'

'Oh.'

The pressure dropped. I wanted to put my forehead on the table, speak at her from under myself, without me there to see. *Sorry, sorry for Rachel and the meaning of Rachel, it's me, just me, my fault, my shit, don't look at me, don't, please, it's me.* I wanted to feel that cool Formica right up in my temples. *Stamp on my toes, Rebecca. Full studs. Please. Help.* But before I could say a thing she'd stood up and stretched her arms above her head and her face was raised to the ceiling and straining with some lumbar muscle ache and she was gone, lost, muttering to herself, *feck that hurts, gah, that fucking wrecks, Jesus.*

Did she mean all that stuff straight, neutral? Or did she want to beat me the way she did when we were kids – scissors to the hair, Collins Spanish dictionary to the head – the way only she knew how? Did she? I wanted her to.

I looked outside. Tash was on the street now, chatting to someone in a hoody with the hood up and the word *SHARKIE* on the chest.

'Who's that?'

'What,' she said, eyes down, phone.

'With Tash?'

She looked behind her. 'Ah *mate.*' She saw them and waved, went outside with her hands in a fin in front of her. 'SHAAAAARKIE! SHAAAAARKIE!' Sharkie took their hood off and Rebecca gave Sharkie's newly barbed head a little rub. I got the bill.

We did our drive, Snake Pass I think they said when we were going through Snake Pass, think that's what they called it, and Rebecca said this was treacherous and it closed sometimes and then Tash got a dodgy tummy. I had a bit of that myself so we headed back. Rebecca drove fast. I closed my eyes.

*

172

After tea we watched *Frozen.*

'You'll like this one Grace,' said Tash.

'Yeah?'

'Yeah it's well deep.'

Frozen. I stayed very still and tried to watch *Frozen*, to let it get me in the gut and for that to just be, without me watching there over my shoulder, or *watching*-watching, problematising. By tin three I was getting somewhere and then 'Let It Go' came on at which point I sang along really loud because we all did, proper belted it, eyes tight shut. When it came to it I couldn't look at all.

Rebecca came through when I was hair-dryering the lilo, tooth-brush in her mouth. She made a *wait a sec* sound, pointed at her mouth and hurried back to spit.

'Just remembered,' she said coming through again.

'What.'

'There's a job going at the library.'

'Oh yeah?'

'Yeah Big Anne's mum told her to tell me to tell you.'

'Big Anne?'

'Yeah.'

'Big Anne?'

'Yeah, Big Anne. Second row.'

'Second row?'

'Google it,' she said, rolling her eyes. 'Look, anyway, she told me to tell you.'

'Oh, right. Thanks.' I looked down. I felt a jolt and then a lift, a little tremor building into this major, thudding, organic thing, this slow-spreading warmth in my abdomen, yes organic not orgasmic but—. I felt real. I felt real. *You can stay. She wants you.*

173

Next day I rang Big Anne's mum and she said could I come in and temp for a bit because Diane's mum had had a bad fall in Eccles. 'Went *right* down,' she said. 'Should I prepare for an interview,' I asked and she laughed and said, 'well you can have one if you like love.' 'A chat?' I said. 'That's fine love,' she said. 'You come in for a chat.'

When Rebecca got back from Revs that night she stood me in the shower room and did my back and sides with her clippers.

'Can't you just give me a buzz?'

'No, Grace.'

'Please.'

'No.'

'Go on!'

She shook her head.

I wanted it, I did. I was feeling bold now. I wanted my perfect undisturbed foot-first head out in the world. That's how we'd been in the womb, me stood tall and gangly, Rebecca head down and ready for the out. I'd been reluctant to come out, debut. They'd had to go in and get me, but now—. Now I was ready. I think I was ready.

Rebecca did the honours, back and sides but curly up top. Then 'wait,' she said and she went out the room and came back in with a little red bandana left over from an eighties night. Tash followed her. 'Eyup!' she said, putting her hand out like wait, now turning back on herself, and then the twinkly bells from 'Borderline' came on in the lounge and Rebecca took the clippers and they were her mic. Tash started running like Bez in 'Kinky Afro'. I was on keys to begin with, keys, then I flung my instrument to one side and I took my position centre-stage. I was Madonna.

Next day I was Madonna on an overripe corridor in Sheffield Central Library. The door opened, a woman and a man. Big Anne's mum was off that day so this was Sandy, Sandy and Kev, Team Leaders. The room was maybe three metres wide and there were three chairs and a table. I took off my coat and talked, stretching up from time to time and rubbing my cervical vertebrae. *Open. Informal. Open, Grace.* I smiled. I shook their hands. Then they took me on a tour. In the children's section a little girl was sat on the floor where the *My First Pet* books were, whispering the titles from the spines to herself in a TV presenter voice.

I watched her in rapture. Sandy and Kev watched me.

I got the job.

That night we had a Greedy Greek special tea and Rebecca and Tash said I could stay for a while, at least till after Christmas when Denise would re-evaluate the situation with her mum. I asked Rebecca if I could give her some keep from time to time and she always shook her head violently, though I'd often tram it to big Tescs or the Aldi further up, stock us up a bit.

Eventually she asked if I'd told Mum – about the job, being here, any of it.

'I haven't really had the chance.'

'Right.'

'I will though.'

'Good.'

'I'll tell her when I see her in person. I don't want to give her the wrong idea.'

She zoned back out. I was looking for her grimace, then and always. Some old, old squirming thing inside me craved that. I remembered it, now we were in company again; we hadn't spent this long together since we were kids. It came back strong that craving and I was hooked, searching for ripples in her apathy, the rage I knew they spoke of underneath, pure twin zero-sum rage, single malt. I knew it was there and I wanted its hit, deserved it, and I had to be the one to coax it out. I'd wanted that before I'd wanted a Rachel, and Rachel was an experiment anyway, wanting a Rachel, having a Rachel. Rachel was the idea of Rachel because something was missing and maybe I could buy it.

That wasn't working out so well, though, that experiment. Whatever Petri-dish want I'd grown for Rachel was still so hesitant and vulnerable and new and up here it was exposed, fucked in a heartbeat. By me and sometimes, even better, sometimes by Rebecca, Rebecca at my wily Iago command. We vanished it, melted it into something more passable, easier, a grimy little gremlin middle-class want, liberal elite, flat white bullshit. Kill it. Dead.

So I was here, doing my back in on Rebecca's lilo, hot water bottle scalding my chest and Rachel was over. Rachel was over. And Rachel was here. She'd made her way up with me somehow, in my rucksack, in my Moleskine, in my face. I couldn't quite shift her.

You haven't told your mother, she'd say, or, more likely, she'd repeat my line back at me, *you don't want to give her the wrong idea,* punctuationless as ever, punctuated by vocation, stylish as hell.

Yes Rachel, 'wrong idea' means I don't want Mum to think I'm back for good, I'd say. She'll get flappy with that information there on her own. I need to be there to chill her out; I need to protect her.

Fantasy of omnipotence. That's what Rachel would be thinking to this. She wouldn't say it. I'd say it for her, and then she'd say fantasies are important and all the rest of it and much maligned and much misunderstood and did I know what a real fantasy was? Fantasies are real; they do real things. Yes, yes I did know.

'Wrong idea' meant I didn't want Mum to be jealous.

'Wrong idea' meant I did.

Rebecca put her phone away.
  'I will. I will tell her.'
  'Fair enough.'

*

I started the job. The library was porcelain toilets with black plastic seats and flush chains, smell of white Hovis and disinfectant, tall ceilings, cold soft water. In the ladies' there were paper disposal bags for tampons with drawings of corseted women. In the staff room above the water cooler there was a poster of a white man wringing his salt-and-pepper hair with wedding-ringed hands. *ACCIDENT AT WORK? AN APOLOGY WON'T PAY THE BILLS!*

In our office there was a work experience girl in bleached pink jeans and silver disco cowboy boots and dip-dyed hair called Alice. There was Madeline with a large feather in her ear and a red and white blazer in the Victorian dance hall style. Simon had a black leather coat and a chequered shirt and a white crew-neck T-shirt and blue straight jeans and black work brogues. And then there was Big Anne's mum. Big Anne's mum had big square glasses with thick black rims. I sat next to her. It said DENISE on the top of her DIY desk calendar but that wasn't for me to decide. This was Big Anne's mum, and the most important preliminary business was mugs.

  'Bring your own mug love or go Primarni in your lunch break, get yourself a nice one cos these ones here are minging—'

  'No they don't do mugs in that Primarni love,' said Madeline.

  'Don't they? God what's the world coming to. I never do town anymore. Where could she go's near here?'

  'B&M?'

'Ooh no love she dunt wanna be trekkin' down there.'

'Oh I don't mind a walk—'

'Sports Direct?' said Simon, waving his, an enormous Sports Direct one.

'Nah I don't think so Simon she's only little.'

'What about that pop-up in the Winter Garden?' said Alice.

'Oh is that the place with the plants—'

'Hmm yeah for summat special but that's more gift like.'

'Wait wait I know love,' said Madeline. 'That little place up Chapel Walk, homewares place.'

I went to John Lewis. Soothing, soothing, soothing, shame.

Big Anne's mum. Big Anne's mum liked The Range. She liked her kids. She liked minestrone Cup-a-Soups but only the Batchelors ones with the croutons and only full fat. She liked to whip the croutons off the top as soon as she put the water in to get the crunch then deliberately not quite stir the remains so there'd be a spoonful of extreme MSG waiting for her at the bottom. In the mid-afternoon she had mugs of Earl Grey with the teabag left in and a full inch of milk. She'd wait for the tea to go tepid and the bag would sit there, lounging on the surface, and then she'd forget about it. As the day passed her fingers would swell and she'd take her rings off, one by one, and when she got to the final one she'd lean back in her chair and give up, start calling Big Anne or Mo, Big Anne's dad.

Work was mostly spreadsheets and staying inbox zero, though Big Anne's mum's real job was to try to get people with money to want to keep the library alive. The library was alive. The atrium had wing chairs and desktop Dell computers and most days it was full of people in need of the Internet and heating and toilets and sleep. These people did not have money.

From time to time I covered the front desk and a member of the public would ask me what I thought of a book and I had to say how I felt, reach in fast for a reaction and the words for it, and in company, and with strip lighting. It was dazzling.

I settled, got into the swing of things. At ten each morning I'd go up to the kitchen with the tray of mugs and teabags – no one put their teabags in the allocated cupboard. 'That way madness lies,' said Simon. There was a photo of J K Rowling there on the corridor that said *Sheffield Children's Book Award: 'J K Rowling', 1998*. 'J K Rowling' had her hair set in layers and a velvet suit jacket and an uninitiated smile. I'd stare at her for a minute then I'd make the morning round and then around twelve I'd take it back up for washing.

The kitchen and the snug bit were where you went at lunch, I soon realised, so I saved my big long walks for the mornings and/or nights. That's where I met Pam, the snug, just outside, top of the stairs. Pam from the racks. She wore long-sleeved blouses made of triangles in mauve and acid green.

'Ooh, if I tickle you now . . .' she said from behind me with a tobacco-stained rasp.

'I wouldn't forgive you,' I said.

'No, not the way to make friends, is it love.'

'One way.'

'What's your name?'

'Grace. What's yours?'

'Pam,' said Pam, and at this I turned my head and she pursed her face into a tight smile, lips closed, before dropping her cheeks back to neutral.

'Hello Pam.'

*

Pam let me lunch with her and Carole. We'd stand around the island waiting for a microwave while Carole made her wraps.

'I know what I'm like, Pam. I'm resigned. I can't go syn free at lunch.'

'Pure carbs, love, these wraps,' said Pam, picking up the packet. 'Pure carbs, bread and bread, folded bread.'

'I know love. I can't help it.'

'You can use all your syns at once, can't you?' I said. 'My mum does that.'

'What would the church have to say about that,' said Geoff from behind the geyser.

'Yes love,' said Carole, 'but I'm a sweet tooth. After six all bets are off. This is me healthy b.' She flapped a white wrap at me.

'Ah,' I said, picturing a cartoon bee in a tracksuit.

'Come look at this love,' she said and I leant in. 'I lay this foil out, see, then me bread, then I'm spreading twenty-eight grams of Philly Light, just two syns that, spreading it out nice and thin, get them edges, then I just cram it up with all the speedy veg I can get in there, so full I need the foil cos the bread's splitting. See?'

'Love it Carole. It's Carole, right?'

'It is, love.'

*

A few weeks went by. Rebecca started staying at Tash's most nights then she cut me my own set of keys, said I might as well start using the bed. I did, and I used the keys, used them with love in my heart. A day would make itself known and I'd get up, lock up and go to work, and when I got there I'd sign my name in a blotchy blue biro and joke and feel alive with the caretakers. Present. Here. Ian and Mick, occasionally Karl. When they found out I was from Leeds I went down a

180

peg or two – *OOF, wuss than London, that*, said Mick – but we were tight now, conspirators.

Ian added my face to his Kingdom of Legends, the name he'd given to the panel behind the CCTV monitoring station. *KINGDOM OF LEGENDS* it said, in a rainbow arc made of sugar-paper letters he'd nabbed from the children's library, and everyone who worked here was an animal as chosen by Ian. If he liked you, if you passed – which meant signing out and in at lunch and putting your womanly things, *you know, your 'things'*, in the womanly bins, *not the loos please, ladies!* – if you passed, he'd stalk you on Facebook then print you out on his home PC, add you to the wall. It was inkjet, his printer, and he used cheapo paper so you came out all streaky and two-tone. It was trendy, very ICA. Anyway, I was a giraffe.

The days came on thick and fast and soon enough it was November, mid-November, late November and I was still here, here at Sheffield Central Library, caffeinating, counting my syns, hell why not, craning my neck at the slightest show of a grey pair of trackies or an undercut. There was a lot of craning. No Ginger, but giraffes are made for craning.

Yes, the weather was creeping in but I thanked my lucky stars because the library heating was violent. It was Victorian, binary, a great big wall of heat, and that was mindless and comforting but sickly, and perhaps all the more comforting for that lacing of sickliness, the intimate dance with suffocation. For me it was. It reminded me of Rachel.

Moleskine Rachel was getting smaller as the weeks went by, tiny now, the little speck you see diminishing out the rear-view. Patrick, too. Sometimes it felt like they'd never existed, like I'd made them both up and dressed them to perfection and fed them with my finest lines. And then abandoned them. Well, I knew

I'd done that bit. That was real. Rejected, cancelled the both of them, the things inside me that were them, all of it, the whole thing, consigned to irrelevance. Some part of me knew that was bad. *You reap what you sow, Grace. Eternal return of the same, Grace.* I held back on the caffeine for a bit when I felt like that.

In any case, Rachel hadn't tried to call. No emails, either. Nothing. She might have sent me a letter addressed in her nice fountain pen to Hornsey Road. Yes, that would be right up her street. But Oliver was living on Hornsey Road. Jessica's Oliver was sleeping in my headboardless bed and word had it he was a cad. Matthew sent a photo of him comatose on the family sofa saying *look what you've become*, and, *we miss you*, and I did reply to that in the end, and to those mounting WhatsApps from Abi and Charlie and Matthew and Adam, replied immediately then archived them so they wouldn't be there to find me.

I didn't reply to Mum. I didn't tell Mum a thing. Rebecca didn't ask again and it went unspoken. We kept the meaning of that hostage. It suited.

Anyway, I had Pam and Carole now and Big Anne's mum and Ian and Mick and I couldn't be in Otley and I couldn't be on Hornsey Road and I was actually OK. It was actually OK. It was just the part where—. The between bits. The weekends. The evenings. The between bits.

Rebecca was with Tash for those and then they were with everybody else. Training ramped up and the rugby club Christmas social calendar was *basically a full-time job, int it B? Yeah.* It wasn't that I wasn't invited to that stuff. I could have invited myself. But I wasn't invited. And I was tired. I was tired.

I told Pam and Carole I liked my me-time and I limited my me-time nights to two or three a week and lied about the rest. When they invited me to Yates or Akbar's Fridays I said no, inventing this thing, *there's this thing I'm doing with my sister, yeah,* so no one would have to feel bad. After work I'd walk as far as I could, at least as far as Aldi, then I'd buy a little bottle of Glen's vodka and get it home and dry and then I'd shot it to the bottom, neat with ice or ice and tonic.

I never really lost myself to sleep, some limbic region of my brain keeping half an ear free and trained on the rubble out the back. Sometimes I heard a distant church bell and that I quite liked – it gave this whole thing a bit of earth and dimension, a bit of end-credits oomph – but more often than not it was a fox out there, a woman fox screaming, or a human drunken woman giving hell to this human rat who she called Jason, and I'd sit up and wait and see if someone needed to . . . If there was someone I should call, if I should do something.

Along with all this I had my ritual awakenings. I woke up stark four times a night, each time I fell from a REM cycle. I wasn't sure what had come first, this need to come back up for air or the knowledge that I could.

*

Dream. I'm in an attic bedroom by the sea, a twin room, with Rebecca. She's in bed with Tash. Our beds are parallel. There's a small table between us with a lamp on it and Rebecca and Tash are kissing. I face the other way but a great big dog gets in despite a door and a corridor and another door. I wake up and it's licking my face.

Dream. I'm at Nana's house. I'm looking for a Bourbon biscuit. Dust is beginning to gather on the sill and the curtains are translucent and the bathroom carpet smells of wee. I'll make you some, I tell Grandad, I'll make you some from

183

scratch, but when I go into the cupboard the flour's infested with weevils.

Dream. I'm working in a hotel. I'm a maid and I also live in the hotel. I keep all my possessions in a green wheelie bin and I keep that bin in a small function room where low-grade cover bands play, where there's the occasional turn. I go in and there's been a flood and my wheelie bin's empty, my bits strewn all over the floor. I'm sad and my feet are wet. Rebecca turns up. She's holding a pair of multipack M&S socks.

'Can I have some?'

'No.'

*

The weather came. The wind, first. That took three umbrellas. One became the wind itself while a man with waterproof trousers stood very still and watched. *Piece of shit*, I said, *PIECE OF FUCKING SHIT*, and I trampled it into the ground. I don't remember leaving it there but I arrived at work without it.

Then there was the snow. We knew the day it was due from *BBC Breakfast*/the *Metro*/those acid-bright skies of recent mornings, pink and prophetic, so: wellies all round. There were two people waiting for the tram that day, a man and a woman. She had gentle creases at the sides of each eye and a dull green raincoat with a peaked hood. She looked like an actress auditioning for a part in a Victoria Wood sitcom. It felt a bit much, too on the nose, but it's true, she did. She greeted the man.

'This'll be a sheet later,' he said, pointing at the road beyond the tramlines.

'A sheet,' she said.

'A sheet,' he said.

184

'Oh my god,' I said.

They turned to look at me. They looked at each other. They looked away.

It started to stick around three. The library closed and Big Anne's mum drove home and I shuffled my way to the bus station. She'd offered me a lift with a glint in her eye, a true glint, but I'd said *no, it's fine!* There were no buses at the station but lots of people and it was festive, in fact. Half an hour passed and a bus arrived. Somebody clapped. We got on slowly with our cash in our hands. There was an advert up, *NOW CONTACTLESS*, though when I asked the woman in front if that was real she shook her head.

'Student single, please.' I held out Rebecca's old student card to the driver, thumb on the expiry.

The driver said something to the windscreen.

'Sorry?'

'Let. Me. Have. A. Look.'

Shit.

'Nice try, love.'

He gave me my adult ticket and I stomped up the stairs and sat at the back. I shoved the breath up long and hard in my nose, out quick. I fucking hated this fucking man and I hated his fucking bus. I should love him. I should make it all symptomatic and belonging to me and then absolutely not mine, not mine, theirs, theirs, theirs down there, down in London, down in the ugly swollen belly of the thing; it was political. But I fucking hated him. I wanted him dead.

We stopped at the end of West Street.

'All off!' he shouted back.

'What's going on?' I asked the contactless lady.

'He's not gonna try that climb, love.'

'What?'

'Lethal.'

'Can I get a refund?' I asked the bus driver.

'You taking the piss, love?'

I made my way home on foot, one step at a time, penguin arms. *Good girl. Good girl*, I said, and *shh, it's OK, shh*, and I hummed. 'Ob-La-Di, Ob-La-Da', I hummed, and 'She'll Be Coming Round the Mountain'. I hummed and hummed till I could no longer hum because now I was singing, wailing, the way I'd sing if Mum were watching, tuneless and embarrassing to make her say *now come on, love, don't be silly, don't spoil it.* Funny face, scowl. And then I felt bad so I started singing well, I sang like a good sweet angel, back in my range, the acoustics just perfect with all this snow because I'd made her turn away now and *Mum. Mum. Sorry I was silly, Mum. I didn't mean it. I didn't mean it. Please watch, Mum. Please.*

*

Work was closed the next day. I got up with the alarm, had a glass of water and went back to Rebecca's bed.

A few hours passed and I must have woken up at some point, woken up and stopped and stared for a bit because eventually that's where I was, still staring. Then I must have got out of the bed. Yes, that certainly happened because I was certainly lying prone on Tash's yoga mat and I was squeezing my face and making these shrieking animal sounds, making these contortions with my face, pained ones I thought might be relevant. I turned over, same again. I flung my arms up to feel the weight of the shoulder blades in the mat. That was nice. I thought about getting up and then I thought some

186

more and some time after that I got up and went to the loo. I did a long wee, had some more water, got back into bed and then I got my laptop out and recorded a video of myself looking at the screen, reading from the screen, trying to capture who I was without me knowing about it. Was this sane? Yes, yes, I think it probably was, *yeah, don't worry but I'm busy just now, just wait a sec, Grace.* I recorded my bobbing flaring hollow face while covering the screen with a Post-it note, so as not to distract myself, and then I recorded myself watching the recording of myself, Post-it covering the screen again. I watched that for a bit, and then I rang Rachel.

*

'Hello?'
  'Hello.'
  Silence.
  'It's me.'
  'I know.'
  'Hi.'
  'Hello. How are you?'
  'I'm good thanks! How are you?'
  'It's me.'
  'Sorry. It's—'
  'Yes—'
  'Sorry—'
  'No, go on—'
  Silence.
  'How are you?'
  'I hate it.'
  Silence.
  'I hate it.'
  Silence.

'Hello?'
Silence.
'Hello?'
'Hi.'

*

We started doing phone work. It felt like she hadn't saved my number because each time I called her she was coy, a little bit hostile and coy, like she was Rachel the actual person Rachel, just answering her iPhone and I was an unknown number, a little role-play. There was something about this coyness that made me love her, the fantasy it lent me of her being her and just out there living her life and well she might be, without me, and then that little moment of *ah, of course, it's time for Grace*. I was fond of that. But I made sure to convey that fondness and all my emotions properly, i.e. obliquely, professionally, lying on the bed so the timbre was correct – leggings at a minimum for ritual and dignity, no descent into PJs, plus socks and sometimes the Gazelles, all lit up with the lavender candle I'd found behind the shower curtain, the one I'd bought Mum last year.

After hanging up I liked to picture Rachel there in her chair, there with the iPhone on the pillow where my head should be. I wondered if, given the phone was right there next to her, she stayed sitting comfortable and dialled someone else. Perhaps she liked to call whoever she'd missed while I was on, and perhaps she said *I was just talking to Grace, you know, Grace, the one I mentioned that time, the one I'd like to do more with*. That was the hope. I'd doze and enjoy her virtual smell as it started to fade: bergamot, lavender, a recurrent sense of concern.

*

'I feel like a child.'

'You don't like feeling like a child.'

'No.'

'Being a child was difficult for you.'

'No, no, I love children, Rachel. They're so savage and unconvinced. I love children.'

*

I told Rachel that Rebecca had a working smoke alarm and no, I wasn't suicidal. *Goodness! Of course not! Yes, yes, no Rachel, I do mean that, sorry. Yes, I promise, it's just really cold outside.* I believed she continued to believe in our progress, the work and the structures we'd worked on, though the connection could be faulty here in this strange vindictive building so I tried to map out expansive narratives, long and baggy, to help give her some time to get the gist. She couldn't really trade in her trademark silences, not on the phone. I gave her my dreams.

*

'So in this dream Mum and Rebecca and me are stuck in an industrial estate on the edge of an airport. We're dragging ourselves along the concrete in the heat and it's like a really nauseating full-sun midday heat, not really in the UK actually, kind of not a temperate-zone heat but more verging on Saharan, dry, and there are these large tower blocks spaced out in a circle and we're in the centre of the circle. The circle's maybe a couple of hundred metres wide, that's the diameter I'd say, mmm, actually maybe a hundred metres, like a hundred-metre track. Anyway, in any case it's quite big and the ground is very flat and as I say it's concrete. We have to stop in the middle of the circle. We're too tired. I'm dripping with sweat I think so I look down and I'm wearing Rebecca's polyester

189

Beauty and the Beast dress she had when she was little. I'm wearing this dress but I'm the size I am now so it's just kind of shoved on, shoved on the best we can manage and the polyester is totally stuck to my arms and it's not really covering my bum properly. It's kind of skirting my bum. I realise this and I'm so ashamed that I squat to the ground. I look down. I'm burning. I'm so ashamed. I'm so embarrassed. And then I look behind us and there's a green screen there because actually we're on a film set and the desert feeling is just coming from these machines blowing hot air and there's this woman there shouting at me to dance. *Dance!* She's very insistent and I'm frightened so I get up straight away and start dancing like she asks, ballroom dancing just like Belle does in the Disney version and then I look at Rebecca and Rebecca's disappeared, Rebecca is absolutely nowhere to be seen at all and I'm darting around looking for her and I can't see her and I'm shouting for her and then I look at Mum and Mum's totally still, looking at me. She's staring at me and as I say she's completely dead still but when I look in her eyes they're—. Dark. Teeming. They're . . . I don't know. Inconsolable. Yeah. Inconsolable.'

*

'So I'm in this institution with PVC windows really high up on the walls and chairs with spindly legs and cream vinyl seats, this really *ugly* old place, like, erm, well, like this building actually, has that prefabricated sense of impermanence. I'm waiting in an anteroom I think, it's like a waiting room and I'm waiting for ages and I'm really on edge and then the door goes and there's Mum, Mum and weirdly enough there's Michael, too. Michael. Michael's in a tabard and he's gaunt and yellow and scaly and he's holding Mum's arm like he's been told to, like he's doing community service but also a bit like it might actually be a fairy tale where he's actually the prince but in a tabard, you know, like it's a test, like I'm being tested, but I think of course that's magical thinking, even in the dream I think that, the dreamer knows, and I can't look at him then. It's too much. I look at Mum and she's wearing this supplied pastel top with three-quarter sleeves and embroidered flowers, crew neck, and her head's right down in her chest and then I see—. I see she's not wearing a bra, her boobs are loose so I go over and I shoo him away and I put my hands in front of her nipples, not touching, just an inch or so away, and I say *SHOO, SHOO.* He shuffles off. I look back at her and there's this big dark bib-shaped shape down her chest. She's crying.'

*

The weather went on; the library stayed closed for a while. There was sleet. Sludge. Sleet. Snow. Sludge. It was difficult to move. I wanted so much just to move. Fast, hard. One day there was a lull and seemingly some additional grit on the street and I got all the way to Iceland. The woman at the till said we hadn't had a winter this bad in twenty-eight years and she should know, the last time it happened she'd gone into labour and the roads had been closed and she'd had to walk to the hospital in her dressing gown and wellies. *How embarrassing,* she kept saying, *how embarrassing, how embarrassing,* and I said *bloody hell, bloody hell,* and in my head there was Rachel: *I'm not embarrassed. Don't be embarrassed.*

'This is the first real winter of my life,' I said as she ripped off my receipt.

'Looks like it.'

'I'm bored. I'm so bored. I'm tired.'

'Try working here, love.'

*

Then I blacked out.

'Going places?' said the litter person. I'd been stood for the tram I think. I don't know how long I'd been there.

'HA,' I said, pulling my hood down my face as he backed away, HA, HA, AH, ARGH, ARGH. Gasp. Judder.

*

'You're experiencing primitive reactions to a hostile environment.'

'Hmm.'

Silence.

'The snow doesn't want to hurt me.'

Silence.

'Does it?'

Silence.

'It really snows. Like, *snow*-snows.'

Silence.

'The hills—. They're honestly, honestly—. It's hard to explain but they're huge. Like, so steep. There's railings on the pavements it's so steep. It's hard to explain.'

Silence.

'It's true.'

'You don't believe I believe you.'

Silence. Mine.

Silence. Hers.

'I—. I—.'

'Grace, I believe you. I believe you.'

CHRISTMAS 2015

On Christmas Eve we did presents at Tash's flat. Next day Rebecca would drive Tash to Jill and Ronnie's, Scarborough, drop me at Mum's on the way. I was going to Mum's. But for now Tash and Rebecca had had a heavy night so I went over in the late afternoon and Rebecca made us short strong cups of Yorkshire Gold. Tash put out the Tunnock's teacakes and we watched *A Place in the Sun* with the fire on, Smudge stretched out in front of it. Watching her there like that made me feel I could do the same. Theoretically. Psychologically. But here I was, piling up my clauses. Well, it was like a hot bath in here. It was nice.

'How is she?'

'She's OK,' said Tash, 'we had a bit of trouble with her bum.'

'Oh.'

'Yeah. She was licking it like a demon for a few days and then I looked, and—. I will say no more.'

'Smudge!'

'She's been having a tough time with the new suite.'

'Yeah, I meant to say,' I said, giving the armrest a squeeze. 'S'nice.'

'Gumtree,' said Rebecca.

194

'She struggled.' Tash leant in for another teacake. 'She's OK with change but not while it's happening.'

Presents. Rebecca got me a Scorpio candle.

'Oh, a Scorpio candle. Thanks,' I said, peeling off the little red 3-for-2 sticker.

'You're the perfect Scorpio.'

'Go on.'

'Sly. Bitchy.'

'We're twins, you div.'

'Now then,' said Tash.

'What's this then?' Rebecca shook her hardback oblong wrapped in Paperchase Christmas cacti.

'Do you like the Christmas cacti?'

'Cute.' She opened her book, started pawing it in slow motion.

'Kelly Holmes.'

'I can see that.'

'You love Kelly Holmes.'

'Yeah she's alright, yeah.'

'It's a book.'

'Is it?'

'Don't be a dick.'

'Fuck off.'

I opened Tash's present while Rebecca fixed Smudge's tea. They'd been together three years now but they still did separate gifts. Joint cards, separate gifts.

'A sushi kit! Thanks!'

'That one got us one last Christmas.' She pointed towards Rebecca. 'B!'

'What?' She came to the door with a sachet of posh: Sheba.

'Was it last Christmas, sushi kit?'

'Valentine's.' She went back through. Smudge raised her little neck and frowned, all damp and strewn out, sated already and imperious with it: *yes, the world is mine.* Tash looked at her with a tight close focus and whispered to her in their caregiver-client divine private language: '*Yes! Yes! For you.*' Smudge did a downward-facing dog then sauntered into the kitchen.

Tash flicked through her apps a sec. 'We took it to Lakeside with us Easter.'

'Nice.'

'Needs sugar the rice and we couldn't find any – *crap* that place – but we chucked a bit of Splenda in there worked a treat.'

'Good to know.'

'You put the rice out on an oven tray once it's done and then you've to cover it to keep it cool. Damp clean cloth ideally.'

'Thanks so much, Tash.'

'Yeah,' she eyed the kitchen. 'She said you'd like it.'

'I love it.'

Rebecca came back then and handed me a Pets at Home stocking.

'Oh. You shouldn't have.'

'Ha.'

FOR MABEL LOVE REBECCA & TASH said the tag.

'Give her a squeeze for me, yeah?'

I smiled and took it from her. Smudge's little name plaque was bumping up against the plastic in the other room, little tongue going for the gravy.

Rebecca was back in her phone. 'Rice vinegar,' she said.

'What?'

196

'Rice vinegar. You add rice vinegar to the rice—'

'Yeah,' said Tash, 'it's not rice-rice. It's distinct—'

'We had smoked salmon in it and what else did we have, erm—'

'*Avocado.*' They said it in unison.

We let *A Place in the Sun* come back in for a few moments. Tash closed her eyes and made her face a cat's, started squeezing her nose and nuzzling at Rebecca's shoulder. With Tash being that bit smaller than Rebecca, and a bit slouched down, Rebecca was in just the right position to put her own nose down into the crown of Tash's head. She inhaled her just-washed hair, still half damp. She kissed her.

I looked away.

I took my phone out, re-collapsed my apps, tried to breathe deeply, knead out the knot that was forming in my belly. I put my chin in my roll-neck. Cashmere. Cashmere from a bin liner I'd found on Shepherd's Hill. I closed my eyes.

'Did she tell you about your mum's email?'

'Hmm?' I opened my eyes, looked at Tash.

'Mother's Pride.'

Rebecca flicked a foil wrapper ball at Tash.

'What?' I said.

'Leave it,' said Rebecca.

'No. Tell me.'

'Tell her, B.'

Rebecca furrowed her brow.

'Your mum sends her this email going *MOTHER'S PRIDE*. List of B's finest achievements,' said Tash, her head still snuggled in Rebecca's armpit. 'Top drawer. Absolute classics. Brownies Sixer. And the *elves*. I mean! Shot put county silver.

197

Man of the match '99.' She paused, sent her face deadpan, fixed on the TV then re-entered the scene with full cuteness, extra snuggles. 'We're so proud of our B!'

Rebecca put her phone on the armrest, her furrow a frown now, and with Tash in prime position for a play headlock and Rebecca not giving her one, it was hard to tell where this would go.

I brought my knees up, nestling my feet together and moving both legs over to the left, the way they break your wind in hospital. My bellyache was setting in. 'Are you and Mum—? Are you two—?'

'Are we what?'

'I thought you were still . . . I just assumed . . . I didn't think you were really in touch so much—. I mean—. I just didn't realise you were that—'

Her face said leave it, final warning.

I ignored my warning. Nothing to lose. My belly was dragging me back down anyway, out of this hot nice room, back into that pained and graceless thing they called Grace. 'Do you see her?'

Rebecca sighed, an automatic one. It didn't quite belong in this exchange. It was the kind you'd do after a flight and you're knackered then the customs queue is massive – tired, bored, captive.

Tash shuffled out to her side of the sofa and brought her face back into neutral, hint of a side-eye. She went into her phone.

Rebecca re-did her bobble, tight. 'We're in touch,' she said finally.

'I—,' I started. I tried, I did. I stopped.

Tash came in here. Tash was the trump. I couldn't trump Tash. 'Right kids!' she said, tickling Rebecca's foot. 'LET'S GET ON IT.'

She got up to put the bhajis on, see to the bubbles.

'Rebecca.'

'What.' A mumble.

'I didn't get an email.'

'Yeah. Well.'

'I'm glad you're in touch,' I said and I was, would have been, if not for the belly. It was spreading right out and round both sides and up my back and neck. Envy? Probably. I couldn't hear to know had I wanted to; she'd turned up the TV.

*

Otley. We drove over, pulled up outside. Rebecca killed the engine but they kept their belts on.

'We won't come in.'

I nodded, gathering my stuff.

'She'll still be at church, so.'

'Can't really wait around.'

'Ron gets funny when we're late.'

Another nod, though as I was opening the door Rebecca said to wait, hang on a sec, undid her belt, leant over the handbrake and handed me a bottle in a sparkly red bottle bag.

'What's this?'

'Will you put some tape on the top there?'

It was the Harvey's Bristol Cream from her fridge. 'Wait. Is this—?'

'Yeah.'

I made to open the tag.

'Don't.'

'I've got some tissue paper I can—'

'Don't make a scene.'

'I'm not—'

'Just—'

'Sorry. Sorry. Yes, I'll give it her. Of course.'

'Thanks.'

I opened the door, went to the boot to get my bag and came back round. Tash wound down the front window.

'Bye then,' I said.

'Merry Christmas.'

'Merry Christmas.'

I let myself in. Mabel came down to say *yes, she's not back from church yet but she's left the heating on for us so don't start.*

'Hi Mabel.'

I kept my coat on and had a look round to see if anything needed taking out before I warmed up. She had a new fridge now, a tall one. She'd sat it in front of the window that looked out onto the yard.

'What's all this about Mabes?'

She shrugged.

I put the kettle on and opened the fridge for the milk, thinking I'd put a splatter down for Mabel, too, butter her up a bit, but there was only a pint of that sour one-per-cent stuff, sourer still for being in the door. Mum didn't like her fridges on high. Too much leccy. I went to chuck it then I stopped myself. *It's not yours, Grace.*

I did do the bin though, the recycling, and was just putting a cloth round when I saw her yellow mohair and her posh wool coat through the glass in the door.

'Bunny!'

'Merry Christmas, Mum.'

'You're here,' she said, her eyes welling up, gazing somewhere only she could see, hands stock-still by her sides.

I took her posh wool coat by the lapels. 'Yes!' I said, giving her a nudge on the nose. 'Let's get comfy, shall we!'

*

We put our slob stuff on and she did me a tour of her new fibre optics: black tree and black-and-white glass baubles, white angel, white poinsettia on the sill.

'Ooh. Classy.'

'Like it? Now I know it's a departure, love. But I thought I'd treat myself.'

'It's great. Très chic.'

'Aw, thanks, love.'

There were a few bits of smellies she'd arranged in a pile down the bottom of the tree, body sets and sparkly exfoliator gloves and the like. Could I carry these bits from Jackie and the girls up to her room for her she said and I said sure.

'I've got this thing in my thumb now, love, just come on.'

'What's that?'

'Aches.'

'What, like arthritis?'

'No, no that's for old people, love.'

'Have you been to the doctor?'

'No, love.'

'You don't want to—'

'No, love.' She'd walked out now. I followed her up to her room.

Her bedroom door was hanging half off, the bottom hinge finally rusted through.

'We need to replace that Mum. That's dangerous.' I put the stuff on her bed then got the little IKEA mini set of steps from the bathroom and reached up into her top cupboard for the toolbox.

'Not now, love.'

'It won't take me a sec.'

She knew not to bother stopping me at this point. I was on one. She was right though. It took us three hours and we almost killed Mabel and Mum had to have a lie-down after that, Mabel too, but it really broke the back of this thing. Christmas was pretty much done, then. I put our curry on and walked to the park in the dark. I sat on a swing. I swung until my chest got tight. It didn't take long. No, not long at all I said to myself, welling up a little at my cadences and then *no, now you shush, you, come on.*

We had our samosas first and I gave her Rebecca's sparkly red bottle bag.

'Oh!' She read the tag and slapped her cheeks with her hands and beamed, started jiggling about from side to side, her face getting all red. 'Did she—?!'

'I think they'll come see you soon, Mum.'

'Did she say that—'

'Don't let her upset—'

'Did she tell you—'

'Shh,' I said, taking her wrist. 'Don't let her upset you.'

'Oh, no, no I'm not upset. I'm not upset, love. I'm not upset!'

I looked down and then askance again to check. No, she was smiling. Fair. So I cleared our starter plates and took the trays back and served up the curry on our oven-heated plates and put the pickle and the yoghurt and the slices of lime on the little round-topped beech IKEA stool and we drank our spritzers and our Baileys and we watched *Billy Elliot* and she cried, her looking at me askance now: *Ah coulda been a dancer,* Billy on the piano then Dad slams the piano; Christmas in the boxing gym with Michael; Billy on the back of the bus. OK, I cried.

*

'Let's go to the new Costa!' she said in the morning.

'Costa? In Otley?'

'Yes!'

'On Boxing Day?'

'Yes, love!'

We walked to the high street. She was right. A Costa. Vape shop, second vape shop, charity shop, sad shop with clip-art sign, closed shop, Costa.

'What the hell.'

'It's mine and Jackie's fave, love.'

'This was the Woolies, right?'

'No love, not this one.'

'No I swear it was.'

'No, love. Woolies was further down.'

'Was it?'

'Yes.'

We ordered the coffees and sat in the corner. There was a triptych on the wall behind Mum's head. On one side was a pile of ground beans ready to be pressed down with the tamper and on the other a flower of aerated milk. In the middle were the words *MAKING COFFEE IS AN ART*. *Art* was in a different font. Serif, italicised.

Mum had a flat white. She knew what one was, love, because there was a graphic above the head of the barista that explained the different proportions of coffee and water and milk. That was how I'd learned what a cortado was, too, though I kept that to myself. I had a coconut cortado.

We ate our foam first, with our spoons, and she told me about the D word.

'I say the D word now,' she said. 'It's my new word. "Delusion."'

'Right.'

'So Ingrid says we've to imagine three people—'

'Ingrid?'

'Ingrid love. She's my life coach.'

'What.'

'Norwegian.'

'Life coach?'

'Otley Courthouse, love. It's my new thing. Tuesdays. She's only a fiver a week love and I'm fed up of Slimmer's, I don't like that new Jane woman at all. At. All.' She wrinkled her nose. 'None of us can be doing with her, this Jane. She's a one, Grace. Amanda agrees now too, love, so it's: me, Amanda, Jackie, Ange, Julie and posh Sue,' she counted on her fingers. 'We've just gone do you know what let's try something new. Oh and I'm forgetting our Zoë!'

'Zoë?'

'Yeah you'd like her. Dead slim. She didn't need to be Slimmer's really but she's got a little lad, Frank he's called, husband's a rotter, left her, left her for some piece of skirt and she's dead pretty you know, Grace.'

'Poor Zoë.'

'I mean she does have this bit of belly after Frank and she's dead self-conscious and we've told her that's *so* normal love. She's dead self-conscious about this belly she's got.' She gazed off. 'Ahh. She's *lovely.*'

'Ingrid?'

'Yeah she comes in from town, love. Train to Menston and then she cycles. Cycles!'

I nodded.

'So last week she's got us with our eyes closed and we're imagining, first you've to imagine your best friend, so I imagine you.'

'Me?' I smiled. 'Not Jackie?'

'I just thought of you, Bun! She said think of whoever just pops up and you're my little friend, love. I know that love, you always write such nice things in my cards and I know you really mean it love. I keep them you know.'

'Oh. That's sweet, Mum.'

'So there's you.' She reached out for my hand. I touched my earlobe. 'There's you. And then a "neutral" person.' This she said emphatically, finger quotes. 'A "neutral" person says Ingrid. So for this I'd say Mags at number five or big fat Debbie and she says choose one so I say probably big fat Debbie. And then she says brace yourselves, ladies, it's time for the hard person—'

'Right.'

'So I've got you and then I've got big fat Debbie and then for my hard one I've got Ginger Whinger, RIP. RIP.'

'Mum—'

'So she has us sitting really still and just picture this Bun, there we all are, we're all on our bolsters and you know she puts the heating on max so we're all nice and comfy and we get to wear comfies for it, you know, just us ladies, all women, so I wear my fleecies love, my actual PJs, and for afterwards sometimes I pack my fluffy boots sometimes just to be extra comfy. I don't even wear a *bra*, love.'

'This all sounds great Mum.' I had my voice but my cheeks were going. My brow. *Don't. Don't.*

'I can actually sit without the bolster. I'm actually the most flexible one in the group Ingrid said. This one time I'm giving her a lift to Menston because it's raining so bad and I just say to her no Ingrid you can't go gallivanting up the bloody Chevin in this, it's a sheet out there, never seen anything like it and she goes oh thanks that'd be fab and then we're at the lights by the Fox and she goes can I tell you something and I go yeah and then, get this Grace, get this, you're making really good progress she says! I was *dead* proud. I was so proud. I'm actually the most flexible.'

I smiled.

'So anyway I'm sat going OHM, OHM, and we're trying to make all three of our three people all the same, like you just say you're all the same to me, it's all about delusion you know so I've taken a bit less off you and I'm adding it to Ginger Whinger and it's all a bit more—. Wait. Wait now it's just flown right out my head. What did she say! Bloody hell. Bloody hell! It's going to do my head in now. What did she say!'

'Balanced?'

'Oh. Wait. "Realistic" I think. Yes, yes! Realistic.'

'Is she calling this Buddhism?'

'It's about non-acceptance—'

'Non-attachment?'

'That's it love. Non-attachment and acceptance.'

'Right.'

'You're a natural-born Buddhist.'

I leant back in the chair, breathed the breath I hadn't realised I'd been holding. Short. Winding. *Don't. Don't.*

'You are!'

I took my spoon, started scraping the remains of the foam from the sides.

'You're like Gandhi love. That's what I tell the girlies. Dead severe. Mahatma Gandhi.'

'Mum.'

'Oh come on love you know what I mean!'

'Mum.'

'What?'

206

'*Agh.*' A tiny muted italicised *agh* just slipped out here amid a breath, something between an *agh* and a *gah*.

'What, love?'

I shook my head, eyes down.

She stopped stark for a second and looked at me directly, just for a second as I glanced up. I saw her teeth, the tiny gap between the front two. That was all, just a flash, but in that flash I saw a sharp quick blade across her neck and then the red-cheeked wide eyes. Side eyes, wide eyes, sad eyes.

'Well. It helps me love. I don't care if it's green, blue or pink if you ask me but you're being funny with me now, Grace, don't you go weird on me.'

I kept my head down.

'I'm cross, now. You'll get me cross, now.'

'Sorry.' A whisper.

'You be funny all you like, love. I'm fine. *I'm* fine. I keep my pecker up and I don't think about the "past" like you. I just think right, here and now, Ange's paninis are ready, kids are coming, let's go, get your apron on, get that Capital FM on and there we go, ba-bam! The eternal present, Ingrid calls it.'

The tears were coming now. I buried my chin further.

'You should try it. Let's see. Hang on a sec.' She got her phone out, put her glasses on her nose. 'I'm sure they've got a course in that London, love.'

'Please.'

'Now come on now love. What's this? Why've you got a face on? I've got you a coffee. We're in Costa's coffee. We're having a nice time.'

Costa.

I'd lost her to Google now.

Costa not Costa's. Costa coffee. Costa. Costa coffee. Costa. Grace, mate. Get a grip.

Still in her phone.

'Mum.'

She looked up and put her phone down, the glasses. 'Right. Come on.'

'I—.' I looked back down. A tear. Another.

She dropped her spoon on her saucer. She sighed.

Silence. Hers.

Silence. Mine.

'Well this is just great. Great. Brilliant.'

I put my head down.

'What do you want me to do? What am I supposed to do?' she said, but it was blurry, like a radio playing in another room. I was nodding I think. I don't know. I was nowhere. Then she came back into focus. 'What have you got to be sad about?'

'I'm not sad. I'm not. I'm happy. Look, I'm happy.' I wiped my eyes with my sleeve down over my fingers.

'All I've done is give. All I've done.'

'Please.'

'All my life.'

'I'm sorry, Mum. Mum, I know.'

'Christ.' She looked up, crossed herself. 'I can't cope with this, Grace.'

'Ignore me. Ignore me. I'm sorry.'

Silence.

I touched her toes with my toes.

She put her chin in her chest.

'I'm sorry.'

'I need a muffin.'

'I'll get you a muffin.'

'*Now.*'

'I'll get you a muffin.'

I got her a muffin. A Costa muffin. A toffee reindeer Costa muffin in a white paper Costa bag.

'Is there a code for the toilet?' I asked the barista.

'Yes. There's a very secret code.' He touched the side of his nose and winked. 'It's so secret it doesn't exist.'

*

I made us a TV dinner, a veggie paella thing with a bit of pre-cooked chicken on top for her. She put her portion on her plate then back in the oven while she did a wee, then she replenished her wine and took the plate out. Sometimes she'd get up midway through the meal and take her food back into the kitchen, give it a boost in the microwave. You'd see her stop and glaze over with a hint of panic in her face then she'd go *mmm*, still chewing, put her index finger up like *wait, wait, wait*, then pause the TV and return to the kitchen. She did now. As she transferred her plate back to the tray, hand wrapped in a tea towel, Mabel ran under her feet and Mum dropped a few grains on the floor. They were darker now and chewy with the radiation. A new yellow. An ochre. Mabel had a sniff but thought better of it. When we were done eating I picked them up with my fingers and took them through with the trays to the kitchen, popping them in the little hand-painted bowl for teabags, the one Rebecca had made at school.

'Can we turn it off for a minute, Mum?'

She frowned. '*Gogglebox.*'

'Put it on record? I just—. Just for a sec?'

'OK. Well, you do it, love. My specs are upstairs.'

'Can't you see the screen without your glasses, Mum?'

'Do it. You do it.'

'OK.' I shuffled past the pouffe to the mantel for the remote. '*Mabel.* Grace! Mabel!'

209

Mabel was scratching at the carpet to get back out. Sometimes she got locked in the lounge all night by accident and couldn't hold on till morning so that, over time, the corner of carpet by the front door had turned ochre too.

She found closed doors triggering and we were supposed to be empathic said Tim the vet though now I was brandishing the remote. 'MABEL.' She bedded in with the claws; you could hear the fibres tear now. '*Mabel.*' I cornered her, picking her up with one hand so the flab fell through between my fingers.

'Support her, Grace.'

'Little sod.'

'Don't hold her like that.'

I opened the door and let her go.

'She's getting old, Grace.'

'Sorry.' I turned the TV off. 'There.'

Mum took a nail file from the side and turned, stretching out her bare legs. She had her chill-out floaty skirt on, still cooling off from her bath and my taste for Pimentón – the bed socks were waiting on the headrest behind her.

'I'm sorry for—. For earlier. I'm sorry.'

'Well, good. Sorry I snapped, but you—.'

'It's OK, Mum.'

'I just want you to be happy. You know that? I do love you, you know.'

'I know.'

'I do.'

'I know, Mum. I'm sorry.'

'Good.' Then she put the nail file and her legs back down and went through to the kitchen and I popped the fire on and pulled my knees to my chest and made a little life raft for myself with the sofa cushions, haul of half-price Laura Ashley we'd got her for her fortieth, battling now with accumulated

Mabel, appliqué bits straggling. Mabel slipped back in and colonised the warm Mum bum patch – *ha* said the back of her unturned head – and through the draught that had caught hold of the door there was the rubber squishing back into place, a tinkle of ice, then Mum again with a vodka tonic and a baby Toblerone. 'Shoo!' She sat down, sliced open the Toblerone and gestured at me for the remote.

'Can't we—'

'I want to chill, Grace.'

I tossed it in her direction but it slipped onto the floor three feet between us. *Godsake.* I uncushioned myself. Clumsy hop. *Here. Thanks.*

She lit the screen up and started scrolling but something had fucked it and it was stuck, maybe the surge in the leccy from the fire, *no, no, that's not how it works, Grace.* Maybe the remote drop. The image was fixed but it was playing the Sky Plus placeholder music, the one that accompanies the menu and lulls your indecision, suspends you in a fantasy of choice, like the one they play you on build-mode on *The Sims.* I wanted to just listen to that, started humming along. I thought of the quartet on the *Titanic. Greasepaint, Grace. Smile. Come on.*

'Damn.' She flung the remote out next to her.

'Let's leave it. Shall we leave it?'

'Grace, can you—?'

'Give it here.'

Another clumsy hop. I turned it off.

'What you do that for—?'

'Off and on.'

She nodded.

She took a bite of her Toblerone. I locked my eyes on the screen. The fire was whirring. Purring. It was getting hot but I was shrinking.

'I am sorry, Mum.'

A nod – mouth full.

'I can't help it, Mum.'

'You can,' she swallowed, wiped her mouth.

Shrinking. My toes had turned to wax.

'You don't know you're born, love.'

Fingers, now. Yellow.

'No clue.'

'I know.' Semi-whisper.

'No you don't.'

'I know I don't.' Full-whisper. *See me* said the fire.

I tilted my head back. One tear. Two. Behind me was the Billy bookcase: two little white christening Bibles; two copies of *Of Mice and Men*, Rebecca's all crusty from a schoolbag squash leak; two pottery angels with copper wire wings.

'Lighten up, love.'

Mabel started brushing against my legs. I slid into the space between the sofa and the pouffe and she dropped down into fifth now, a deep, kernel-popping purr, her presence firm. I pressed my forehead to my knees.

I heard Mum's vodka and the Toblerone touch down on the side, and then I felt her hand on my shoulder, two little squeezes. 'Shh.'

*

There was a car in the night. I pulled the curtain. It was Dawn, Dawn the Red Twingo. It was Rebecca.

She hovered for twenty, thirty seconds then there was that nervous drop in power. *Zhoom.* She was alone. I watched her haul her little wheely case for a moment then I moved away from the curtain, body drained of blood again and rooted like the films, a great authentic performance of paralysis

– black-and-white, Satie keys – except I was wearing Mum's snowflake dressing gown and her Center Parcs nylon slippers with their static electric rasp and I noticed I was also wide-eyed, mouth slightly open like a child. More *BFG*, then, the animated eighties one: Sophie in *The BFG*.

A few seconds passed. She must have come inside now but of course she had her stealthy agile way with objects and logistics, hand-eye stuff; I didn't hear her.

I took off the slippers and moved over to the door, left ajar for Mabel. She chose me when I was here, curled her little bum tight as a scroll, fur impossibly glossy up here on my bed – 6 a.m. or thereabouts, once her night shift was up. She'd settle just north of my toes because I was cold as in cold and cold as in mean and cats loved that and cats knew humans weren't gods I'd heard and Mabel knew me. I respected that. I left the door ajar.

I stopped on the landing, plugging back in from this reverie when oh, fuck, that was Mum. Mum was down there. Whispers.

'I—. I—.' This was Mum.

'She'll be fine, Mum.'

'I—. I can't believe it, love. Don't you think it's weird?'

'I guess. I dunno.'

'Don't you?'

'Dunno, Mum.'

'She's been at yours all this time?'

Silence.

'I can't believe it, love.'

'It's fine.'

'Is it?'

'She'll be OK. You know what she's like.'

'What's she said?'

213

'Mum. It's fine.'

'What's she told you?'

'It's fine. She's fine.'

'Is it?'

'Yeah.'

'Has she said anything to you?'

'What about?'

'I don't know. She's been spooky—'

'Mum.'

'She's weird again.'

Silence.

'It's just what she's like.'

'Is it, love? Dya think? Is it?'

'Mum. It's fine.'

'I—'

'It's fine.'

'OK, love. OK. I'm jus—. It gets me all *funny*.'

'It's fine.'

'You're OK, love? How's Tash?'

'She's fine, Mum.'

'How's Jill?'

'Fine.'

'Ronnie alright?'

'Fine, Mum.'

'It is naughty, love. You're here. My little love in the night!'
She lowered her voice. '*My favourite*.'

Silence. A muffle.

'Do they know you're here?'

'Yeah, like I said, I gave my panto ticket to Gina, Ronnie's
Gina.'

'Oh, oh yeah you did say. You did say that.'

'Yeah.'

'So no rush back tomorrow?'

'Yeah. No rush.'

'Come here, love. Hug for your old—'

'Mum—.'

Silence.

Whimpers, Mum's, and then a charged silence, the booming kind that brings about a key change, and then a key change. '*Sorry! I*—. Oh god. Oh, love. Oh. I—. I'm sorry, love.'

Silence.

'Why is she like this?'

Silence. A sob. The tap went, glass on the side. 'Here.'

'Thanks, love.'

Silence.

'Do you think she'll come round?'

'She'll be fine, Mum.'

'Do you think this is it?'

'What, you mean like is she back-back?'

Silence. Mum was nodding so hard I swear I could hear her neck.

'Do you think—? Do you think I'll ever—? Do you think she'll—?'

Silence.

'I don't worry about you, love. Not now, love. And I mean, well, you've got your *friend* and I love Tash, I see Tash as a daughter—'

'Mum.'

'Oh, love. I said—. I said I wasn't going to get in a state, I wasn't going to get upset and I, I promised myself no, *no*, now don't get upset—'

'Mum—'

'No, no let me finish. Let me. I know you and me, down the years—'

215

'Shh. You'll wake her, Mum. Chill out—'

'*Let* me. I know you and me, down the years . . . I know, love, but I get it now, you know I do and I just wanted—. I wanted to tell you in person, love. Love's love, love, and I get that. I do.'

Kleenex on the side. Kleenex out the box.

'Thanks, love.'

Silence.

A little giggle. 'Gosh. What am I like!'

Silence.

'I told you about Ingrid, love?'

'Yes, Mum.' Rebecca seemed to go back to the sink again here. The tap ran for a while, in to the kettle.

'Oh you're *here*. You're here. You're my little love, you're my little pal.'

Silence.

A muffle.

'I know I've got you, love.'

'*Mum.*'

'But—. But now, now I've lost—. *Now I've lost her—.*' She made a high-pitched noise here, aftershock. Another long silence. A nose blow, a muffle. And a sob. I put my head in my hands.

'What's wrong with us?' She was whispering now.

'There's nothing wrong with us, Mum.'

'She can't bear us.'

Silence.

'Do you blame me?'

I went down.

*

Rebecca saw me first. She looked at me the way you look at some indecipherable noise in the dark, you can't see for shit but you know it's a threat. She was stood right under the big light, her pupils slits.

'Go to bed Grace.'

Mum turned round.

'Look what you've done to her.' Rebecca shook her head.

'Me?' My heart was pounding.

'Stop it! Stop it, girls.' Mum was flapping her hand.

'Yes, you.'

'Please, love.' Mum put her hand on Rebecca's wrist. She pulled away, turned, strained her teabag on the side of her mug and paused there, back to us.

'What do you want from us?' She said this to the counter. Her back was screaming.

'I—. I—. Rebecca—.'

'Look at her.' Rebecca turned now and looked at me and I pulled my eyes towards Mum.

Silence. I looked at Mum, tried for her eyes but she was somewhere inside herself, I couldn't find her, so I looked at the floor then at the little pottery bowl in the middle distance, the steam rising from the teabag.

'Sort your shit out, Grace.'

'I—.' I looked at her now. I put my palms out in front of me. 'Listen to me. I'm trying to—.'

'I'm off to bed.'

'Please Rebecca.'

'I'm *tired.*'

'Please.'

'No. It's not a fucking safari, Grace. You're in my flat and no, it's not enough. I get you a job and no, you're still—. I don't even know. What's your *problem*? What do you want?'

I looked down. 'Fuck. That's not—.' I thumped myself in the forehead. 'I—. I—. Fuck.'

'*Language.*'

'Sorry,' I touched Mum's arm. Fingertips. Little stroke.

Rebecca stared at them there and recoiled, heaved with frustration.

I breathed out hard through my nose.

'Give us a break, Grace.'

'You never let me—. You never tell me how you feel—. I don't know how to—. *Jesus.*'

Silence.

'Sorry.' Quiet now, almost inaudible.

'Why are you here?'

It was quiet now. A rich quiet, dense. The air grew thinner and then the clock came back in, the clock was ticking again, had been ticking all this time and we were here in the kitchen. It was getting on for two and my feet were gone and my fingers but I couldn't afford to care and Mum had sat herself down on the floor now, on Mabel's unused bed, back flush to the radiator, still on low to stop the pipes from freezing and Mabel was in here now, Mabel was nudging at her feet. It was fucking cold.

'I—. I don't know. I don't know,' I whispered, tiny whisper, eyes to the heavens.

'Well you best work that out.'

A moment. Ten, fifteen seconds. No one looked at anyone. Bar Mabel. Mabel was staring at Rebecca. Rebecca gave Mabel a pat then she picked up her bag and her mug and tried to get past.

'Rebecca,' I said. 'Look. I love you. I fucking love you, you div.'

Mum put her head in her hands. 'Please,' she whispered.

'I couldn't do it. I couldn't stay here——.'

Mum tugged hard on the dressing-gown tie. Emergency stop.

Rebecca took a sip of tea.

'Can I?' I pointed at it. She nodded, handed me the mug and I held it for a moment in both hands, shuffled up against the radiator, took a sip. Mum took the bed socks drying on the radiator and tapped me on the top of each foot, slipped them on me one by one. I took another sip of tea. I handed it back. I pulled away.

A few seconds passed, almost a minute. I counted the beats. Then Mum put her hands out in front of her from the floor, made little pick-me-up movements with her fingers.

'Alright, Mum,' said Rebecca, noticing her now, looking down. 'We've all had a few.'

'Come on Mum,' I said. 'Can't take her anywhere.' I took her hand. She did a little tippy-toe dance as she stretched, clasped her hands together and beamed, catching Mabel's tail just a touch with her foot.

'*Riow!*'

'Oh! Oh! Sorry, love.' She bent down to stroke her. Mabel ran away.

'Christ. Mabel's having a fucking mare.'

'Language.'

'Sorry, Mum.'

*

Next day we drove up to Weston, the three of us. We decided to surprise them so I went in there first, Rebecca and Mum waiting down the side. Grandad had pushed an MDF sign into the grass out front. *Santa Stop Here.*

Knock. Wait. Knock again. Ring. Knock again. Wait.

'Look who it isn't,' he said, opening the door.

'Iiiit's Santaaaaaa!' I rustled my bag for life, shook my hips. He put his hand on the side of my face and paused.

We went through.

The place was a state, all this stuff from the garage and the eaves and god knows where piled high, every surface. Old Lilliput Lanes, plastic shovels for cat litter, miniature battery-powered fans, tiny cans of Irn-Bru.

'What's all this, Grandad?'

'What's what?'

'This stuff.'

'Stuff? Cheeky sod.'

'I don't understand.'

'There are things you don't understand when you get to my age.'

'I—'

'You say hello to your nana.'

I went through into the lounge. *Fiddler on the Roof* had just come on and Nana was singing along, quite pearlescent, the nails at least. Powder-pink jumper. I kissed her hand. She didn't look at me. She didn't move.

'What's up with Nana?' I said to Grandad, taking our wines off him.

'What?'

'What's up with her?'

'WHAT.'

'Never mind.'

'WHAT.'

'You sit down,' I said and I went to the kitchen, WhatsApped Rebecca *come in.*

I wandered back into the lounge and sat down.

'Cheers!'

'Cheers, love.'

Nana zoned back in. 'Oh! It's Grace!'

'Cheers, Nana! Merry Christmas!'

'Meeerrry Christmas!'

Then the doorbell went.

'Ooh,' I said.

'What's that, love?'

'Someone's at the door, Grandad.'

'You get it, love.'

I got up, brushing the lounge door behind me then *Pink Panther* creeping up to the front door. Mum, Rebecca. Fingers to our lips. Then: one, two, three . . .

In my peripherals I saw Grandad splash his red down his front and Mum go rushing back to the kitchen for some white to neutralise it and Rebecca giving Nana a kiss then going back through for more glasses, for the flutes, for Prosecco, but I was looking at Nana. She was smiling. Watching her Virgin Mary and smiling. She took a fag, last in the pack. Lit up.

We doled out the Prosecco then Rebecca and me made butties. Bacon. Grandad's first, to account for the sometimes (always) subpar first, second for Nana. I reminded Rebecca of this law; I was the second twin. She biffed me on the nose. *Pass me the butter.* Right, butter. Butter, good quarter of a pack of Lurpak, always from foil, foam it up then fry on high until the water's gone and keep going and going till you're left with gold and crispy. Touch crispier for Nana. The bread's a small white Danish loaf, pre-sliced, the skinny stuff, the bacon streaky Danepak. Always. When the bacon's ready you pile it in the corner of the pan and press the bread into the butter for a few seconds to soak up the fat, just the one side, the inside side, there'll be little shiny black bits there for Nana's but no bother. Perfect.

We walked in with the plates.

'Turn it over please. It's disrespectful.'

'What?'

'Jewish.'

'Oh.' I took the remote and turned on Gold, *Dad's Army*. It was the one where Mainwaring's drunken brother Barry wants their father's pocket watch and they put Mainwaring's drunken brother Barry in the wardrobe and then Mainwaring's drunken brother Barry is a phantom moving wardrobe. They watched transfixed. We watched them eat their bacon.

'Let me,' said Grandad when I took the plates back through, coming in behind me and pulling on his Marigolds from the plastic pole by the bin. He loved washing up.

A cow sounded in his pocket once he'd foamed up the pans. He was just about to rinse and then this cow.

'What's that?'

'Animal Farm.'

'What?'

'Animal Farm.'

'Nope.'

'Animal Farm.'

'Farmville?'

He took the phone out of his pocket, started jabbing at it.

'You have to take the gloves off Grandad.'

'I've just put them on.'

'You have to take them off to make it work. It can't feel your fingers. You have to—'

'I'll glove you in a minute.'

'Grandad.'

He gave me a flick and I gave him a cuddle then I took his phone off him and put a photo of my scowling face as the screensaver. I googled *Fiddler on the Roof*.

'What does a fiddler on a roof do Grandad?'

'Go on.'

'A fiddler on a roof tries to scratch out a pleasant simple tune without breaking his neck.'

'Well done. Well done our lass.'

'That'll do, donkey.'

'*I'd do anything for you dear, anything—*'

'Shh. Let's have a nice port wine, shall we?'

Rebecca had to get off, had Buck's Fizzed her Prosecco and vetoed the port wine for her drive. 'I have to get off, Grandad, drive back to Scarborough.'

'She's at Tash's, Dad.'

He nodded, vacant.

'Tash, you know. Tash. Jill and Ronnie? You know, Tash.'

'Tash, Grandad,' I took his empty glass off him, put it on the side.

'Tash,' he said, like it was a word game, like he'd said leg or blue or tomato.

'Tash! You know, Tash, Grandad.'

Rebecca was blushing.

'*Tash*, Dad.'

'Easy for you to say.'

She said she'd give us both a lift back but I said I wanted to walk, get a bit of air, see her in Sheff tomorrow or soon and she nodded and her and Mum got in the car.

*

223

I walked slowly, stopping for a while in the middle of the bridge. I watched the water crack open on the weir, Garnett's paper mill sitting dead in the background. *What do you want from us? Why are you here?*

I didn't want a career. I didn't want to transact. I didn't want to master a vocabulary. I wanted mystical communion. But you don't get what you want. *You don't get what you want, Grace. That's not how it works.*

I'd had a choice. I could have stood right here on this bridge with my hands on my ears, waiting for the courage to take them off and listen but I'd run. I'd got on the bus. I'd got on the bus out of here while the eggs smashed on the window – *SCAB! SCAB!* – and I'd released the little popper on the dusty nylon curtain and I'd pulled it to. *IT HURTS. No. Don't look down.*

Maybe you had to be on the bus. Stay on it. Take your faulty sovereignty, take their money, get on your knees in a white fur gown then get on a couch and pay it all back. Maybe you could never get off the bus, you'd always be there traversing the Midlands on a National Express or an East Coast/East Mids overpriced train, freaking out and not. . . And maybe that was fine. Maybe you were eternally Billy, Billy en route to ballet school, pounding your fists on the back window to hear what they were trying to tell you: *WE'LL MISS YOU. WE'LL MISS YOU. REMEMBER US.* A swan nudged a twig. *Take two*, Grace. *Take two. This time Billy.* I'm pounding the glass. I have *fists*. Give me a decade and I'll dance for you. But I'm not getting off my bus.

I watched the lockets tied to the mesh, the swan curl its neck into its wing. I cranked up 'Back to Life'. I went home.

*

224

Mum got up at six for her Macmillan coffee thing down Bridge Street. I listened to her shower and wee, her slippers flap back and forth across the kitchen, back and forth, Go Ahead! apple slice a-rustling, *Iams, Mabel!* And under all this she was pacing something out, some feeling. It felt light. Itself.

I left her a picture of the three of us: Mum with her banana hair and me in my big square glasses and a little bit of space and then Rebecca with a spanner, just ready and waiting in case something broke, and I put us in a love heart and then I drew Mabel, fat scowling Mabel on the outside looking in. I gave her a speech bubble. *Roar*, she said.

JANUARY 2016

I went back to Sheffield and back came the snow. Second wave. Farce this time. *Foot-long icicles! Four-foot drifts!* I told the London group chat. *Nahhh* they said and so I sent a cut and paste of my shiny cherub face atop Mont Blanc.

[Sardonic face] (Charlie).

[Vom] (Michelle).

[Aubergine] (Adam). Adam liked an aubergine.

I had one month left at the library. I spent the days with Big Anne's mum and Pam and Carole and in the evenings I got off the tram opposite the old Henderson's factory and climbed the hill to my new friend Gary's, Gary the fruit and veg man for some fun object to play kitchens with: Jerusalem artichoke, celeriac, once a glut of premature blood oranges of which I ate my weight. Then the rhubarb came. Gary was out gritting the pavement that day in double denim – acid-wash upper, faded grey skinnies – plus mid-calf caramel Uggs and a parka on top. He rested his spade a moment as I got my breath back.

'When's this shit going to end, Gary.'

'I think it's hot. End times. I'm into it.'

'Not for me, babe.'

He shrugged. 'The heart wants what it wants.'

I went in. I bought a rucksack's worth of rhubarb, cleared the place out, and a pot of posh crème fraîche and some chicory. I liked this colour scheme; I liked the rhyme. Google. Hmm. Muscovado, bag of walnuts for a pretty little chicory walnut brittle and fuck it, *yes, I'll have those cut-price cacao nibs at the till, yeah, go on then. Chuck 'em in.*

I came back out.

Gary rested the spade on the wall, slipped his hand into my open rucksack while I had a rearrange, pondered my weight distribution for the hike back home.

'Thank *youuu*,' he said, sliding a rhubarb stick under his coat.

'Play safe, kids.'

He winked. 'You've really gone for it tonight, hun.'

I pretended to paint my nails.

He put his mock analyst's pipe in. 'The chicory seems to me to be an indication of what people in my profession call a sufficient libidinal attachment to oneself.'

I gazed into the gods, voice dreamy. 'What, you mean, I love myself?'

'*Yes!*' He pulled his parka hood up. 'Am I a good enough mother, hun?'

'You're fucking Mary, babe.'

He cocked his head, eyes to the heavens, faux-Renaissance painting.

'See you tomorrow?'

'Mwah.'

*

Evenings were Gary and kitchen play; weekends the Showroom Cinema. I'd make small bags of fruit and nut and cacao nibs and a hip flask – layer up hard just in case they went too far

229

with the air con which was always – then swagger my way to the Showroom, and if I had a meltdown I'd Uber it. The meltdowns were often, now, I was learning, and they happened in a style I termed the Grace Classique: showy laced with shame, in the dark in public, wild and invisible then hit the lights for a melodramatic tableau. It was a look.

Showroom tickets were £4.50 for the under twenty-five and I'd never get that again, not even the ICA weekday matinees, not even Peckhamplex. So I put myself in the Showroom and I mainlined. I watched everything going, anything, and I branded it my re-education, the one where I made the rules, though Rome wasn't built in a day. When I saw a little Palme d'Or logo or that cute little Berlinale bear I still got a flutter in my belly but I tried not to succumb. I tried to watch everything with an open face and an open mind and the calm that could not but accompany such a bargain ticket price. I was calm or I was ruined and, as I say, we were learning, here, and nine times out of ten we were Ubering.

I encouraged all this. I'd project, project, project, see myself in everyone, and if the soundtrack floored me, which it mostly did, I'd wait for the credits then take photos of the credits with my phone then add them to the Spotify playlist I had named 'emote'. *Erm, Shazam?* said Matthew. No.

If some rogue element of critical analysis popped into my head I let it. *Hi, yes, hello, I know you. Hello. Maybe later.* And sometimes the urge to respond was big, to draw or write or best of all message Charlie or Abi or Michelle to say *GAH, are you on this? Get on it.* Sometimes that urge was insatiable, and that was a way to know there was somebody in there making meaning. I'd get her back out in time. For now, when I thought about where all this had ended last time, all this thinking, all this intellect, pushing me off, away, tearing me in two, I still lost my breath. I squeaked and clasped my face. I gasped into the dark. It was a quarter-life version of a teenage howl, a scream, which is what should have been happening all along. So, that. *Billy, Grace. Fists.*

*

And then, then there was Ginger.

I bumped into her one Saturday afternoon, fresh from a screening of *Carol*. Ginger. Ginger from the train. You couldn't write it but there she was. She really was.

For our reunion I wore Rebecca's trackies with tights underneath and the talismanic Mum bed socks off the radiator plus an off-brand heat-tech gilet and the Bet Lynch coat. *The heart wants what it wants.*

I was at the little ledge by the loo where they kept the upturned Kilner water jar and I'd filled my plastic bottle and was downing it, my throat parched from the air con and the liquids nil by mouth I always impose for an hour or so before a film, wee prevention strategy. I was downing my water, downing it, and then there was a finger on my shoulder, a pinky. I might have jumped but my body knew that finger.

I turned. Yes. Ginger, red flannel shirt and box-fresh Reeboks. She was dancing. She had her arms in L shapes out in front of her and she was rotating her shoulders and her hips, tiny and perfectly controlled movements with her toes, weight through the balls of her feet.

They played music in the bar here, and often it was movie-related music and that's what was happening now, 'Theme from *Shaft*'. The bloke behind the bar turned it up and Ginger spread her arms out then to clear some space and it was a little bit like a *GOAL* movement of the arms where the hands start lifting upwards to say *wheeeeyyyy get up,* yes *mate,* but she didn't go quite that far. She was just making some space to have a late-afternoon dance of a Saturday. I joined her. The barman had a little shake too.

It faded out. We were both enclosed in the dance still, silent for a couple of seconds while she moved her smile from down on the floor up to my face. I knew she'd want to make that move and I could see even without seeing her face how much pleasure she was having in the delay. She was choosing what to do and it was a pleasure to watch and wait – her arms, thick and strong, leaving the edges of a ribbed cotton T-shirt, and her hairline, downy, drowsy, partly sweat but mostly that still-wet wet you get from the shower. She finally raised her head and there was her jaw. It was beautiful. It was meaningful, the way the structure of a bone is meaningful in the aftermath of acne, when the face has survived the skin.

'This is mad,' I said.

No. I summoned you, her face said, *it's all as is meant.* She pointed at the heavens. 'It's Grace!'

I smiled. My heart was knocking on a heart attack but so be it. I couldn't do anything about it. I didn't want to.

She held my gilet zip. She winked. Then she shouted for Vicky.

Vicky was the woman on the sofa with her laptop out and her headphones on, Ginger's headphones, the red ones. She looked about fifty. Silver hair. Big red jumper with white letters: *THIS IS AS CHRISTMASSY AS IT GETS.* In front of her on the coffee table was a reusable carrycot coffee cup. It was open and I thought to myself she's definitely lost the top off that, happens to us all, and I put a pin in that thought in case that was a Vicky-ish observation to make, in case that was a way for us to bond. Here was the time to find out, and as we moved towards her I made sure to look inside. Hot chocolate. *Right.*

She stopped typing, took off the headphones and held her right elbow with her left hand, circulating the right wrist. She smiled at Ginger. Furtive. Permissive. *Ahh*, it said. I thought. I hoped. *Aha.* There was a lot of tension exuding from that wrist. Vicky took hold and it dissolved into space – efficient, sage – and this was the baseline feeling of Vicky, her energy. It was irresistible. I crossed off my coffee cup gambit, and the *oh, I see you're drinking hot chocolate, I like hot chocolate, too*, putting my bag down and leaning over and making to put my water bottle away. I wanted Vicky to look at Ginger, to transfer whatever needed transferring, without me watching. *One, two, three.*

'Hi,' I said, coming back up. 'I'm Grace.'

'Grace,' said Vicky, on with her other wrist now. She let it go limp and focused all of herself on this greeting. 'It's *good* to meet you. It's great.'

'You too,' I said, hoping my face wouldn't betray my ignorance though I clocked it then, yes, Vicky was the woman who got the *LRB*. Vicky and Ginger. I looked at their fingers for rings. No. Little blush. 'RSI?' I pointed at her wrist.

Vicky nodded. 'Nightmare.'

I moved my pointer to her laptop. 'Are you a writer?'

She smiled. 'Ha. I wish.'

'PhD,' whispered Ginger while Vicky put her hand to her brow for the shade, head down. Ginger sat on the armrest and leant over towards her, stroked her on the wrist.

'Ah! Wow. What's your topic?'

'Algae.' Eye roll. 'For my sins.'

'Amazing.'

She sighed. 'Yeah, I used to think that too.'

Ginger smiled at her. 'It's Grace off the train, Vicky!'

'It's Grace off the train.' Vicky shook her head, shook herself off, back in the room. She smiled at Ginger. She smiled at me. 'Sorry, Grace. Deadline. Head's like—' She did a little poof explosion with her lips. 'Come sit for a bit.' She shuffled up and patted the space next to her with her palm.

'Oh no. No, I know what a mare it is. I don't want to interrupt.'

'Please do. Save us.'

Ginger laughed.

'Save her from me,' Vicky added, stroking Ginger back.

The blush hit me hard here. I'd been doing so well but no. *Damn.* Massive. I ducked back down and rooted in my bag again. More blood rushed to my head but I kept my head down in the bag for a bit because then it would look like I'd gone red like the normal red, like a rush of blood to the head.

I came back up. Vicky was seeing off her hot chocolate, palm still firm and energetic on the leather next to her. *Sit.*

'What you having?' Ginger did a mock pint with her hand.

'Oh. I, I really do have to go, really. There's this thing.'

'Aww. Go on,' Vicky said. 'Ten minutes.' She reached into her pocket for a fiver, handed it to Ginger. 'Get her a half.'

'No, no, really—. I've—.'

Vicky winked at Ginger and Ginger went to the bar. She patted the sofa again. I sat down.

We had this half an hour and I learnt this. I liked Vicky. Vicky liked me. I liked Ginger. Ginger liked Vicky and Vicky liked me. I liked *Anomalisa. Did you like* Anomalisa? Ginger didn't get it. Ginger liked *The Lobster* and Grace loved *The Lobster* but Vicky wasn't a fan. '*What?!*' Here me and Ginger shared that private blissful shared incredulity you get when you get in a triangle and the third person doesn't have to die, no, the third person's the necessary third. I knew triangles.

'What did you see?'

'Hmm?'

'Just now, what did you go see?'

'Oh. *Carol.*'

I took my empty to the bar, put my rucksack on to leave.

'What's your number, Grace?'

'Oh. Erm.'

She tore off a bit of menu and wrote her number. 'Message me?'

'Oh. Yes. Yes. I will.'

Vicky went to put her headphones on. 'Have a nice time with your sister,' she winked. Ginger ruffled her hair again.

'Thanks. I, I will. You too.'

*

I walked up West Street, through the packs of biceps and sockless loafers. *DYKE*, said one to a chorus of *wheeey* but my heart and cheeks were Teflon. I gave them the finger without turning then I ducked into West Street Tesco Express. I bought a cinnamon swirl in a cellophane bag. I bought two.

*

A few days later I saw her again. I went to sort the petty cash and there she was, in the Post Office queue, wearing an M&S uniform and holding a little red *sorry we missed you*. Strictly I hadn't started thinking about her yet, how and when to message. I hadn't felt the need. Also I was shitting myself. I guessed my mind had decided to protect us from me for a bit, maybe as long as a week, though TBC. TBC. It was legitimately busy at work, financial-year-end approaching and that had nothing to do with me but I did have a Diane's mum handover to do.

'Here's Grace,' she said, turning slowly with her teeth there on her bottom lip as I joined the queue behind her.

'That's me. What you doing?'

She flapped her red card.

I flicked it then bumped my forehead with the heel of my hand.

'Ha.'

Till number one, please said the tannoy and the LED said *ONE.* The number one man popped his head up, looked at us, a slight hint of a sigh.

'After you.' Ginger fanned the route, her card turned palm leaf. I did a miniature curtsey.

I waited for her outside. Here she was with her parcel. ASOS, it was, soft, quite big and as she came through the door she chucked it at me and I caught it, squishy like a pillow. I threw it back to her. She put her face in it. I laughed.

*

Next day we went for lunch at a Taiwanese place down the Moor. I got there early and went inside, trying to stand a few paces back from the menu up above the hatch so I wasn't in the way though I was highly in the way right away and I couldn't see the menu in any case, not even with my glasses so that was that and then Ginger came. Ginger was outside, waving. This one was more subdued, this wave, still essentially regal but more subdued; this, this and us, this thing, it wasn't an accident now so I guessed it was that. It was a hot potato that hint of shyness. I'd caught her ASOS bag and now I caught the potato. I did an am-dram come hither with my left-hand finger. In she came.

I said hi and she said hi too and then we didn't really talk at all to begin with because we were ordering. It was hectic. I ran to get us the seats by the window and she followed with the polystyrene and the chopsticks, putting her bag under the table then spreading her fingers down and out on the surface in front of her, taking a little breather.

'Bit mad in here,' she said.

'It's good though.'

'Yes. Yes. It's excellent.' She drummed the table for a second, her pupils concentrating on the rhythm in her head.

'Earworm?'

She released a little laugh. 'Something like that.'

I opened my chopsticks. I wanted to hand her them so she could tap the rhythm out of her system with the chopsticks, make those chopsticks into little drumsticks and then I could be her accomplice and maybe she'd got stuck in her head and she didn't know quite what to say and maybe I should crop up here and say something, do something, help. But then I came back to and the rhythm was a rhythm, curious and rich and I found I was just listening, making little micro movements with my nose, little spontaneous upwards circles.

Ginger had small hands and small nails and the whites of her nails were pretty short but not uniformly, the right-hand ones all marginally longer though still not long enough to catch a keyboard key for a click. *She must play the guitar. Maybe the ukulele? Hmm. No, guitar.* She had short sleeves today, this odd length that ended up about an inch above the wrist bones, might have been machine shrinkage but felt more deliberate, the way it can be nice to have wrists even in winter sometimes, to see your wrists, to air them. The jumper was on its way from sienna to oatmeal. Her hair was like glass.

'Your hair looks great.'

'Thanks,' she said, taking a bobble off her wrist. I hadn't seen that bobble there. All that looking and the bobble had just slipped on through. She fashioned herself a topknot and smiled lengthways, pursed but thriving with this sprightly kind of energy, her dimples popping, then she cradled her fingers and stretched up and out and sighed. 'Just dyed it.'

'You can tell. It's—. Hmm. Erm. Hmm. What word am I looking for. . . Erm. Glossy, I think.'

'Grace! I thought you were going to hit me with a banger there.'

'Ha. Hmm. How's—. Erm. No. Brain freeze.'

Her dimples popped again. She went into her phone for a sec. 'Cherry red?'

'Ooh. I like that.'

'That's the shade on the pack.' She showed me the website. 'It'll do.'

We ate. She didn't want to use her chopsticks she said.

'Oh yeah, kind of culturally—. Kind of tricky territory.'

A laugh-frown. 'I'm starving, so—'

'Inefficient.'

She nodded.

We ate our bean curd and rice and Sriracha and chilli oil and a salad of cauliflower, chickpeas and dill and she said yes. Yes! Yes, she played guitar and yes *I work at M&S, four-fifths now though, not full-full weeks and also yes I dance, I dabble, got to keep these knees in order, good work, Grace!* Then the man behind the counter came over with some fortune cookies. Ginger still had a bit to go but he needed the table back.

'What's yours?' I asked as we tapped them on our mats.

'Oh dear.'

'What is it?'

'Doesn't matter.'

'Go on.'

She wrapped the bit of paper/plastic back into a tiny scroll and pushed it at me slowly with her air-snooker cue, mimicking a tricky shot, all this in slow-mo then straight back to regular eating at her non-cinematic speed. She ate slowly. She was perfect. *YOU WILL FALL IN LOVE.*

I read it, closed my mouth to hide the lips and side-eyed for the both of us then wrapped it into a scroll. It sat there in the middle.

'Nice sentiment?'

She had her mouth half full. *Suppose so* said her eyes. No, actually more *spose*. Lighter. Sweeter.

'I find these dodgy to be honest.'

She swigged her Lipton. 'Why's that?'

'They're a bit problematic aren't they?'

'You kids! What are you like.' Cap back on the Lipton. 'I get what you mean though.' Pause. Three seconds. 'So. Vicky.'

'Ahh, Vicky.' A slight dryness in the back of my throat. 'I love her.'

'One of the nicest human beings you will ever meet.'

'Hear hear.' Big swallow. Nope, still there.

She handed me her Lipton.

'Thanks.' Smile. Swig. *Shall I put the cap back on or do you want another swig* gesture.

I want another swig gesture.

I handed her the bottle. 'I love her energy.'

'She's a peach.'

'Are you—?' Cough. 'You know.'

Ginger let her fork hover over her final strands of rice for a moment, started to herd them to the corner, watching her hand with a frown that enclosed her reaction to the frown, nodded slightly then got halfway to a smile which then morphed into a nibble of the bottom lip, always the bottom lip with Ginger and I wanted to know that about her, to name it. I was with her, throwing all my weight behind her while she worked out what to say. *It doesn't matter what she says. It doesn't matter. Stick with the feeling.* Then the person from behind the counter came over like *can I take your container now*, aka *it's busy can we move this thing along* and she acknowledged him with a little movement of the fork and the eyes. She said *yes, sure, sorry* in the form of a *sorry, mate*, an open-hearted *genuinely sorry, mate, give us a sec* and the counter person looked down and moved to the table across.

'Are you OK?' I asked.

She collated the last of the rice and put it in her mouth. It turned out an ambitious mouthful. Her cheeks bulged. She laughed out her nose. 'Bloody 'ell,' she said, 'made a right pig's ear of that.'

I shook my head.

'You're lying.'

I laughed. 'I'm not! I enjoyed it.'

'I haven't answered your question.'

'You—. You don't have to answ—.'

'I do.'

I took out my Oyster/bank card holder thing.

'It's kind of complicated and it's not,' she said. 'Can I leave you with that for now?'

I nodded. I couldn't look at her now.

'On me,' she said.

'Oh, no, no, I—.'

'Shh. My treat.'

A day or so went by then:

Blue Moon breakfast? I'm on a late shift

Yes!

I gave myself an air-quotes 'cold' and we met up for breakfast.

This time she was there when I arrived, back in her aubergine fleece, raincoat over her arm, stood by the cascade of current and bygone fliers at the entrance: yoga mums, ESOL Sheffield, Lescar jazz. We hugged, and as we came loose she said she'd panic-eaten and she was sorry but she was definitely going to order some extremely milky and sugary thing and she strode us over to the counter.

She started whispering a menu commentary to herself. She seemed preoccupied, like maybe she'd panic-eaten then smoked or panic-eaten but not very much then coffee. Then she turned her volume back up and what was she saying now, she was saying she always broke the day in early and she liked to do that with something bitter, preferably a grapefruit. 'Red though, never white. Never, ever white.' On this I disagreed and I flagged it then I let her go on and she said 'So, yeah, grapefruit and the sun, and if it's raining I like something smoky. If it's raining I have a lapsang.'

She ordered a cappuccino.

'I'm just going to—.' She pointed at the door for the loo.

'Mmhmm. I'll take these to the ta—.' I pointed to the table in the corner.

'What can I get you, love?'

'Oh. Erm. Hot cross bun, please.' Hot cross bun and a two-wo/man cafetière.

241

'You sit down, love. I'll bring these over.'

'Oh. Thanks.'

I sat down. I felt myself want to get my phone out. I didn't get my phone out. I got my phone out. Then she came back in and sat herself down, unzipped her fleece and took her glasses out her pocket, little rustle of her keys in there, then this other person, not the one we'd ordered from but a different one with a newish baritone, sixteen or so and gorgeous, glaze of oil on the forehead, came over and said they'd burnt my bun. My bun was stuck and it was the last bun. Was that OK?

'Oh,' I said. 'Oh, mate. Happens to us all. Don't worry.'

'Dan said to say would you like a scone?'

'Yes, yes please,' I said and a few minutes later here were the scones. Two of them. Two once-upright, once-uptight things that'd exploded in the oven. *Flour, butter, sugar, currants. Flour, butter, sugar, currants.* Now it was me freaking out. *He bought us two scones and that's because he thinks we're together. He thinks we're together. Grace!* The stencilled cocoa on Ginger's cappuccino stayed put through all this. She'd paused to admire her scone.

'I want this scone.'

'Eat it.'

'When you get to my age. . .'

'Don't be silly. You're—'

She reached her index finger out towards my mouth. 'Ah ah ah!'

'What!'

'Don't say it.'

'You don't know what I was going to say.'

'What were you going to say?'

I did a lasso action with my hands, jutted my chin forward.

242

'Ah! Tease. Go on! What were you going to say?'

I shook my head.

'Tell me later.'

I nodded. 'Here.' I handed her the pickle tray, a pickle tray except with different kinds of jam. She was raspberry. I was blackcurrant.

'Grace, do you want me to ask for some cream?'

I shook my head.

'Correct.'

We lathered our scones and I told her about Mum, a précis.

'So yeah, she's gorgeous. I love her to bits. But, well—. She's, well, she's my mum you know and well, I guess, that's—. It's always going to be complicated.'

Ginger was nodding. Her nod was such a knowing nod, so absorbing, so willing and embracing and involved that I left that complicated without its d, though I couldn't really say it was me doing the leaving. Co-credits. We had a pause. Two, three seconds. Then I told her about Ingrid, Ingrid at the Otley Courthouse.

'Oh! I love stuff like that.'

'Cute right? It's a lot.'

'She sounds like a peach.'

'Yeah.' Pause. 'Yeah. She is.'

'Easily bruised but very sweet.'

'Ha. That's nice. I like that.'

'Fun, right? I play it with the new starters.'

'I can see that.'

'Ha. Say more.'

'Like, you mean at work, right? I can imagine you're an absolute babe with new starters.' Wait. Oh. Yes. Blush.

'Oh stop.' Faux eyelash flutter, fingers through her hair.

'I mean it.'

'Ha.' Sip of coffee.

'What am I?'

'Hmm?'

'What fruit am I?'

'Hmm. I'm deciding.' Deadpan face. Looked over at the door. Looked back at me. Little smile.

'Decided?'

'Give me a sec!' She poked her head as if to say *rusty cogs, I am old.*

I put my *shh* fingers out to her now. 'Got yours!'

'Ah! Tell me.'

'Lemon,' I said. 'You're a lemon.'

'Oh dear.'

'No! No, Ginger. It's good.'

'Good?'

'Mmhmm. Lemons are good. Refreshing, versatile if you have some imagination. And—.'

'And?'

'Violently inappropriate when misused.'

'Yes.' She leant back on her chair legs. 'Love it.' Toppled back forward. 'I'm a lemon.'

'What am I?'

'Hmm.'

'*Ginger!* Please!'

'You're a tough one.'

'Can I be a grape?'

'Well generally you can't self-designate them's the rules but, go on.'

'Prefers to move in a pack of like-minded others.'

'Right.'

'Small and kind of pointless when alone.'

'Grace!'

'Monotonous, tiring.'

'I've only known you five seconds,' she said, smiling broad, palm flat on the table, 'but you're wrong.'

We stayed for an hour or so and then we stayed a bit longer, ordered some recuperative post-sugar teas. It was dingy out and chilly now, the Blue Moon being cavernous and therefore beautiful and therefore cold and also eco-friendly/vegan and therefore even colder, and then when the tea arrived it was lukewarm and they'd served it in glasses. I wrapped my fingers round mine and Ginger took her lighter out and lit the tea light on the next table, brought it over, cradled it.

All this weather made me worry about the weather, and despite our teas and Ginger's tea-lit calm I was edgy. I'd started blabbering. I was talking about Patrick and as I talked him out to Ginger I found he wasn't a stranger or an emblem or a myth or the gremlin under the bed but just real and passed and gone, and as I talked I realised I wasn't blabbering and blabbering didn't really belong here in this tea-lit corner of the Blue Moon café with this person who chose apricot jam. I had something to say and it was simple and truthful and real.

While I spoke she made a little circle of currants on her plate, a circle and then an s and then a square.

'Sorry,' I said. 'I'm kind of intense in the morning.'

'Don't be silly.' She leant both elbows on the table and loop-the-looped with her spoon and the eye contact was sustained, an expanse, and she smiled. It was chucking it down now, the patter echoing.

'Oh,' I said, breaking her gaze, checking my phone. 'I wonder if it'll set in—.'

'Grace.'

245

'Hmm?' Semi-whisper.

She took my hand. 'There's nowhere else you need to be.'

We let the rain clear up a bit then we left, wandering over towards the Peace Gardens to watch the jets. There was a toddler in Thomas the Tank yellow wellies so we watched her, too, and then we pulled our raincoats further down our bums and perched on the side, letting the dampness in the stone do its worst. She showed me Jay. Jay was her brother and he lived in Tooting and had long straight dark hair just like hers with flecks of early white in it and a magenta-coloured ribbon at the base of his neck and silver polish on his nails and a dreamy silk hibiscus at his ear. Jay and Chris had just broken up. How long, I asked, six years, she said, but he was going to be OK.

'Look at his hands. They're perfect.'

'Yes,' she said, a pause. 'He's going to be OK.'

I looked at hers.

She spread her fingers out.

I took her left thumb between my thumb and forefinger. 'He'll be OK.'

A pause. *Hold it. Hold it. Stay here, Grace.* Wah! Too much. Release. Now I was looking at my hands, my nails, saying mine were crappy, all this playing kitchens, I said, lots of washing up you know and my Marigolds split and the Fairy does me in and the weather, got this blow heater off Argos cos my sister's place is freezing and it sucks all the moisture, it's a devil, and she smiled slowly and smiled again and suggested I buy some Body Shop hemp and if I liked playing kitchens and I liked recuperative teas, to which I nodded vigorously, she said try boiling cardamom and orange rind. Try using fennel seeds.

'Oh! Hold up. We've got a load in at work,' she said, 'I'll give you some next time I see you.'

'Oh! Perfect.'

She looked at the clock up on the town hall. 'I have to go,' she said. 'Come to Marks?' she said. 'Tomorrow? Come see me.'

'I will.'

She pecked me on the cheek. She ran.

I watched her disappear. Then I went into Browns for my wee, loitering at first like I was meeting someone so they wouldn't tell me off, plaiting my legs and sending blessings for the pelvic floor workout. It was an extraordinary wee. Up there with my finest. Top five. The weight in my shoulders and arms moved down towards my fingers and when I wiped I was soft and warm and delighted.

Ask for Angela said the toilet door.

'We're good,' I whispered. 'We're good.'

*

The scone plus the coffee plus the tea plus the wee plus a hike up the hill to see Gary turned out a bit much in the end. To start with I was walking on air, though round about the Arts Tower – when you come round the corner and the full force of all of Sheffield's wind gets in your face – I started feeling like the wind was some godly wind and this was the part in the silent film where her eyes go wide and it's REVELATION. *She'll move through you like this wind. Soon enough she'll see so much of you you'll disappear. You'll dissolve. There's nothing of you. There's nothing to keep you in place. Retract, Grace, leave it, take yourself off to the rubble out the back of Rebecca's and stage a little ritual fire. Burn it off.* But when I got to Gary he hugged me hard, a hug that said let me play Rachel. Trust me. And

I nodded because I knew now that Rachel was in everyone. 'The only thing needs burning is these pigs in power, babe,' he said, to which I said huh and he said shh with his finger then he bore his bicep. 'Never surrender.'

So I didn't surrender. I had a think-in. I imagined us up, transformed us into art. Art to move me out of my own way. Art for the sake of life. I thought about Marina and Ulay. I thought about FKA twigs and her ropes. I thought about the blue Matisse dancers with the hands that weren't quite touching. I thought about Mike Leigh. And then I called Michelle.

'EYYY!!!! GRACE!!!!'

'Been a while.'

'Tsss. Been a *minute*. Where were you?!'

'Well . . .'

We had one of those ecstatic WhatsApp chats, tipsy without wine, real-time. I told her about Ginger. I told her everything. She was in Lagos at Abi's aunt's place and *EYY, come see!* She gave me a virtual tour and there was Abi's aunt who wore string vests and flip-flops and a Rolex as a matter of faith and principle said Michelle and we all danced and then Abi's aunt went off and Michelle firmly, firmly vowed to be the same contradiction and glam in this world if not IRL then in spirit. Then the connection went so we reverted to text.

GET ITTTT she said. [*End-spectrum Black flamencos x3*]

[*Pastiest yogi, woman form*]

[*Fortune cookie*]

Ha.

*

Dreams: Grace and Ginger.

Performance one. Ginger is the doula and I'm giving birth. We make it so my waters break in Debenhams. She paints a glossy jelly on the fronts of my thighs, wallpaper paste, and then I drink a pint of out-of-date milk and wait for the bloat while we make our way to the store. She says to ham it up with big sounds and arm movements. I know I can do that: am-dram human pain. Ginger is a kind of Alison Steadman, kind of annoying and into bunting and royal weddings and lovely and very brilliant. We're asked to leave.

Performance two. We buy this slice of muslin, six by four, and draw an oversized woman on it in black marker pen, a woman in a wedding dress. We use the bulk of the ink at the bottom of the dress, weighing her down. Further up the lines get vague, undetermined, and then the tip turns dry. We wrap me in the muslin and sit me in the church. Ginger is the priest and has this glass in her hand that we've painted red and there's food-coloured water sloshing over the sides, vermilion. We're asked to leave.

Performance three. I'm living in a van in the Homebase car park. Ginger is the store manager. She opens up and lets me in and I'm free to heat up and mingle and rest. There are all these big tall DIY wardrobes all mocked up and bathroom suites and fields of lights, lights hanging in the middle of the air, and I'm walking round and round in circuits. Then Ginger runs after me and grabs me and tells me she's found a rat. She shows me it, slap in the middle of the bed I've just been resting on. I clear my throat and scream, and then I scream again to try and do it better. I look closer. Wait (wink at Ginger), this isn't a rat. This is not a rat! This is a plastic rat, a fat dead slapstick plastic rat in the middle of the bed.

We laugh and laugh and then I wake up and I cry a bit and then I laugh some more.

*

I ate my morning porridge with the window open. There was a Geordie woman out on the rubble waiting for her Scottie to take a shit, her toddler on the turn. *Mummy's even bought you some mac and cheese. Are you going to have that for your tea? And maybe even a* Rolo *yoghurt! What do you think?*

*

I started paying daily lunchtime trips to M&S. Whether or not she was on shift I went in. I liked browsing round Nana's special tins of jellied chicken, tongue, the cans of mince Mum used for Delia cheats cottage pie. I liked the M&S Food Hall smell and the way it moved out of the Food Hall and into the jeans and trousers and gym wear and beyond, to the front of the shop, where they'd soon put swimwear and linen shirts for twenty-nine pounds fifty. It was an ecosystem. A warm bath.

On Ginger's days off she left me little clues and Easter eggs to find her with, messaging when a new line she thought I'd like was added to the sale rail. That was often. The customers at her store, the Fargate one, they were older and few and they'd been few for years because of Meadowhall (the tram out there making it so simple) and getting fewer and fewer as Fargate collapsed in on itself. It was heaving when the funfair came up but then people were buying German beer and bellyache. In any case the stuff that ended up on sale was always arty and cool.

Our finest work was an XXL gold puffa jacket, twenty-five pounds. I ran to the store in my Bet Lynch coat and flung it on the adjacent rail and she held that coat of many colours – it was the world, the colour of everything – she held it by the shoulders behind me with her head bowed ceremonial and I bowed my head correspondingly ceremonial and we dressed me in the gold puffa jacket and I paced out an offstage pace, checking my mic and Ginger had to hold the rail to calm down. It was a warm bath and an orgasm and Ginger was watching and I never wanted to take it off.

This is a colleague announcement . . .

'Whoops, that's me,' she said, 'team meeting.'

'See you tomorrow?' I put the hood up.

She brought the hood back down with both hands. 'Tomorrow.'

I took it off. I walked it to the till.

'Sure about this, lov?' (Wakey accent.)

'Yeah.'

'Hmm,' she said. 'Put it on fer me.'

I put it on.

'Oh, no. No, I can see it now. Yes, lov, I can see it. Nice pair o' black skinny jeans and a black roll-neck and boots. Ooh yes. OK. OK, lov.'

'Sometimes you've just got to go for it!'

'Well—. No. No, I won't say it.'

'No,' I said. 'Go on.'

'Well I did see you come in here, yeah, and I thought you looked a bit, you know . . .'

'Go on.'

'Quirky. Quirky, lov. I see you with our Ginger. Quirky!' Wink. 'And I think you should keep that. Don't listen to people, lov.'

'I agree.'

'Don't you listen to 'em.'

'I'm getting long in the tooth now. Don't you worry.'

251

'Just enter your PIN for me, lov.'

'Oh, thanks.'

'How old are you then?'

'Guess.'

'Ooh.'

'Go on.'

'Sixteen? Seventeen?'

'I'm twenty-three.'

'Well I never. BRIAN! Brian, come here, look at this.'

'Oh yes. Looks great, love. Go for it. I had my doubts, but . . .'

'She can handle it Brian, go on.'

'I saw you come in and I thought: aye, here's a one.'

'Guess how old she is, Brian?'

'How old are you love?'

'Twenty-three.'

'Bloody hell, you kept that quiet.'

'What's your name?' I asked, smiling.

'Me? I'm Sheila.'

*

My last week at the library came round. I'd learnt some things about work. I'd learnt you should fuck up from time to time, for the camaraderie. You had to do it with feeling and moderation. If you send a medium parcel out for fifteen pounds with public money instead of repackaging it into two small parcels then you should buy a multipack of Bourbon biscuits to atone. And anything goes when it comes to the kitchen island. Anything, except panettone from the previous year. *That's just offensive, Geoff* (Pam). *Wouldn't use that fer an ashtray, Geoff* (Carole).

It was a matter of balance, choreography, there would always be more than one person in the room, all things had a price, and no, you didn't have to be in it, not in it-in it, but you were always in it. I finished off my spreadsheets; *no such thing, they never end* said Big Anne's mum, *no such thing,* shaking her head. *Diane's handover notes? Ah, OK.* I finished Diane's handover notes. *Honestly, I really have run out now. Do you want another brew?* 'PAM! *Pam, Carole,* get in here. Give her something to do. If she feeds me another Earl Grey I'm gonna burst.' Pam and Carole let me type up and laminate the new signs. First I did them in Garamond, then Georgia, then Baskerville, then Garamond again, and finally Gill Sans. Gill Sans!

DO NOT POUR YOUR COFFEE GROUNDS DOWN THE SINK

PLEASE TURN OFF THE LIGHTS

ARE THE LIGHTS OFF?

ARE THE LIGHTS OFF?

ARE THE LIGHTS OFF?

ARE THE LIGHTS OFF?

*

We had my leaving drinks at the social club down Ponds Forge. There were lots of plush red velvet chairs and posters on the walls, Bradley Hand, these ones, and permanent green foil decorations hanging from the ceiling. I liked it here. I liked

253

the way they dimmed the lights after ten, and the pale weary face of the Liverpudlian bartender with the soft fine hair and the soft fine accent, and the subsidy gin. Pam held her elbow static on the table for much of it, pinning it down with her opposite hand and circulating her wrist. 'Fucking RSI.'

GOOD LUCK, they said in the card, nearly A4 it was, a nice big colourful card with an A4 paper insert too so everyone could sign, all smudged up with multicoloured biro. Pam drew a star. They gave me some chrysanthemums and when I got home I cried.

*

I started packing the next day and it got to midday and then Ginger came back. *Come see me*, she said. *Sorry for quiet, will explain.*

I got the tram to town in my gold jacket. I walked down West Street. I saw Rebecca out by Revs, having her break-time fag. Well, Rebecca saw me.

'WHO THE FUCK'S THIS, THE URBAN SPACEMAN?' she hollered.

'FUCK OFF.'

Funky dance (me).

Funky dance (Rebecca).

It was freezing at M&S. There was a glitch with the fridges so they'd put the air con on max. It got up in my nose and I was blowing and sneezing all over the shop.

I found Ginger. She was restocking the ales. This was the best aisle for skiving, tucked away and out of the remit of the CCTV, though really Ginger had worked here for ten years and nobody gave a shit, not about her, not anymore because she was a world-class manager, always won the star jar. We hadn't discussed that yet but we would and it was clear. She was Ginger.

I fingered a 9 Hop Kent Pale Ale.

'Oh yeah. Those are excellent.'

'I'll buy us some,' I said and she smiled and held me out a four pack. I took it from her and then I felt another sneeze coming on. A double. A treble. 'I'm sorry.' *SNOOOOOOK.* 'Shit. Sorry. I'm disgusting—.'

'No.'

I pointed at my dirty tissue. *Surely?*

'*No.*' She shook her head and smiled. 'Never.'

'OK. You're wrong but I believe you.'

She walked us round the corner to the bakery. I followed.

'Look at this new range of hot cross buns!' She swept her hand across the new range of hot cross buns. Apple and cinnamon. Mini hot cross buns. Chocolate. She picked a packet up and traced the white stripe of the cross with her finger with the care of a connoisseur.

'*ACHEW*!' Blow. 'Jesus. I don't know what's wrong with me. I'm all—. Clammy and weird.'

'You've got a cold.' Pause. 'Hmm. OK. Let's try . . .' I followed her down tea and coffee, oil and vinegar. 'Look at this imported pottery bottle of Spanish olive oil! Look at this bad boy. We're in Spain! Mmm.'

I did a mock bottom lip.

She mocked my mock bottom lip.

'I've only got ten minutes left. Go buy these and wait out front?'

I nodded.

'Wait!'

I turned.

255

She put her finger in the air and disappeared back to the booze aisle, returned with a bottle of whisky, took the ale off me. 'Medicinal.'

'I don't like—'

'You will. Trust me.'

I turned back.

She joined me a few minutes later with her burnt orange Eastpak.

'Give me—.' She put her arm out for the whisky and the little bag of veggie Percys I'd snuck in there, Percy Pig and Friends because, well, broad church. I handed her it and she put it on her back.

'Are you sure?'

She nodded. 'I like the weight.'

'Where are we going?'

'We're going to ours. If you want—?'

'Yes. Yes.'

*

She walked us up to Sharrow. Nether Edge. We walked past Gary and Gary's mates Tom and Ali down Dempseys – *hi babe!* – and under the underpass and up the hill that lines the cemetery and then she turned us left and took my hand. We were on this intense wide avenue lined with limes, enormous lime trees on steroids and great big villas with steep Tim Burton gables, steep and severe but magical.

Ginger looked at me.

My face said *look at these bay windows and—. The canopies—. And—. And—. And the trees are so tall, how did you make the trees so tall! And the rhythm of the houses and trees! What the fuck—? How the fuck—?*

256

She squeezed my hand, pointed at theirs.

'What the fuck! You *live* here?'

'Sorry.' She smiled. 'I couldn't help it.'

'I can't believe you live—.'

'Complicated and not? Remember. I thought I'd save the surprise.'

'Explain!'

'Come inside?'

I followed her to the gate.

'Ginger.' I was knotting up.

She turned.

'Can you—? Is Vicky—?'

'She's not in.' She paused. She looked down. She bit her lip. 'Bloody *hell. Ginger, get a fucking grip.* Sorry Grace.' Pause. 'I'm really fucking this up. Fucking hell. I'm nervous!'

'Don't be nervous.'

'Wait.' A pause. 'Vicky and me are—. Right. We're together. We live together. We share our lives. But—.' She took my hand. 'You look worried.'

'I'm not—.'

'I promise I'll—.'

'I'm—. It's none of my business—.'

She held the ends of my fingers. 'I want it to be.' Whatever it was in the ends of those fingers was down in the pit of me now, soft and warm where it mattered. 'I was going to tell you before, Grace. I just—. I wanted to show you in person so you wouldn't have to imagine it. Sometimes I think that can be harder. That can be cruel I think. I might have—.'

'It's—.'

'I did the wrong thing. I'm sorry.'

'No. No. No, you didn't.'

'It's OK. It's OK. I'm sorry. I've fucked it up. I'll get an Uber back for you if you're not ready.'

'No. I think I—. I think I get what you're saying.'

She looked at me.

'Actually can you explain? Can you—?'

'*Ginger.* Jesus lord. Throw the woman a bone. Sorry, Grace.'

I was smiling now. I held on to the gate, fingered the latch.

'We're platonic. We love each other, but—. It's not like that. We have partners.'

'I understand. I think.'

'I—. It's—.'

'I want to.'

'I want you to.' She made a gesture with her head, towards the door. *Shall we?*

I nodded. A pause. 'Wait.'

She turned around.

I pointed at the house. 'What the fuck?'

Her dimples popped. Open smile. Broad. Little glide with the toes. 'Follow me.'

*

She put the key in the lock. *Ready?*

Nod. Nod.

We went inside.

First there was the hall and the size of it, its size and its parquet floor and its panels. 'Oak,' said Ginger, slicking back her hair like a prospector. There was a telephone table with those two famous pictures of Barbara Hepworth, black-and-white postcards. In one of them she was peering into a hole. In the other she was stood at a lathe making dust.

I walked in slow motion to the bottom of the stairs.

I took the end of the banister and looked up the stairs.

'I know,' she said. '*Monarch of the Glen.*'

'I'm feeling Kirsten Dunst in *Melancholia.* I'm feeling very Kirsten.'

'Huh?'

'Like at the beginning, the wedding.'

'Haven't seen that one.'

'Well. God. I can't believe you *live* here.'

'Well. This is it.'

I went to put my jacket on the rack, the gold of my big gold jacket just beginning to nestle this lovely bright blue Scandi mac and then she stopped me.

'Don't get giddy,' she said. 'Communal hallway. We're just the bottom floor.'

'I knew that.'

'Poo. You didn't! You didn't, did you? Aww. I thought I'd fooled—'

'OK I didn't. But I still win. You had an advantage. I didn't have my—.' I took my glasses out my inside pocket, popped them on. Now I could see there was parquet, yes, but the parquet was ropey, quarterly clean at best.

As she faffed with the door, triple lock, she explained Vicky's family were—. She turned around and rubbed her thumb against her four fingers.

'Ahh.'

'Her mum passed last year. Only child.'

I nodded. 'So you own this—?'

'Mortgage, but—'

'Impossible.'

'Possible. Keep dreaming.'

'Wild.'

'Come play.'

We went in. Shoes off I felt and I took mine off and she ducked to get hers. She'd double-tied the laces for work so she had to crouch right down and her knees clicked.

'Dicky knees!'

'I'm an old bat.'

'No no I've got those too. Listen.' I went down and up again a couple of times.

'Aaaand squat.'

'One, two, three and squat!'

'One, two, three and squat!'

Here we were squatting then a cat came in.

'This is Biscuit,' said Ginger.

I put my knuckle out for Biscuit to rest Biscuit's chin if they so chose and they chose, did that little circular action against the bottom of the jaw.

'Ahh,' said Ginger. 'You have a cat.'

'Yes. Mum does.'

Biscuit moved on from me and was walking round Ginger now, coating her, and the M&S nylon was perfection for that. Biscuit was moulting. That meant there'd be a spring.

She handed me a spare pair of slippers and went to get changed. 'Feel free to snoop,' she called back after her and I said yeah? and she said go mad.

I went into the lounge. Eight-foot chiffon curtains pooling slightly on the floor. High white walls. Yellow Anglepoise next to the TV. Succulents on the mantelpiece and Morris-y tiles and a pair of Moreschi slippers, Italian leather slippers, just slightly pigeon-toed there by the hearth and then up on the

260

roof, up on the ceiling these white glass light shades the shape of ostrich eggs and, and on the walls antique circus posters – a rhino in a blue jerkin, a gentleman wolf with sweet red lips – and taupe linen blinds behind the chiffon and dark slate sofas and pine floors and pine stairs and pine windows. It smelt of Pears soap. *What the fuck! What the fuck!*

She called me through to the kitchen. A dresser. A clothes rack suspended from the ceiling with a rope. A great long table recycled from a church with recycled backless church pews either side. And devil's ivy. Draped all over. Hanging from the ceiling. Everywhere. Chains of hearts hanging from the sides of the window and devil's ivy 'Ginger,' I whispered. 'This is everything.' I didn't know plants but this was everything.

On the table there was a little wooden pipe and an old silver pillbox for her green and a hunk of peeled ginger the size and shape of a thumb, half a crumpet and a dilapidated Council Tax bill.

'Sorry,' she said. 'Rush this morning.' She picked up the ginger, tossed it high into the air and caught it. 'But this we can salvage.' She nipped back through to get the whisky out the rucksack. 'HOT TODDY?' she called back.

'YES!'

Ginger at home. Ginger at home was Birkenstocks for slippers; mahogany ones with fluoro green socks poking out the ends, Nike joggers. Ginger at home was hot toddies then beans with ginger and garlic and chilli and ground-up coriander seeds and fenugreek and fennel. She had a little pan for toasting spices and my instrument, she called it, a huge big stone pestle and mortar. I was in charge of the grinding.

'This smells of god. This is god and she's a woman.'

261

She came over and sniffed with her zester, brandishing it like a wand. She was on the butternut and lime zest crumb. Wedges. 'Mmm,' she said and she hovered, her breath at the nape of my neck, her finger in the small of my back. *Fuck.*

She pulled away. 'Leffe?'

'Fuck yes,' I said and I noticed she'd suspended a head of washed lettuce upside down in the sink. I couldn't take my eyes off that lettuce trunk. Handsome, somehow. Proud.

We went through to the lounge for a Leffe while the butternut oozed out its sugar. Ginger flopped, put her feet out on the L of the sofa and held on to a pillow, a Habitat one with little kissing zebras. Mine had elephants with little red birds perching on their bottoms. Someone buzzed the communal door in search of her lost cat Pippa. Ginger went out into the hall and I heard her pick Biscuit up from behind her, give the woman a compensatory cuddle.

We ate, we ate, we ate, *we ate.* Then she rolled us a spliff and I watched her make a batch of impromptu brigadeiro, spatula-ing it into a second-hand jar of sterilised Golden Shred, wiping the rubber hard across the rim, licking. We ate it with a teaspoon, sharing, then we took the green through to the lounge and she played us some ditties with her guitar and I sat without my body, sat over by the radiator then moved onto my back, my feet in the grooves, moving the soles from time to time when they started to burn. She took a long time with her sentences now, let the stuff of them trickle out into the space, and that space was insulated.

She lay down next to me. She was looking at me.

'Know who you remind me of . . .?'

'Who?'

'Adèle.'

'What, like Adèle from *Blue is the Warmest*—?'

'Mmhmm.' She took my earlobe. 'The bit with Adèle eating that meat thing in the square with that boy,' she whispered.

'Mmhmm.'

'The bit with Adèle with the spaghetti, that bit at the start.'

'Mmhmm.' *That click and splutter, the pouchy cheeks, those thighs.*

'Those thighs,' she traced her finger.

'Pippa!' The woman from before called into the dusk, pulsing rhythmic plastic fork against plastic bowl. 'Pippa!'

*

'Let's go through?'

'Yes.'

There was a Poäng chair in the corner.

'A Poäng!' I said under my breath.

'Po-eng not po-ang,' she whispered, drawing a line down between my shoulder blades. I rolled my shoulders down and forward.

'Oh. Oh no,' I said, my voice trembling, 'I've been saying it wrong all this time.'

'How were you to know?' she whispered in my ear.

I hung my head. I whispered now. 'Yeah. Not sorry.'

She moved away and sat on the bed, put her hand next to her. We sat under a blanket the same colour as her fleece, also fleece. Maybe it was more stewed plum. I felt she was accident-prone and I was an accident, or something adjacent to that. And she was adjacent. Or I was. She put her hand under the fleece, her fingers under my elastic.

*

263

5 a.m.

'What can I do for you?'

I pulled the duvet up and over my head, breathed quickly into the imprint of my face. I was cold the way I do cold, a cold I understood, now, cold with that loss of heat peculiar to a person dancing with her shame, or simply felled by it, who needs some time to stand back up but someone's there and watching.

Ginger came under, took my thigh in her hands and started rubbing, first one and then the other, put her hand back where I missed it.

'What can I do for you?' A whisper now.

'Parent me.'

She shook her head. She moved down.

*

8 a.m.

Ginger woke up first. She kissed me on the forehead then went through to the kitchen. I heard her open the mini freezer compartment in the top of the fridge then nudge the door back into place, lift it slightly to get it flush without breaking the door itself. Some of the plastic was missing she'd said last night.

She walked back in to the bedroom with a jug of Ribena and ice.

'Jesus.' I put my beak in the air like a bird.

'Ribena. Ice.'

'Thank you.'

'Aaaand. Bananaaaaaas,' she said, doing a hands up from her dressing-gown pocket.

'I can't handle them smushy, Ginger. You have them.'

'No, smushy's best for a hang. You need the sugar.'

'OK.'

Then the smell of burning.

'SHIT!'

She'd fucked the crumpets and they'd run out of bread so could we have Warburton's from the freezer, she said, thick so the bread stays melty and raw in the middle, the orange stuff? Yes, yes, we fucking could.

She brought out a dinner plate with the toast in a rack and in quarters, said she couldn't handle when you get the condensation on the bottom of the toast, liked it dry as dry and halfway cold before you buttered.

'Fucking weirdo.'

'Shush,' she said, scraping a bit of unmelted butter with her finger and hovering it out in front of my mouth. I stuck my tongue out rapid and put it back. 'Tease.' Smile in the corner of her mouth. Dimples. 'Not eating?'

'Bit vommy. Maybe a quarter,' I said, taking one dry and nibbling. 'Ugh. I feel like shit. I'm a shell.'

'You're hanging.'

'I'm a shell.'

'You are now.' She kissed me on the nose.

'Ha.'

'This needs honey,' she said, going back through and returning with the bottle, a squeezy one, drawing out a shy smiley face onto her slice.

'That me?'

'Yes.'

'Can I have some?'

'Yes. Here.'

I took the honey, poured a drop onto my index finger and licked it off. *Mmm.*

265

She took the bottle and poured me another drop. Another. Another. I felt I'd spent my life trying to ward off this moment, the moment I couldn't stop pouring sugar on myself, and now it was here and I wasn't even doing the pouring. I was done. I was away.

'Tea?'
'Yes please.'
Ginger stood up to make us tea, shivering a little as the heating clicked off. She put a fleecy jumper on, one arm first and the head, contemplated her other sleeve for a moment before seeming to decide she liked the wad of fabric right where it was, cushioning her underarm. I branched my fingers out in the air. We waited in silence for a moment then she held the back of the Poäng, her knuckles white, and when she let go it wobbled then it quickened.

She came to my side of the bed. I was sat up. She put her palm between my shoulder blades, pressed a little, let go.
'What you doing?'
'Just checking.'
'Hmm?'
'Just checking you're real.'

We had turmeric tea. Then she sat at an angle looking at me, knees up, elbow resting on one knee, her face in the heel of her hand, the cushion of flesh at the base of her thumb holding up cheek and head. Slowly, surely, the string on her turmeric teabag turned yellow.

I stayed very still for a moment, pulling the duvet up over my head and breathing into it so the heat would percolate a bit.

I came back up.

She put her mug on the side.

We went back down.

*

I had three days left. Rebecca and Tash came over for a leaving lunch.

Tash was wearing a navy playsuit and a long grey Zara cardigan.

'I like your playsuit Tash.'

'Show her the back Tash,' said Rebecca.

Tash lifted her Zara cardigan and showed us the hole for her lumbar spine.

'Ooh. That's different. Lumbar cleavage,' I said.

'Tenner, ASOS,' said Tash.

I made sweet potato fritters, lemony leeks with feta and dill and green beans in a caper vinaigrette.

'Here, look at this B. It's Nigel Slater,' said Tash.

'Just a light midweek supper,' I said, stroking my Nigel beard.

'Alright, Nigel!' said Rebecca.

'It's syn-free this if you leave the cheese,' I said to them both. They'd joined Pam and Carole's group now.

'Thanks Grace,' said Tash.

'How's it going?' I asked.

'We've lost ten pounds,' said Tash.

'Amazing!'

'I was cynical, wasn't I Tash,' said Rebecca, 'but I wouldn't miss it now.'

'Wouldn't miss it,' said Tash.

'Wouldn't miss it,' said Rebecca.

'Tell her about last week B.'

'Last week? Oh yeah. This woman couldn't bring herself to eat her pack-up come lunchtime—'

'She goes yeah, just can't do it, it always goes so soggy and warm, and then this other woman pipes up and she goes oh my god I have the solution for you love, you get yourself down Asda love and you can get these plastic blue things what you put in the freezer, so what you do is you put them in the freezer, and this other woman butts in and she goes, they do them at Aldi! She's losing her shit. They do them at Aldi! They do them at Aldi!'

'Wouldn't miss it.'

I went to get some berries out the fridge.

'We'll miss you,' said Rebecca.

I turned around.

She nodded. Tash held her hand.

*

I had two days left. Ginger rang and said she'd help me move back down, fancied the trip, would go hang out with Jay in Tooting for a bit, too, and I could stay, I could stay at Jay's if need be. I asked after Vicky. Vicky was off to Aldeburgh for a Wi-Fi-less deadline push. Great I said, perfect, though I still needed to do a proper clean of this place, make it nice for Rebecca.

'Can I help?'

'Really?'

'I'll bring the rest of the whisky.'

'*Yes.*'

I begged some shouty industrial kit off Ian and Mick – *BANG, VANISH, POWER, OUSSSST* – then went across to Castlegate

B&Ms for some floral tabards and rubber. Medium pink for me; small and yellow for Ginger. Then Ginger came round in some old pyjamas with her bicarb and a toothbrush. And her portable speaker. And the whisky.

We did a proper clean and as the whisky went down we got a bit carried away and it became a deep clean and deeper still; we took the place back way beyond my time in it, back to its inception and when I say deep I mean deep. I told her about Michael. I told her about Rachel. I told her what I knew. It was hard to hear all these I-statements clattering about but I have to admit that I made them. And when I say clattering I mean yes they were clattering but then Ginger was there and the whisky. They fell like feathers.

*

She stayed that night and in the morning, early it was, before the shops opened, six, she said she had a surprise and she went through to the fridge and she'd bought us M&S packed lunches for the train: little plastic boxes of peanuts and roast cauli and red onion and sweet red pepper and giant couscous and kale and roasted garlic slipped out of its skin and tahini dressing and fresh lemon zest. Fruit salad with apple and kiwi and orange and lime. Chocolate mousse. And the forgotten packet of Percy Pig and Friends.

We showered in turn then I put on a pair of chandelier earrings and Rebecca's old pair of white Reeboks and a big Fred Perry polo and some glitter bomb socks. We got the train.

*

Rebecca WhatsApped somewhere north of Grantham with a Humans of New York photo, a pensioner in a floppy hat with heart-shaped sunglasses and a long silk dress, carnation pink, and yellow ribbed socks and big black shoes, men's brogues. *You*, she wrote. I sent back a range of watery emojis. The crab, the lobster, the fish. Michelle sent a little cascade of voice notes, winkle picker clicks, new job she had, new job as a product MANAGER not just content but product, product, so there she was in her winkle pickers taking Curtain Road by storm, bus suspension at the edges of her diction. *Ducksoup*, she said. *Eight*.

Ginger didn't come to Ducksoup. Jay had had a bit of a crisis with Chris and I said *you go. Honestly, go.* She kissed me and I walked down Shaftesbury Ave to Ducksoup. Charlie, Matthew, Adam, Jessica, eventually, eventually, majestically, Michelle. We talked about work, love, not working, the cis-able-hetero-patri-archy, the crude appropriation of intersectional discourse, the structure of work itself and how it all got up in the psyche and what was going on with neoliberalism and the shifting sands of global corporate power and care, yes, care, what about the way care work was undervalued and 'intellectual labour' and 'emotional labour' had got kind of weirdly baggy and dodgy as concepts and FUCKING AUSTERITY. We talked about white debt. We talked about Palestine. We talked about olive oil versus rapeseed. We talked about oxygen in every which way. Everyone was thinking and sharing their thoughts. We knew as little as we did and fuck it, fuck it, we were fucking geniuses too, geniuses, geniuses, fuck it, fuck it, and then *BUBBLES* I said and we had bubbles and cheese and black pepper cinnamon biscuits and cured meat and more cheese and more bubbles and we sang and got lairy. I drank a carafe.

'SPEECH!' said Michelle, tinkling her glass.

'Thank you,' I said, standing up. I took a sip of wine. 'As a young woman I wasn't thinking. I wasn't thi—. Very well, very well. I was—. I was alone. I was so—. I was so alone.'

'May I?' said Michelle.

'Michelle, no! I'm—. I'm still a young woman. I—. I think we all just need to be eccentric. Be eccentric! Expand. Duplicate. And then—. And then—. And then—.'

'And then—.'

'Michelle! Wait. No. No. Yes. No. OK. I'm done.'

I got an Uber to Tooting.

*

Ginger held my head over the bowl. I had another shower.

'Did I call you from the car?'

'Yes.'

'Did I make a tit of myself?'

'No.'

'Don't lie.'

'No.'

'Did I do a burlesque Leeds accent?'

'Yes.'

'Fucksake.'

'It's OK.'

'Is it?'

'Yes. Don't worry.'

'I'm worried.'

'Don't worry.'

*

We had coffee then Ginger went out for eggs and bread and Jay and I hung out. We talked. He washed up his last night's

272

dinner, *you don't have to do this, no, let me, let me help*, then he rolled us a joint and I ate some of the melon from the fridge and I put us on more coffee, waited plunged poured. His oat milk coagulated but we stirred it again and continued. He told me about Chris. I'm really depressed, he told me. I put my palm on his lovely outie navel. He put his palm over mine.

*

We watched Larry David for a bit then Ginger and me went for a trip. We took the Northern line for a million years, up to Belsize where I showed her the godforsaken deli where I'd first landed in this trash heap, *ha*, she said, *you love it* and I did and I very much absolutely did and I didn't, and on we went to the Freud Museum. I wanted her to meet Rachel.

'This is—' she said in the room with the chair. We stood in silence for a moment, looking at his chair, looking at the back of it, looking at all that shit on the desk.

'Horrific?'

She looked at me.

'I know,' I said. 'But the heart wants what it wants.'

She smiled. Her dimples.

We sat outside for a while instead, nursing a couple of semi-instant self-serve coffees on the green plastic chairs in the garden.

'I don't want to be down here.'

'Shh,' she said. 'There's time.' Then she handed me a head-phone bud, put the other in her ear and she went *ready*. I nodded. Daniel Bedingfield '02, 'Gotta Get Thru This'. I thought I would die.

I saw a squirrel. Ginger saw a snowdrop. We kissed. It started to rain.

*

We headed to a little French place, Sylvie's, for lunch. There was some Alaskan salmon fillet on the pavement and a chicken carcass left to the rats, already chewed right down.

I pointed. 'I don't want to be here. See.'

'Shh!'

We went in and ordered and Sylvie came out from the back and I kissed her on each cheek and we sat. Sylvie stood leaning on the handle of a long stick I guessed she kept for the hard-to-reach windows. She wrapped both hands around the top and rested the edge of her cheek there.

'I need a new chef,' she said, breathing fast and hard out of her nose, her face locked.

'Have you put an ad out?'

'For a chef? No.' She tapped the floor. 'For someone who knows how to *feed* you have to call down.'

'What do you mean?'

'You have to go outside and find them on the street. But you can't go looking, not too carefully. You have to call and wait.'

'How do you know when you've found one?'

'Oh, you *know*,' she said. 'You know. But it's difficult. First you must learn to be alone.'

Sylvie had a knee-length taupe skirt made of great swathes of fabric and a navy polka dot cardigan done to the top, flat pumps and short russet hair. She was expensive but unglamorous. It would have been graceless to call her Parisian, though she had a face of great concentration and was artfully imprecise.

'Well. You need to get on the street.'

'No. I'm still waiting. RALPH! Ralph!'

Ralph came out with a tray of small plates: houmous; paprika-stained yoghurt; oily little slithers of aubergine; jalapeño croquettes on silky garlic mash; pearl barley; lemony

274

rocket; whipped goat's cheese; liberal wedges of wholemeal sourdough, delightfully underbaked.

Sylvie disappeared.

'Tell me what you're going to do,' said Ginger, handing me the bread.

'What do you mean?'

'What are you going to do? Are you going to take your room back?'

Ralph came and topped up our glasses on the house.

'I don't know.'

We finished our meal and walked back out past the bones on the floor. The light was dimming.

'Gah,' said Ginger, cradling her belly. 'I'm so fucking full.'

'Like you had to activate your airbags and they haven't come back down?'

'Not at all.'

'No?'

'Like I love you and I don't want to leave.'

*

We walked for a bit, went to King's Cross and down for the Piccadilly. Ginger took my arm. There was a red metal casket embedded in the wall with two fasteners and the residue from three or four strips of tape, a few *TESTED FOR ELECTRICAL SAFETY* stickers, and on the front there was a forest-green sign with white letters: *Emergency Gap Jumper*.

I got on the Tube.

MARCH 2016

Hornsey Road. I let myself in. Oliver had moved out now. The British Heart Foundation came to take his stuff away. Two men arrived and put little yellow stickers on his drawers and his desk and his gym equipment and then they took it all off, silently and quickly. I cleaned the mould off the wall, fished out the condoms that had slipped down the side of the bed. Unused, mostly.

Nobody was home, though my stuff was still intact, huddled under the bedroom window, five IKEA bags plus a few big Aldi ones for charity. I walked them up to Crouch End Shelter for the climb then I took a Christmas Grandad cheque to the Post Office. I had a mare with the machine, went to the man at the desk. I recognised him from his little leather bracelet, the khaki heat-tech under his shirt.

'Did the machine not let you fill in the amount yourself?' he asked.

'Maybe. I didn't try. It came up as a quid.'

'I don't blame you.'

'I remember you. You helped me change the address linked to this account.'

'When?'

'God. Maybe two years ago? Do you remember?'

'Yeah.'

'Really?'
'Yeah, yeah I do.'

*

Oliver had gone and Jessica lived here now, and Eli too. Adam had found Eli in GAY, so Adam was, yes! Yes! And Eli moved in and now we were five and often we were seven. Daniel and Coco who were friends with Jessica had moved in upstairs and now their lounge was above my bedroom and Daniel talked loudly and sometimes they fucked but not enough, *not enough, sad face* said Jessica and sometimes he went out and that's when Coco cried and I had to take my framed postcard triptych of fallen women off the wall, make three little taps on the ceiling. *I'm here. It's OK. I'm here.*

Daniel came round a lot. Him and Matthew played squash up in Hornsey then they'd run back and sweat a double squash-sprint sweat on our kitchen stools and drink tins with Daniel's belongings. Sprawled out all around him, they were. Racket, phone, disintegrating packets of Orbit gum. And then Coco would come down and stand with her bum resting on the kitchen counter. *You can sit! It's OK.* She was serene, closely negotiated though with a slight shortage of breath.

Boris was dead. Almost. We kept his corpse for an ashtray. But Matthew and Jessica were very much Matthew and Jessica. In the mornings they'd wake up and shower and breakfast and laugh. On Sunday nights she made trays of roasted vegetables. The courgettes she salted first and they were tremendous. Those were the courgettes for a real week at work in a realistically recompensed job, courgettes you share with somebody you're capable of loving. She was warm. She was precious. She was soothing. She had a very soft way of walking into a room, any situation. She let people simply imagine the density of

279

her problems. She took good photographs. She took baths. One night she had such an intense bath it turned the toilet roll to pulp and sent water streaming down the tiles. I sat in the kitchen, head in my hands. 'Why can't she turn on the extractor Matthew?' He laughed and ruffled my hair. I couldn't even write about it. Jessica was just the flow of time. Jessica was ritual.

So this was Hornsey Road Part II, velvety weekends of photogenic food and occasional sex and I could only get out of the way but *go forth*, I said to everyone, *I've got someone waiting*. I told them everything. And Matthew, Matthew darling, sweet angel, I had enough in my overdraft for one month of rent. That was fine. I sat in my room with my new Tilda Swinton *Kevin* slippers – triangular toes, fuchsia silk, tight, lively things – and I went to Crouch End for a daily Dunn's then I sat in my room with my peanut-buttered pumpernickel and my MUBI subscription and I painted my nails and I waited for Ginger. Inextinguishable flutter in the gut. Waiting for Ginger.

I'd watch a MUBI that made me feel dodge, too much Maurice Pialet or the like, and somehow I'd forget I was leaving and then I'd think, *ah, yes, you're leaving*, I'd remember, and I'd think about all the thrilling things I'd take with me this time, only really dubiously mine, finders-keepers mine but mine all the same: the sieve, the clothes horse, the lemon juicer. I'd miss this all too, rabbit hutch cohabitation. I'd miss stealing the Dove and the pepper and the garlic cloves, I'd miss being tight and a thief and then lavishly generous. But the possibility of Ginger was why I was here, why I'd moved here, the attraction that London had for people like Ginger, that's why I thought I was here, that's why my heart chucked me down here in the first place, I liked to think these days, I liked that narrative, but Ginger was in Sheffield.

So I did my bit, paid my bills, chucked my food by its sell-by date, was obliging and flexible and not too prurient, headphones on at night. And in the day I'd dance around in my psychotic slippers. I was leaving.

*

I buzzed my hair and in the mornings after everyone had left I put my back against my radiator, up on max, and I looked for work, work back north, crossed my toes for something arty, something soulful and then as the days went by just something, just something at least and you couldn't be a chooser, and Big Anne's mum was irreplaceable. *SLIM PICKINGS* I told Ginger, *[alarmed emoji]*, *SLIM AF* but *yes, Grace, magical thinking*. I looked at deposits on little flats in Sharrow. I looked up M&S salaries. I googled the Park Hill developers in a fit of adulation and then I closed the tab quick, wiped my browsing history.

I was very serious, very sincere about the imaginative work of a job application. I was very sincere and my cover letters were brilliant, dramatic monologues, masterpieces. Though after sending them off I'd remember what Holly had told me, that the people in HR who read these things were more often than not underpaid and undervalued mothers in their thirties, often balancing out a maternity or three, or else underpaid undervalued women or men or women or nb in their forties or fifties or sixties and, *well, I'm going on, Grace, but essentially none of these groups want that shit.* Nobody would likely care to be reminded of the febrile mess of twenties life they'd all now managed to break out of, some of them only very recently. I begged to differ. She shook her head.

I did another stint with baby Sara and Sara's mum Saba. That was nice. That was fun. No. In fact it was deep and important; Sara was the new Rachel. I found them on the street en route to Tesco Express and they'd had another baby, Zaf, and they were moving to Bournemouth now and they could do with a hand.

Sara was working on her words now. She didn't have many yet, but even so you could tell she would turn out brooding. Her wry little face gave her away; she knew how this language business worked very well indeed but Bartleby, that was her vibe. Respect. She was pretty much indifferent to me. I was her facilitator, her PA. I loved it.

'Green juice?'

Vacant.

'Banana?'

Vacant.

'Dora?'

Nope.

The one thing she was really on with was the iPad. She knew how to unlock it. She knew how to get home. She knew the rainbow button for pics and videos. Saba left her little waving videos to help me calm her down if she went funny. Some of the videos had Sara in them too. In one she was a few months younger and drooling and Saba made her waltz by holding her underarms. She *loved* that one. She laughed her little head off. 'Who dat!' I'd say and she'd ignore me.

Sara's mentorship was very intense. I was anxious to credit her specifically and massively, write it all down after our sessions. She taught me the very limited room for manoeuvre I had and would always have with some people, that some human relationships were simply damage limitation no matter how hard you tried; she taught me to stick around when someone's there because they might need an emergency poo, they might need you so don't be a dick, and don't intimidate or patronise because people shut down, people disappear into their iPads when you do that. She taught me that I could feel radically exposed, incapable of connection, but that didn't mean I was radically exposed or incapable of connection. OK, that was Ginger. But Sara, Sara built up my appetite for mundanity. I was far too keen on these great affect-laden arcs of development, and sometimes life was just dull, dull for twenty, thirty minutes, for twenty-four hours, for life, who knew, who knew what cliff edge could await you but hey, *Peppa Pig*, hey, Percy Pig and Friends. Hey, another poo. It was all here for you.

*

We had a little party for Sara's birthday, a farewell to London and a Sara birthday. She was dressed as Jasmine from *Aladdin* and had glitter on her face.

'Oh, it's Jasmine!' I said.

'Yes, it's Jasmine,' said Saba, wincing, the new true baby Zaf on her chest. 'But we're having open conversations about what that means. Sara understands there's freight to this. Tea?'

'Yes please.'

'Jasmines come in all shapes and sizes, don't they Sara?' said Saba.

'Yes!' I said.

Zaf stayed asleep, unexcited but thoroughly there. He had a knitted cap on his head, made of a plump pink thread and tightly, regularly woven. There was no chance of any air there, no gaps.

I put Sara on my hip and we did a birthday dance.

Don't just tolerate yourself. You can do better than that, I wrote in her card.

She was two.

*

And then Pam rang. Diane's mum had gone for good and Diane too and we need you back said Pam. Full-time now. Proper.

'Can you take it?'

'*Yes.* YES.'

*

I arranged a flat dinner to make my announcement but when I left to get some bits I hadn't gone far before I had to stop. The thing with my neck was here, this old ancient thing, dicky neck cropping back up from the archives. And I couldn't get a working understanding with the creases in the backs of my knees and the balls and sockets where my legs became my pelvis. I had a milky taste in my mouth and a rich patina on my tongue and my palate. I had to stop and sit on a bench.

'Ex—. Excuse me,' said two little voices, almost in unison, just a millisecond out of sync.

I looked up. I was sat opposite an eight-foot wire fence and behind it there were two boys in royal blue jumpers, five or six. One of them pushed a yellow highlighter out through the gap and it scattered across the pavement.

'Will you get my pen?'

I picked up the pen and stood up.

'Are you a boy or a girl?'

'What's your name?'

'What's your name, lady?'

'It's not a lady.'

'What are you two called?'

'I'm Yem—'

'I'm Andy.'

'I'm Yemi.'

'Hello. Guess what mine is.'

They looked confused. I was confused too. I'd meant to ask them for my gender but the name part had thrown us all off.

I handed Yemi the highlighter and went back to the flat.

Eli picked up some bits instead, stuff for Jamie's fifteen-minute prawns and a couple of bottles of Casillero del Diablo. He did the shopping and then he cooked. It would help his anxiety to have a role, he said. Eli was nineteen.

When we sat down and the food was gone and we were all a bit drunk I said 'Eli. Tell me. I don't know you at all! Tell me things.'

'I was thinking,' he said, clearing her throat, Adam idly stroking his wrist, 'I was thinking today about the poverty of my vocabulary for talking about architecture. Like, I look up and I think, I'd really like to know what it is that I'm looking at.'

He blushed then, sank back into his wine.

'Oh babe,' I said, semi-whisper. 'There are words enough.' I was a whole new person now and Eli was Eli so I distributed the last of the wine and then I flung my arms in the air. 'A toast! A toast to Eli and Adam and Matthew and Jessica. A toast.'

There were my wrists, my Casio calling time.

I'M LEAVING! I did it! I got the job! Fanfare, fanfare, trumpets, streamers, open-top inner-city champagne tour. But in fact they were all over it. They'd clocked this from the start. There were *CONGRATS* balloons and *SORRY YOU'RE LEAVING* balloons all blown-up already, waiting in Adam's room. Eli paraded them in, had bought them especially. And then he said we have a gift for you. Oh my god! Little hoop earrings. Framed *Lobster* poster. Matthew's Chang vest washed and ironed. *Oh my god! A transitional object! Oh my god! Wait.* I had to stop there. My chest had gone titanium. I was frothy at the mouth again. My stomach *wrecked.*

The four of them huddled on the sofa, prepped for *Blue Planet* and I took a load of Jessica's codeine. I called for her and she sat on the edge of the bath, flannelled my brow. I was bleeding.

*

I went shopping, Haringey TK Maxx: wellies, walking boots, ultra-light down, ultra-ultra-light down. XL hot water bottle, Thermos small, Thermos large, golf umbrella. It was coming up April maybe and a freakish nice April they were predicting at that but I was taking no chances. I bought a stack of Perspex boxes. I started packing.

I called Peak Estates and Amol the Lettings Guy gave me a virtual tour of a flat, video thing. It was on Bank Street, this place on the top floor. It faced a brutalist car park and he showed me. Between each tier of concrete was a dark patch that you could watch light up when a car moved through. Magical. I wanted to lie on those concrete ledges. I wanted to live in that flat. And there was a TV included and it was light and you could hear the cathedral from here, he said, *atmospheric, love.* Amol was keen to draw my attention to that, the TV in particular, not the light or the bells quite so much as the *TV included, this one, yeah, and a DVD player too, love*, though when he pulled that player out I could see from 175 miles away it was dusty. *DVD player there, love,* he said again, the disc smiling patiently. I said oh, great, though, something like that. I was keen. I took it. *When can you start paying rent? Next week, love? Yes.*

I called Rebecca.
    'Where is it?'
    'Bank Street.'
    'Right.'
    'More the cathedral end.'
    'Dodgy.'
    'It's fine.'
    'Hmm. Well at least there's Big Tesco.'
    'What?'
    '24/7.'
    'What?'
    'For when you get robbed.'
    'Shut up.'
    'Dodgy as.'
    'It's on the top floor.'
    'Flying home, then?'
    'Fuck off.'
    'How much?'
    'Two hundred.'
    'That all?'
    'No. Like the agent's two hundred. Five hundred rent.'
    'Does that include bills?'
    'Bills?'
    'Yes.'
    'Yes.'
    'What, so bills are included?'
    'No.'

'Shit. Bills on top?'

'Yes.'

'Right.'

'It's a bargain.'

'It's not.'

'It is. I've been paying nearly twice that for some shitty little dump down here.'

'Are you fucking kidding me?'

'Nope.'

She ran the hot tap.

'Rebecca?'

'Yes.'

'Don't say it then.'

'Lol. Yes. Well done. Congrats. Congrats.'

'Congrats Grace,' she said.

'Thanks!'

The colander came in now, out from the back of the cupboard.

'Wait. Wait a sec. I'll call you back.'

One, two, three, four. Five mins. Seven mins. Ringtone.

'Well fucking done.' Tash was in the background: *WOOOP! WOOOOP!* 'It's fucking mint.'

*

The last day in London I went to the Barbican. I saw two women kissing on the Tube, one with yellow trousers like Rupert Bear and a wet-look leather coat with sheepish trimmings and a shiny gold bag full of red and yellow Strepsils. The other had corduroy straight-leg trousers frayed at the hems and a little bit short with bottle-green boots and a beret.

288

Snow boots. *JEAL. JEAL. You're not done with this. We're not done here, Grace! You're not fucking done here. Fuck.* And then I remembered London was, what even was it, within you without you and here. Always here. Dying, fading, impossible. Here.

I had a walk and a Leon and a mooch and a whimper as these thoughts of loss came up, and went, and came, and as I was truly leaving I saw Rachel on the promenade, whatever that central strip of sloping floor was supposed to be. She was larger than life and she was luminous. At first I thought it was just an intense resemblance – the light was moody, it was the Barbican – but no, it was Rachel, it really was. I hid in my gold hood. I fetched my glasses out my pocket. *Wait, wait, wait.* No. It wasn't, no. It wasn't Rachel. (It was.) I wrote *RIP RACHEL* on a fresh page of Moleskine. I scribbled it out.

*

Simon from the library came down on his Thursday off, drove me up in his van. We packed up and he nipped to Tescs for a bottle of pop and I waited with a fag by a tree. I'd put my headphones on for some ambient end-credit feels, Orbital 'Chime', was reading a notice pinned to the bark concerning the legal interests of the Hornsey Pensioners. An old man stopped by my side. He gestured to me, his hands cupped over his ears, a wide grin on his face.

I took off my headphones.

He started talking in French.

'Désolé. I'm British—. Well. I'm not. Hmm. I'm not French.'

'Are you learning French?'

'No. No, I—. Music.'

'Ah. You're from Britain. I'm from Beirut.'

'Oh. Gosh. What's it like?'

'I haven't been back for more than thirty years.'

'Oh. Sorry. Of course. Gosh. I should have—. Sorry.'

He gestured to the end of my fag for my apology. I gave it him. He smiled and took a drag. 'Are you sure you're not French?'

'No. I'm sorry. I have a few words, but. No. I'm sorry. I really am.'

'It's a shame.'

'It's a crying shame. I believe it. But. I'm European. I am.'

'I knew it.' He held out his hand and I held out mine and he kissed it.

'Oh my!' I said, pretending to blush.

'We'll miss you when you're gone,' he said.

Evening voice notes to Michelle. *I'm in S1. That's like Westminster. I'm on the top floor.* I sounded cogent. The cathedral chimed. Opposite was the brutalist car park. This was my flat and still empty so my voice became the sound of the flat being empty but inflated by the sound of my voice and critically I could bear it. It was mine. I was a new woman. *I'm a new woman,* I told Michelle, I told them all. *Heavenly child emoji. Octopus. Lightning bolt. Aubergine.*

*

Then it was Friday and Rebecca came round and I used my nice clean oven turning spinach wraps into spinach tortillas and we had tortillas and milky tea with a pint of milk she'd brought with her for a gift, that and a cross-head screwdriver.

I unpacked my fancy goods there in front of her so she could call me a dickhead, *do your worst, mate.* A selection of complex carbohydrates, fregola and such, white miso, black garlic, dried lime, tamarind, holding them up to her in turn and narrating. 'Bloody love tamarind,' she said.

Then Tash rang her – *surprise!* – and Tash was downstairs and we buzzed her up and something fishy was afoot and up she came, up the stairs, and there in her hand was a cat box and a kitten. *OMG. OMG. OMG!!!* Smudge had had an illegal

291

baby and we smuggled her in right then and there and she became my illegal guru.

I named her Maxine, Max.

Max liked bare feet. She liked to push her right paw up onto the human sternum and make a very gentle patter, the sound a ball pool makes to greet a happy child. We hit it off. And that first night I had gins in tins and she had kitten milk and we watched DVDs. *Harold and Maude*, *Minnie and Moskowitz*. I wasn't lonely, not anymore, but if I were I'd be able to admit it, I thought, wrapping her sweaty peaceful sleeping tail round my finger. I wasn't lonely. I was Moskowitz. Pretending as though I was Minnie. Waiting to be Maude. *Yes*, said Max, nodding sagely. *Yes*. And when she did her inaugural poo in the morning and didn't we all I raked away her poo and took out the little food waste bag, moist and aromatic. She went under my feet as I got to the door and I nipped her tail and she yowled and looked filthy. *Don't look at me like that*, I said with my face, turning away. I looked back over. She looked at the ground. I did a star jump. She stayed looking down. I squatted, found her face. She stayed still and then she lifted her face slowly and purr. *Purr. Purr.* I picked her up and took her back over the threshold.

*

On Saturday Rebecca drove us to Leeds IKEA, carried my shit because she couldn't deal with my crappy handling. *Thanks. I'll buy you tea*. We walked through at speed and then sat with the blue-green evening-lit Leeds over her shoulder.

We ate in silence. I had the salmon, sacrilege but I did it to wind her up, bants. She videoed it. I wolfed mine down and then watched her with her meatballs and her Daim cake. I spotted her moles. I'd forgotten her moles. I had one slap in the centre of my head and she had two, one on each cheek. I arranged my salmon bones like a little house then she took our trays to the depository and dropped me off at the flat. I'd bought a stainless steel salad bowl. I'd bought coat hangers made of wood. I'd bought a wooden chopping board and I would oil it, just like the instructions. I'd bought a Poäng chair. I built it and I angled it out towards the world.

I slept.

On Sunday I went to see Ginger.

*

I walked up there. Trek, but I wanted to be there with my body all the way. I tried to go as normal, have my feet hit the tarmac neatly, suavely, but I couldn't see my shadow. I was a puppet with an absent-minded handler. The freakish bout of good weather they'd predicted had hit and it amplified everything, all the sounds that come with a Sunday morning – crying, humming, pounding – and all the crap, the tat and pulp. An odd unseasonal serum coated the lazier cars and all sorts of straggly flotsam had gravitated there – tissues, leaves, dust and fags. It was stunning.

*

Knock. She opened the door in bumblebee stripes and a pair of cycling shorts. I put down my bag. She took my shoulders with her hands. She looked me in the face, looked me up and down. She nodded. I went inside.

*

We went to bed and we stayed there. And then when the sun started to fade we walked down the Eccy Road to M&S. Adults buying bottles of wine for dinner parties. Adults buying freekeh and Sicilian thins and Pie d'Angloys. Adults buying Chantenays and Tenderstem. I filled up my arms with the evidence.

It was warm still on the walk back, despite the fading light. Mediterranean. My leggings were black and they clung. My legs were burning.

'Ginger?'

'Hmm.'

'I think I—.'

'Me too.'

*

Dream. Mum's away; I'm looking after Mabel. It's spring outside and I've power-washed the yard and bleached the outhouse and the door's wide open and it's all sweating off the smell of old tomcat. I'm sat on Mum's iron bench and I see Ginger's hair in its topknot now, skirting the top of the trellis, and she comes round and stands by the open gate and she's beaming, and that's our beginning.

Acknowledgements

The mothership. Saba, Rachel and Tele. Katy, Katie, Mark, Jack, Paul, Lara, CHRIS. Michelle. Yosola. Nicky. Jen. Laura and Chris R. Vicky.

In Sheffield the AOS bunker. Catherine T. Lunch-hour pals, lost pigeons, our man at the Hungry Buddha and the men downstairs who always kicked us out with such wit. Thank you to the lovely people at the Showroom and at Union Street, and Post Office Gary you'll never know and Joanna for the aubergine, mango and Thai basil and eventually Abi for helping me let go.

In Otley Mrs Cunniffe and Wells Cole I blame you! It was worth it. Emily H I love you. Countless X84 drivers for opening up the world. SO many others. You know who you are and if you don't I'm working on it.

The book people. None of this without you, Eleanor. And POPPY, thank you. The team at Chatto big love. And booksellers far and near you're everything and the people at the White Review and the Eurostar seat allocation system. The people who read this on submission, thank you. Philip, you are so kind. And Anisa Makhoul, you are a g-e-n-i-u-s.

Nana and Grandad, Grandma, Dad and Big Louise.

Last and first Mum, Louby, Twin One, Dotty (keep on keeping on) and Mabel (RIP) xxx